PRAISE FOR R.J. PATTERSON

"R.J. Patterson does a fantastic job at keeping you engaged and interested. I look forward to more from this talented author."□

— **Aaron Patterson**, *bestselling author of SWEET DREAMS*

"Patterson has a mean streak about a mile wide and puts his two main characters through quite a horrible ride, which makes for good reading."

— **Richard D.**, *reader*

DEAD SHOT

"Small town life in southern Idaho might seem quaint and idyllic to some. But when local newspaper reporter Cal Murphy begins to uncover a series of strange deaths that are linked to a sticky spider web of deception, the lid on the peaceful town is blown wide open. Told with all the energy and bravado of an old pro, first-timer R.J. Patterson hits one out of the park his first time at bat with *Dead Shot*. It's that good."

-*Vincent Zandri*, *bestselling author of THE REMAINS*

"You can tell R.J. knows what it's like to live in the newspaper world, but with *Dead Shot*, he's proven that he also can write one heck of a murder mystery."

— *Josh Katzowitz*, *NFL writer for CBSSports.com & author of* Sid Gillman: Father of the Passing Game

DEAD LINE

"This book kept me on the edge of my seat the whole time. I didn't really want to put it down. R.J. Patterson has hooked me. I 'll be back for more. "

— **Bob Behler**, *3-time Idaho broadcaster of the year and play-by-play voice for Boise State football*

DEAD IN THE WATER

"In Dead in the Water, R.J. Patterson accurately captures the action-packed saga of a what could be a real-life college football scandal. The sordid details will leave readers flipping through the pages as fast as a hurry-up offense. "

— **Mark Schlabach,** *ESPN college sports columnist and co-author of Called to Coach Heisman: The Man Behind the Trophy*

ALSO BY R.J. PATTERSON

Titus Black series

Behind Enemy Lines

Game of Shadows

Rogue Commander

Line of Fire

Blowback

Honorable Lies

Power Play

State of Conspiracy

The Patriot

The President's Man

The Haitian Assassin

Codename: Killshot

Chaos Theory

House of Cards

False Flag

A Deadly Game

Brady Hawk series

First Strike

Deep Cover

Point of Impact

Full Blast

Target Zero

Fury

State of Play

Seige

Seek and Destroy

Into the Shadows

Hard Target

No Way Out

Two Minutes to Midnight

Against All Odds

Any Means Necessary

Vengeance

Code Red

A Deadly Force

Divide and Conquer

Extreme Measures

Final Strike

Cal Murphy Thriller series

Dead Shot

Dead Line

Better off Dead

Dead in the Water

Dead Man's Curve

Dead and Gone

Dead Wrong

Dead Man's Land

Dead Drop

Dead to Rights

Dead End

James Flynn Thriller series

The Warren Omissions

Imminent Threat

The Cooper Affair

Seeds of War

Polar Vortex

Lunar Deception

Operation Nightfall

© Copyright 2024 R.J. Patterson

First print edition 2024

Published in the United States of America

Green E-Books

PO Box 140654

Boise, ID 83714

OPERATION NIGHTFALL

THE PHOENIX CHRONICLES
BOOK 12

R.J. PATTERSON

For Ron Counts

A blessed father and husband with a big heart and a big future ahead of him

ONE

KUALA LAMPUR, MALAYSIA

Brady Hawk clutched the steering wheel of his BMW M3 coupe, his eyes locked on the red Alfa Romeo Giulia Quadrifoglio weaving in and out of traffic just ahead of him. The M3 engines whined as it found another gear, forcing him and his colleague Dallas Ryder back in their seats. Street lights flickered past as they roared down the road. Just as Hawk drew near, the other vehicle sped into a roundabout before entering a drift that didn't stop until the car was facing west, a virtual left turn.

"I thought this guy was a hacker, not a Grand Prix race car driver," Ryder said, his right hand clinging to the grab handle over the passenger side window.

"Everyone has their secrets," Hawk said.

"A secret is that you jam to Taylor Swift behind closed doors, not that you can drive like a Hollywood stuntman."

The M3 slowed and then its tires barked as Hawk zipped between a couple of cars while making the turn in the round-about and continuing pursuit of the Alfa Romeo.

"Did you read the profile Morgan gave us?" Hawk said, referring to Magnum Group director Morgan May's briefing. "Quantum Glitch has never been caught."

"Then how would we know he can drive like this?"

"We don't, but it shouldn't come as a surprise since he's been so elusive. You don't avoid capture from more than a dozen governments pursuing you without having some set of special skills."

"Well, let's change that little fact in his profile."

Hawk jammed his foot on the accelerator. "Working on it."

The engine found another gear as the M3 rocketed past a long line of cars and drew closer to the Alfa Romeo.

With CIA resources limited and leaks galore plaguing the agency, director Robert Besserman decided to let Morgan's covert team handle the task of dismantling The Alliance, the shadowy organization intent on disrupting global markets and creating geopolitical turmoil. While The Alliance's ultimate endgame remained unknown, it was apparent to those in the U.S. intelligence community that the leaders wanted to create an environment conducive for a person or cabal to seize greater control over various countries and regions. Morgan's team, led by Hawk and his wife Alex, had thwarted several attempts by The Alliance to control everything from telecommunications to the financial market. The organization seemed well-connected and unrelenting in its quest to take control, making the Magnum Group's mission seem akin to putting out an endless string of fires rather than eliminating them altogether. And with Jun Fang almost untouchable while directing the organization's movements from the shadows, Morgan decided to pursue all leads, no matter how small.

But Quantum Glitch was anything but small. In his own right, he was a major target. The hacker had been responsible for some of the biggest viruses unleashed on the internet, including several that attacked global financial institutions and brought trading to a halt. He excelled at crippling major networks and large corporations, forcing them to bend a knee to his demands. However, his real threat was in creating backdoors within legitimate programs. If he was in league with The Alliance, no system was safe, no program protected enough to escape his fury.

And at the moment, Quantum Glitch was the only viable lead the Magnum Group had with ties to The Alliance, thanks to a tip from the director of British intelligence. He had passed along the hacker's whereabouts to Besserman, hoping the U.S. had more assets in the region than MI-6 since it was experiencing pressure to capture another terrorist who'd sought refuge in Malaysia. If Hawk lost Quantum Glitch, U.S. intelligence was doomed to another cycle of simply reacting to The Alliance's whims rather than putting the organization on its proverbial back foot. Hawk opposed The Alliance's aims out of sheer principle. But the older he got, the more he wanted to do his best to keep the world as safe as possible for his son. He'd never been more determined to take them down.

As they approached another roundabout, Hawk sought to force the issue as he squeezed between Quantum Glitch and the car behind him. The tight fit enraged the driver behind Hawk, but he didn't waste any time responding to the man's middle-finger salute and long blast of his horn.

"What are you thinking, Mia?" Hawk asked over the coms.

Mia Becker, the team's tech wizard in the field, started to respond before her breath hitched. "I was—I'm—I'm not sure."

"Come on, Mia," Hawk said. "Give me something. What's his destination?"

"I'm still trying to figure it out," she said. "He doesn't fit into any box, which is making it rather difficult at the moment to determine where he might be going."

"At this time of night, I think it's safe to say he's not headed to the airport," Ryder said.

"That eliminates one possible destination," Hawk said. "But I was thinking the same thing. Mia, we need something, anything."

"I'm combing through some databases right now, trying to figure out where he's staying tonight."

"Think that's where he's headed?" Hawk asked.

"It's nearly midnight there," she said. "Where would you be headed if it were this late?"

"The only sane answer is bed."

Ryder chuckled. "Tell me you're married and have a kid without telling me."

Hawk shot his partner a side-eyed glance. "Tell me you're single without telling me."

The Afla Romeo made two trips around the circle before whipping the car back in the same direction from which it came. Hawk followed, refusing to give up even an inch in the pursuit.

"I got it," Mia shouted over the coms.

"Got what?" Hawk asked.

"He's staying at the Merdeka 118 building," she said. "He's registered there at the Hyatt, which occupies the top floors."

"Think that's where he's headed?" Hawk asked.

"He's going in that direction. And if he can lose you, he's not that far away. So, don't lose him."

"Copy that."

Hawk maintained his focus on Quantum Glitch's car, which continued down the stretch of four-lane road, darting back and forth between the lanes in an effort to distance himself. But Hawk was up for the challenge, matching the Alfa Romeo move for move. As they drew closer to the Merdeka 118 building, Quantum Glitch risked everything by squeezing between a pair of street cleaners rumbling side by side. Hawk looked at the gap but realized that trying to shoe-horn the wide-bodied M3 into the winnowing gap was about as smart as a screen door on a submarine. He laid off the accelerator, leaving him and Ryder to watch the Alfa Romeo's taillights become smaller as they vanished into the night.

Hawk slammed the steering wheel and let out a string of curses.

"I would've tried to sneak through those two sweepers," Ryder said, pointing at the trucks impeding their progress.

"You would've been a fool," Hawk said. "Getting sandwiched

between those two behemoths would've assured that we lost him."

"I would've made it through," Ryder said matter-of-factly.

Hawk grunted. "There's a reason I drive when we're together."

The two trucks blocked both lanes of southbound traffic for the next three minutes, drawing the ire of the dwindling number of drivers out at that time of night. But eventually, the trucks went right at the next roundabout, reopening the road. Hawk pushed the accelerator to the floor, the engine growling as the M3 zoomed down a clear stretch.

"Mia, how far away are we from the Merdeka building?" Hawk asked.

"You're about five minutes away, give or take a few minutes based on the traffic lights," she said.

"Why don't you make them all green for me?"

"That's not impossible most days, but right now, I haven't hacked my way into the Kuala Lampur transportation system. So, you're stuck with what you've got."

"Then can you tell me what room Quantum Glitch is staying in?" he asked.

"He checked in under the alias of Mark Moore—room 11854," she said. "I've got you a room reserved and sent the info to an app for you on your phone. You should be able to scan the app at a kiosk when you walk into the lobby and it'll grant you access to the top floor."

"Copy that."

Hawk and Ryder hammered out a plan of attack for once they reached the building. Hawk would go in first and try to flush out Quantum Glitch, who was staying alone, according to the intel British intelligence had passed on. Ryder would remain in the hallway in case the hacker somehow subdued Hawk.

"I don't think it's fair that you're going to get all the glory on this one," Ryder said.

"What kind of glory are you talking about?"

"Brady Hawk, the man who captured the world's greatest hacker."

Hawk waved dismissively at the comment. "We're a team, Ryder. If I get any glory, it's shared with you. But I don't care about any of that. I just want to interrogate him and find out what The Alliance is up to. Quantum Glitch is just a small cog in a big wheel. You know that as well as anyone."

"But this is child's play for you," Ryder said. "A hacker versus a trained operative. It's not even fair."

"In case you haven't been paying attention, this guy isn't just *some* hacker. He's never been caught for a reason. And if I impart any wisdom to you as a young operative, it's this: never underestimate anyone."

"But, come on, Hawk. You know this is gonna be a walk in the park. You don't have to play coy with me."

Hawk glanced over at Ryder and narrowed his eyes. "Never. Underestimate. Anyone."

After reviewing their plan once more, Hawk pulled up to the building. He wagged a finger at an eager valet before rushing inside. Using the app Mia had sent him, he scanned it at a kiosk, and the machine spit out a pair of keycards. He handed one to Ryder before they hustled over to the elevator. The elevator used exclusively for the top floor hummed as it flew up through the shaft. A man wearing a keffiyeh and sunglasses looked straight ahead, moving only to scratch his nose during the rapid ascent.

The elevator stopped on the floor just below the top and the man exited. Then it continued to the top and the doors parted. Hawk and Ryder surveyed the small lobby and then looked for the cluster of room numbers containing the one assigned to Quantum Glitch.

Hawk pulled out an endoscope camera and used it to peer beneath the small slit under the door. He scanned the room and then turned to Ryder.

"He's in there," Hawk whispered.

Hawk removed a small black box from his ruck and flipped a

switch. A series of lights blinked and the machine whirred to life. He placed it in front of the keypad and then a small click. The faint noise drew the hacker's attention. He spun around as Hawk charged into the room.

The man hurled a short-fused flash bang at Hawk and ducked behind a couch. The device bounced off Hawk's chest, and he spun and dove to the floor. The metal clanked against the tile floor in the entry way before exploding with a thunderous boom. Smoke poured into the hallway as Hawk tried to reorient himself. He got up on his hands and knees and looked around. After squeezing his eyes shut, he opened them again, his vision still blurred, his ears still ringing.

Ryder tapped him on the shoulder. "I've got this."

But then another explosion. Another flash bang, followed by a series of gunshots.

"Ryder," Hawk called as he re-entered the room, a gun in his hand.

The acrid smell wafting in the air on the smoke made him want to gag.

"Ryder," Hawk said again.

As the smoke lifted, Hawk found his partner lying on his side unconscious.

"Come on, Ryder. You're okay," Hawk said, shaking him.

Ryder opened his eyes and squinted as he looked up at Hawk. "Where is he?"

Hawk scanned the room but didn't see Quantum Glitch. "I don't know."

After staggering to his feet, Hawk trained his weapon in front of him and moved through the thinning haze, clearing each room in the suite. Then Hawk felt a strong breeze and noticed the room quickly clearing.

"What the hell—" he said as he stared at the floor to ceiling window made of glass. A large section had been removed, allowing in the high winds. The gusts pushed out the smoke, but it also rocked the building. Hawk could sense the Merdeka 118 building swaying.

Then Hawk edged closer to the window and peered out into the night. Street lights illuminated the street below. Hawk's breath hitched when he saw it.

"Come here, Ryder," Hawk said, motioning for his colleague. "You're not going to believe this."

Ryder stumbled over to him, using Hawk to stop his momentum. Both men peered out of the hole in the glass and watched as Quantum Glitch glided to the ground in a parachute.

Ryder sighed as he put his arm around Hawk. "Like I've said before: Never underestimate anyone."

Hawk cursed and then set his jaw before activating his coms.

"We lost him."

TWO

ROBERT BESSERMAN SAT ACROSS FROM PRESIDENT Charles Bullock, who was loosening his tie while releasing a long exasperated breath. On the flat-screen television against the wall, a political operative named Kip Hughes was on a cable news channel talking about how the president was going to destroy the country. Bullock shrugged at the comments and then gestured toward an aide, who turned off the lights.

Bullock pointed to the screen as an aide cued up a video. "I know why Jun Fang is so rich. He's got an uncanny ability to make you believe whatever he's saying, even when I know it's utter bullshit."

He nodded at another aide and the video began playing.

"Just watch," Bullock said.

A title page flashed on the screen, signifying it had been catalogued by the FBI, before Jun Fang's image appeared. Fang stood on an empty sandy beach, his back to the water. His stringy black hair whipped in the stiff breeze, revealing a higher hairline than usually visible. He wore a short-sleeve polo shirt and board shorts, a surf board planted nose down in the sand behind him. The

9

backdrop was nondescript, something Besserman recognized was by design. Fang clearly didn't want to be found by anyone.

The image narrowed as it slowly zoomed in on Fang.

"If you don't already recognize me, I'm Jun Fang, the head of JF Industries," he said. "You might be wondering why I'm making this video. The truth is, I wish I didn't have to, but sometimes you must stand up to the blatant lies that are being propagated by powerful people. The lies got so bad that I feared for my life and had to fake my death. But it's no secret that I'm actually alive— and I intend to fight back against the oppressors who have tried to silence me."

Bullock signaled for the aide to pause the video. "Fang is unbelievable. He's going to play the victim. Just watch."

"That's what makes him so good," Besserman said.

Bullock gestured to continue and the video resumed.

"When I founded JF Industries years ago, all I ever wanted to do was give people a better life, especially those who found them-selves as one of the outcasts in society. I wanted them to know what it was like to grow up in a loving home. I wanted to create innovative products that improved the lives of others. The fact that I amassed a fortune along the way was a pleasant byproduct. But everything took years of hard work. None of it happened overnight. However, there are governments trying to tear me down overnight, if not erase me from the planet altogether."

Fang shuffled over to the surfboard, resting one of his hands on the side of it.

"But I'm not going to let that happen, not only for my sake, but also for yours. The governments of the western world have amassed far more power than they should be allowed to have, putting us all at risk. If a billionaire with enough resources to fight against these criminals holding political office like me can be targeted and brought to my knees by these unjust systems of power, what will happen to you when they come for you? How will *you* be able to fight?"

Fang spun the surfboard around, revealing a target painted on the bottom side. Then the camera panned over to a bikini-clad woman wearing a pair of protective glasses and training a pistol on the target. Fang walked over toward the woman. He gestured toward her and she emptied her gun into the surfboard, which appeared to be about thirty yards away. Fang and the woman walked together toward the surfboard to check the accuracy of her shots.

"Now, my friend Mei Ling Wu here understands just how dangerous unchecked governments can be," Fang continued as they walked. "Her father and mother were both imprisoned in camps because they held political views that opposed the president at the time. Growing up without both parents in the home for several years and being shuttled around from home to home until their release reinforced the idea that governments have too much power when we must bend a knee or be forced to lose our loved ones and our way of life."

Fang indicated the target, which showed Wu had drawn a smiley face with bullet holes. The camera panned to her and she smiled.

"If you think you are safe," she said, "think again. Mr. Fang and JF Industries will be doing all they can to make the world a better place, a world free of a government lording its power over us and enslaving us."

"That's right," Fang said as the camera swung back to a tight shot of him. "Fascism has a different face these days, one that's difficult to recognize. It's why we must all be vigilant to recognize it and point it out when we see it."

The video paused and then lights came back on.

"There's a few more minutes of this bullshit, but I think you get the gist of it," Bullock said.

Besserman nodded. "What was his ultimate point?"

"All our security analysts believe he made the video as a precursor to something he's about to do," Bullock said.

"But aren't his hands still tied?" Besserman asked. "The last update I got was that the British government was bringing charges

against him for child trafficking. His little orphanage business—
and his little bit in that video about helping kids find homes—was
nothing more than a cover for him to traffic children as well as
siphon the best ones off to train for a special group of secret
operatives."

"According to the British consulate, charges are pending
against him but the investigation is still ongoing. They believe
there's much more beyond the orphanage, so they're probing a
little bit further."

Besserman pursed his lips, thinking for a moment before
responding. "If he's making a video like that, he knows
something."

"What do you mean?"

"I mean this wasn't just a video to help remake his image. He
definitely has designs on doing something. Whether it's the
launch of a new product or his way of angling to regain his
freedom in the UK and the world beyond, I don't know. But he's
plotting something, and this was his way of setting it up."

"What do you think he could be planning?"

"I don't know," Besserman said, "but I'm sure you read in
your security briefing that The Alliance had allegedly employed
the services of the infamous hacker Quantum Glitch."

Bullock nodded. "I read it, but I'm not real familiar with his
work."

"He's made a household name for himself in the hacker
community by staying in the shadows and never getting caught."

"Then how come we aren't pursuing him?"

"We are," Besserman said. "But he's very good. Nobody
knows much at all about him—though I should say nobody
knows anything at all. We only have one grainy photo of him that
could be any number of hackers, so his identity is a well-guarded
secret. We don't even know his country of origin, political leaning, anything. He will do anything if you pay him enough
money."

"And The Alliance has vast resources, don't they?"

"From all accounts, yes. And that's especially true if Fang is dumping his own personal money into the organization."

"Why don't we have him yet?"

"Like I said, the guy is good. We had two agents in position to capture him last night, but he managed to escape from his hotel room at the Mederka 118 building—jumped through the window and into the night with a parachute on."

"Any idea what this Quantum Glitch guy could be working on?"

Besserman shook his head. "The thing about him is that he's not just a hacker. He can get into banks and steal money almost at will. But he's more a principled criminal. Consider him more like a vigilante than anything else. If there's been an injustice—or a perceived injustice from his perspective—then he will get involved. So, he can hack, yes, but he can also code, write nasty viruses and embed them in systems designed to infect everyone. And no matter what his motivation, make no mistake about it—the man is very dangerous."

"Could Fang use him to put a Trojan horse virus in one of his products?"

"That's possible, but also predictable. Watchers would be able to spot that right away and Fang would lose all his credibility. And remember that The Alliance requires funding. And without a successful venture, the organization is dead in the water."

"How do you recommend we handle this?"

Besserman drummed his fingers on the table and sighed. "Nothing changes. We keep doing what we've always been doing when it comes to Fang, which is keep a sharp eye out for him. In a perfect world, we'd capture him and bring him in for questioning, but he's got the resources and the smarts to stay in the shadows."

"What about his bikini model? Think we can get anything out of her if we put the squeeze on her?"

"I think any attempt to detain Mei Ling Wu and question her would only play into Fang's hands. It's pretty clear to me that Fang's going to utilize her to carry his message to a massive audience. She's known for her modeling pictures, but she's also a social media influencer with a huge following, somewhere around eighty million people. So, there might be other ways to leverage her for our purposes. But I wouldn't directly go after her as a way of getting to Fang—unless we have to, of course."

Bullock nodded knowingly. "It sounds like you have a good handle on how to approach this."

"I'm trying to stay on top of it, but it's a fluid situation. And Fang could make me look foolish an hour from now if he launches some cover attack somewhere."

"No, I think you're doing exactly what needs to be done—and what can be done. But that's not the only thing I wanted to talk to you about."

"There's more?"

"Yeah," Bullock said with a sigh. "You heard anything yet about a program called Operation Nightfall?"

Besserman shook his head. "Want to read me in?"

"We don't know much about it, but the FBI and the NSA has been hearing chatter about it over some of the networks they're monitoring. I'm surprised you haven't heard anything yet."

"Maybe it's working its way up the chain," Besserman said. "I'm usually not briefed about radio chatter. Threats have to be fairly concrete before it's brought to my attention."

"Of course," Bullock said. "Makes sense. I'll send over whatever I've got on it so you can check it out for yourself. Not sure if it matters, but I thought you'd want to be aware, if you weren't already."

Bullock thanked Besserman before the CIA director left the meeting.

Once Besserman reached his car, his phone buzzed with an incoming call from a number he didn't recognize. He hesitated to answer it but figured he better in case it was one of his assets needing his help.

"Director Besserman," said a man with a thick German

accent, "thank you for taking my call. This is Klaus Schreiber. Do you have a minute?"

Besserman was somewhat relieved there wasn't another fire to put out, the enthusiasm in his voice reflecting it as he responded to the German director of intelligence.

"Of course, Klaus. Anything for you."

"Excellent," Schreiber said. "Now, I heard a rumor that you weren't going to be at the intelligence summit in Venice next week. Is that true?"

"I was considering not going and—"

"Just stop right there," Schreiber interrupted, speaking at a rapid pace. "I don't want to hear any excuses. We need you there. I know you think of European intelligence as an entity that stands alone. But the truth is we need the U.S. intelligence community. And most importantly, we need you. If you come, it's going to signal that we're serious about stopping these terrorist attacks. And not only that, but it will let these terrorists know that they're facing a united front."

"Okay, okay, Klaus. I'll be there."

"Good," Schreiber said. "I have some other important things to discuss with you."

"What kind of things?"

"Things I can't talk about on the phone. Things about The Alliance. Understand?"

"Got it. See you then."

Besserman ended the call and then saw he'd received a text while he was talking with Schreiber. He opened it up and read it. One of his embedded assets had a lead on Quantum Glitch.

At least something's going my way today.

THREE

SALT LAKE CITY

Alex Hawk blew a tendril out of her face as she collapsed into a chair outside the terminal to her flight. While she enjoyed working for the Magnum Group with her husband, they recognized that little John Daniel required more attention. The rascally six-year-old was a bundle of energy who woke up every morning like someone had stuffed dynamite into his shorts. He bounced from activity to activity, the combination of his curious nature and short attention span making her feel like she was parenting the Tasmanian Devil.

She looked at J.D. and smiled, his eyes wide and wild as he crouched on the chair. She reached down into her purse to look for a coloring book and crayons, something she knew might only occupy him for a couple of minutes before he grew bored of it. After grabbing the items, she glanced over at the chair where J.D. had been only to find him missing.

She jumped to her feet and scanned the area, just like she might on a mission. Whenever she was out in the field and something went wrong, she knew how imperative it was to stay calm. But she wasn't out in the field. She was in a busy airport teeming

16

with travelers rushing from one gate to the next—and J.D. was nowhere to be seen.

Alex swore under her breath, promising to teach him a lesson as soon as she found him again—*if* she found him again.

Where the hell did he go?

She figured she couldn't have been looking in her purse for more than fifteen seconds, leaving her to wonder how he could disappear so quickly. It wasn't like this was the first time he'd pulled a stunt like this, but it always baffled her. His ability to vanish so quickly made her wonder if he wasn't a natural-born operative.

"J.D., where are you?" she called.

The plea for her son was a desperate one. Some of her fellow passengers waiting at the gate looked up at her and then scanned the room in bewilderment. Alex knew it made her look like an inattentive mother, but she didn't care. Parenting a child with as much energy and mischievousness as J.D. required setting aside your pride and simply doing whatever it took to get the job done. She long since realized that she would never earn style points for her parenting like all those mothers who marched around their well-behaved, well-dressed brood like obedient ducklings. No, those women had never encountered a kid like J.D.

Alex felt a slight pinch on her heel, causing her to jump and then squeal. She spun around and looked down to find J.D.'s little head with his messy brown hair and big blue eyes staring back up at her with a cheeky grin.

"J.D.!" she said. "What are you doing down there?"

He giggled as he wormed his way out from beneath the chair. He jumped to his feet, and Alex brushed off all the dirt and crumbs that had become attached to the front of his shirt while lying on the ground.

"Please don't do that to Mommy again," she said. "You scared me."

"You didn't like that?" J.D. asked, his bright eyes dimming, his smile gone.

"You can't hide from me like that when we're in a place like this," she said, her tone softening. "Do you understand?"

J.D.'s eyes welled up with tears as he nodded and then buried his head into her chest. Alex wrapped her arms around her son and pulled him close.

"It's okay, buddy. You're fine. Mommy loves you."

J.D. sniffled, wiped his eyes, and then drew back. He smiled and then climbed on top of the chair next to her. With a quick glance to see if his mother was paying attention, J.D. leaped onto the floor, immediately falling and then rolling before jumping back to his feet.

"What do you think, Mommy?"

"Good job," she said. "But let's not do that right now. You almost knocked that lady over."

"Oh, he's fine," an elderly woman said. Her voice cracked as she spoke, but the smile on her face supported her encouragement of his playfulness. "He's just a boy being a boy."

J.D. went from watching the woman back to his mother. "Can I do it again, Mommy? She said it was all right."

Alex shrugged and dropped her reading glasses from the top of her forehead onto the bridge of her nose. "I guess so. Just be careful you're not running into people."

J.D. pumped his fist and then clambered back onto the seat before taking another flying leap. He stretched his arms wide as he soared from a height of two feet onto the floor, a broad grin plastered on his face.

Alex dug out a highlighter and a few reports she'd shoved into her carry-on bag and started perusing them. Without a hands-on project to occupy her time, Morgan had asked her to review some of the Magnum Group's standard operating procedures to see if there was a way to tighten the loop on the dissemination of information. Too much intel had leaked out from their office, and Morgan recognized it was a threat to the safety of her team, especially the ones on the field. She read a paragraph or two before checking on J.D., who found an activity that seemed to arrest his full attention. She was deep into the files when she a husky voice interrupted her train of thought.

"Alex Hawk, is that you?" a man asked.

She slid her glasses on top of her head and glanced up at the man. "Sid Weston. What are the chances?"

Her husband had introduced her to Weston years ago when they first started working for Firestorm under J.D. Blunt's direction. Weston had assisted on a few missions in between assignments for the CIA. Working as a covert operator for the agency, Weston was a highly skilled asset, though neither of them had heard anything about him since they started working for the Magnum Group.

"Sometimes the stars just align," he said, flashing his trademark smile, one that was as warm as it was genuine. "What are you two up to?"

He nodded at little J.D. as he took another leap.

"How'd you know he was mine?" Alex asked. "I've only flown with him one other time."

"Well, he looks just like Brady, but he's got your eyes. So, where are you two headed?"

"Just going somewhere much warmer," she said. "Put our toes in the sand and dip our feet in the water."

Weston looked up at the destination on the screen above the terminal. "They've got sand in Atlanta."

She chuckled. "Not the kind I want. We're just connecting through there."

While Alex didn't suspect Weston, she had determined never to tell anyone her final destination in case someone else was listening or watching. It had the potential to come off as rude, but she determined that when it came to her and her family's wellbeing, she would rather be wise than polite.

"Where are *you* headed?" she asked.

"I've got some business over in Asia," he said, also being somewhat vague.

She didn't press him for any more information.

"How's your son?" she asked. "Isn't his name Steel?"

"Good memory," he said before nodding toward J.D. "He's actually just about like your son."

"And Sarah?"

"She's good. But she's been run a little ragged lately."

"Oh, I can relate."

"I bet you can."

J.D. jumped off the chair and crashed into Weston's leg.

"J.D., what did I tell you?" Alex said, her eyes bulging as she cocked her head to one side. It was as polite of a scolding as she could give with such a calm tone.

"Sorry, Mom," he said.

Weston knelt next to J.D. and helped him to his feet. "You're all right, big man. If you want to slow your momentum when you fall, you need to jump to your feet faster. Want me to show you how?"

"Yeah," J.D. said.

Alex smiled as she watched Weston demonstrate his technique, while J.D. watched wide-eyed. When he finished, J.D. practiced the move, rolling and then bouncing up to his feet with a big grin.

"Good job," Weston said, clapping with encouragement.

J.D. shrugged. "I like my daddy's way better."

Weston arched his eyebrows, unable to suppress a smile. "You've definitely got your dad's bravado."

J.D. scowled. "His what?"

"Bravado. Chutzpah. Swagger."

"I don't even know what that means," J.D. said as he climbed back on top of a chair and leaped off again.

"Well, you tried," Alex said.

"He'd get along famously with Steel. Maybe if the stars align again, we can get them together one day."

"That'd be fun," she said.

"J.D., come here," Weston said. "I've got something for you."

J.D. hustled over, eyes wide. "What is it?"

"Captain's wings," Weston said. "You ever had a pair of these?"

"No."

"Well, here you go," Weston said, pinning it to J.D.'s shirt. "Keep these with you at all times. They'll help you jump higher."

"Let's see," he said, scrambling to the top of a chair and leaping off.

He hit the ground hard and rolled before popping up to his feet.

"I think I went higher. Did you think I went higher?"

Weston smiled and nodded before he glanced at his watch. "Okay, gotta run and catch my flight. It's been great seeing you."

"Same here. Good luck."

Weston turned to J.D. "See you, big man."

"We're going to Aruba," J.D. shouted out.

Alex gave her son another piercing stare but didn't say a word. She'd have to deal with his mouth later.

"Have fun," Weston said as he turned and looked at Alex with a wink. "Build some nice sandcastles for me."

Then Weston spun and hustled down the concourse toward his gate.

Alex wanted to remind J.D. again that he wasn't supposed to tell anyone where they were going. It was for his safety. But she could only blame herself. She should've never told him in the first place. Sometimes, she just couldn't ignore those big blue pleading eyes.

She turned her attention back to the documents in her lap and put the incident out of her mind.

FOUR

PARIS

AFTER LOSING QUANTUM GLITCH IN MALAYSIA, HAWK, Ryder, and Mia retreated to a safe house in Morocco to wait for any possible sightings of the escaped hacker. They didn't have to wait long. A day later, a CIA asset embedded with Russian oligarch Alexander Nikolaev, an illegal arms dealer who owned a legitimate natural gas company, said she had some information about Quantum Glitch. CIA director Robert Besserman told her to set up a direct meeting with Morgan May's team to reduce the chances of the intel being leaked or intercepted. But it wasn't just any random asset—it was one of Ryder's former flings, Sadie Marion.

Despite the passage of two years and the divergence of their paths within the U.S. intelligence community, Ryder still had feelings for Sadie. He'd wanted to stay with her, but when they talked about the fact that they'd have to either ditch their careers or split up, she said she wasn't willing to give up her job for him. Ryder would've happily done so, but he didn't get a chance to tell her what he wanted before she revealed her feelings. While he couldn't blame her, Ryder couldn't help but admit that it hurt.

The fact that she was now the mistress of a Russian oligarch meant she was tied to him for as long as the agency deemed necessary. And if Nikolaev wasn't the one to break it off with her, she'd likely be looking over her shoulder for the rest of her life. That fact alone dashed Ryder's hopes that he would one day get back together with her.

But then he saw her walking toward him at the riverside cafe along the cobblestone streets of Paris. Sadie's shoulder-length blonde hair shimmered as it bounced with each step. She wore large sunglasses and a wide-brimmed hat, giving her both an air of anonymity and a hint of mystery. Women who dressed like that in Paris typically attracted attention, though he knew she didn't want any.

She walked right past him, discreetly dropping a business card on his table. Ryder didn't react, waiting until the man on the other side of the street trying to secretly snap pictures without her knowledge left before moving. Then Ryder followed the instructions on the card, to meet her at the back corner booth at a cafe around the corner. Ryder followed instructions and was the first one to the table. Sunshine streamed into the skylight overhead, brightening up the shop. Hazelnut and chocolate roasted coffee beans filled the air, an aroma that Ryder found almost intoxicating. He studied the menu for a couple of minutes before Sadie finally entered, her knee-length green skirt flowing as she strode toward him and sat down.

"Let me know if anyone comes in after me," she said, her back to the door. "I know this goes against agency protocol, but I need to at least give off some semblance of normalcy in case that creep tries to photograph me again."

"Is he paparazzi?" Ryder asked. "Because I can take care of him if you want me to."

"I'm not sure who he is, but it's a little unsettling. He followed me for five blocks. I had to double back a few times to lose him, but I'm pretty sure I lost him."

"I saw him following you," Ryder said. "If he walks in here, I'll have a few words with him."

"Just don't," she said. "I don't need your machismo to protect me."

She didn't touch her sunglasses or hat, both still providing her with some level of protection.

"Okay, okay," he said. "Relax."

She offered a beleaguered smile.

"I miss seeing your beautiful eyes as well as that smile of yours," he said.

She waved dismissively. "Stop trying to butter me up, Dallas. You know nothing's going to happen. Why are you even trying?"

"I guess you just don't understand."

"I don't. And quite frankly, I don't want to at the moment. I need to tell you what I know. Get in, get out, get on. Got it?"

"All right. All business. I get it. So tell me what you told Besserman."

"If someone were to photograph me with you, Nikolaev would probably feed me to the sharks. But if I looked like I was enjoying myself, he'd disembowel me before turning me into chum."

"Point made."

Sadie scanned the room one final time before she leaned in close. Just as she was about to speak, a waiter approached their table and asked for their orders. They both ordered espressos, remaining quiet until he went behind the bar to make their drinks.

"So, I happen to know all the comings and goings of Nikolaev, mostly because I have to know his schedule better than he does in case his wife comes prowling around."

"Prowling around?"

"I don't know. That's how he describes it. He detests his wife, but he needs her political connections. And he's convinced that she would divorce him if she found out. It would also mean the end of my very fruitful assignment."

"Have you stopped any of his deals yet?"

"No, but that's not what we're trying to do. The agency has captured three of his buyers, which is ultimately what I'm there to do. Pass along the names of the people he speaks with and then let someone at the agency take it from there. You might recognize some of the names, some big in the world of terrorism, others just small players. But that's why the meeting with Quantum Glitch stood out to me. It jarred me, to be honest. It's unusual for him to meet with anyone like that. And since I know that the agency was hunting him, I thought I should let Besserman know about this opportunity."

"Do you know why they're meeting?"

She tucked her hair behind her ears. "No, but I think it has something to do with a conversation I heard him having with Jun Fang."

"Wait. Nikolaev is an associate of Fang's?"

She scrunched up her nose and shrugged. "I'm not sure I'd classify them as anything more than acquaintances, but Nikolaev is always trying to expand his operation. Maybe he heard that Fang was looking for something. But if Nikolaev is doing Fang a favor, I can almost guarantee you it's some kind of test to see how trustworthy my favorite oligarch is. So, whatever you do, you can't screw me on this."

"I wouldn't dream of it. The last thing I'd want to do is—"

"Yeah, yeah, yeah," she said. "I know. You don't want me to get hurt."

"So, when and where is this meeting taking place?"

"That's the thing. I don't know."

"You don't know? I came all the way to find out that you don't know?"

"Don't get your panties in a bunch," she snapped. "I don't know *exactly*, but I can tell you when they're meeting and give you an approximate location before giving you a more specific one."

He scowled, but she continued, apparently reading his thoughts by answering the obvious question on his mind.

"I gave him a good luck coin," she said. "It's got a GPS tracker embedded in it and will last up to six months. He just thinks it's something I gave him as a good-bye gift to remember me by. But it's letting me know his exact location."

"When is this meeting taking place?"

"Tonight."

"Where?"

"Well, he's on the Greek isle of Amorgos."

Ryder stared at her incredulously, tilting his head to one side. "Amorgos? What the hell good does that do us if they're meeting tonight?"

"You'll know where Quantum Glitch is."

"You think they're going to meet at some seaside villa that he owns?"

"No, but I know they won't do anything out in the open. There's a good chance that they will meet on Quantum's turf, his terms. I heard them talking on the phone. I think Nikolaev thought I was asleep. I was lying on my side and eavesdropped while Nikolaev only listened, furiously scribbling down instructions from Quantum. Right after they discussed their rendezvous time, Nikolaev retreated to his study and closed the door, shutting me out of the conversation. But based on what I've read about Quantum Glitch, he's too private and wouldn't dare risk being seen in public."

"There's a reason he's never been caught, though we almost caught him—but that's another story for another day. There's no guarantee that Quantum's going to be there tomorrow when we get there."

"No, but it'll at least be a starting point, which is better than what you've got right now from what I understand."

The waiter returned to the table with their drinks and hustled away again.

"I wish you would've given us this information earlier," he said.

"It wouldn't have mattered. I didn't know where he was going until his plane landed today. For some reason, he kept this meeting secret from everyone on his yacht's staff. And I couldn't have you meet me in Venice where I was with him. Whenever I'm with him and I go out by myself, he sends two bodyguards to tag along and watch me. You don't understand just how deep I'm in with him right now."

"But he lets you just jet off to Paris?"

She smiled and nodded. "It's his way of indulging me for indulging him."

"I don't know how you do it," he said, shaking his head.

"It's not easy, but I do it because I know it's for the good of the country, the good of the world."

Ryder reached his hand across the table and touched hers. She drew it back quickly.

"Ryder," she snapped.

"Sorry, I just—I just miss you and—"

"Damnit, stay focused, will you? For both our sakes."

He sighed. "Well, thanks for the information. I'll be awaiting confirmation of the exact location whenever it's time for his meeting."

"I'll text you from my burner phone," she said. "But I must warn you that whatever is happening, it's going to be big."

"What do you mean?"

"The only other piece of intel I gleaned while eavesdropping on Nikolaev's conversation with Fang was that The Alliance was about to unleash its biggest operation to date."

"That's saying something given the stunts Fang has tried to pull recently."

"Yeah," she said. "Fang called it Operation Nightfall."

"Did he mention any other details?"

Sadie shook her head. "Nothing. But I thought I'd give you a heads up in case you hear that term again. Something big is going down."

"And we'll be ready when it does," Ryder said before pausing, "*if* it does."

"Thanks for the coffee," she said before sliding out of the bench and disappearing out the back door, leaving Ryder to pay for the drinks.

She's the one with the Russian oligarch's credit card, but I'm the one stuck with the bill.

Ryder forked over the money to the waiter and left a few minutes later, following the same route Sadie took out the backdoor. He went through the alley, sidestepping several garbage cans overflowing with trash. The mix of fresh croissants, roasted coffee, and restaurant trash almost made Ryder retch. His stomach was already gurgling when a man smoking a cigarette while leaning against a wall at the end of the alley sucker-punched Ryder in the gut.

Ryder's knees buckled as he pitched forward and fell on the ground. The smoker raised his boot heel and prepared to crush the back of Ryder's head with it. But he rolled over in time to see the impending attack and spin aside. With the man off balance, Ryder yanked on his foot and then spun into a position that gave him a clear shot at the side of the man's knees. Ryder unleashed a vicious kick, cartilage groaning and creaking as his foot drove hard into the man's leg. He yelped in pain and tried to scramble into position to fight, but he couldn't move his leg, dragging it aside.

Ryder seized the advantage, charging the smoker and forcing him against the brick wall. More cracking of his bones as his head snapped back. Blood oozed from his head and down his neck. Ryder made the bleeding symmetrical when he drove the base of his palm up into the man's nose. More cartilage, more groaning. The man had a thick Russian accent and pleaded for mercy. But Ryder knew better. The man had been sent there to kill him. And while whoever had done such a thing would possibly do it again, it wouldn't be this guy.

Ryder jammed his Sig P365 rigged with a suppressor into the man's chest and pulled the trigger twice. The smoker crumpled to the ground, blood blooming from the entry point on his white shirt. Ryder shoved the lifeless body to the ground before searching for his wallet. He didn't have any identification on him, so Ryder took a picture of the dead man's face before covering his body with trash in the alley. Someone would find him soon, but Ryder wouldn't be to blame. He doubled back down the alley toward the back entrance to the coffee shop and headed toward the bathroom to clean up. He cleaned his hands of the blood and exited through the front door.

After traveling two blocks, Ryder called Hawk.

"That took you a while," Hawk said.

"I ran into some trouble in the back alley."

"But you handled it apparently."

"Yeah, but we've got something else that demands our immediate attention."

"Oh," Hawk said. "Did Sadie tell you where we could find Quantum Glitch?"

"Not exactly, but I know where we need to go," Ryder said.

FIVE

AMORGOS ISLE, GREECE

HAWK STOOD ON THE BALCONY OF HIS HOTEL AND looked out across the choppy Mediterranean Sea. The salty air whipped across his face and tousled his hair. Leaning forward on the railing, he drew in a deep breath and watched a pair of fisherman sling a net out across the water. Their way of life was simpler, devoid of all the trappings that accompanied his. Hawk couldn't help but feel a twinge of jealousy, not only for himself but for the majority of the Western world. The advances of the modern technology may have brought people together in unfathomable ways, but it had also stolen quiet moments like the one he was witnessing. But that's why he did what he did. As frenetic and unsettling as life had become for most people, he knew the evil that sought to disrupt what precious peace remained would be more pronounced if he and others like him weren't fighting it.

As Hawk scanned the beach, he noticed an elderly couple making their way along the sand, pants legs hiked up and cuffed to avoid getting wet. They held hands and occasionally stopped to look at one another and laugh. He hoped he'd get to do that one day with Alex, just two old souls lost in the moment.

His phone buzzed, jolting him back to reality. It was Alex.

"I was just thinking about you," he said as he answered.

"Good things, I hope," she said.

"Always."

"You'll never guess who I ran into today while little J.D. and I were catching our connecting flight in Salt Lake."

"Who?"

"Sid Weston."

Alex recounted the interaction to Hawk, including J.D. blurting out that they were going to Aruba.

"I know you met him a couple of times, but he wasn't my favorite person when I was training with the SEALs," Hawk said. "Something about him always seemed a little bit off to me."

"Did he ever do anything to you?"

"No, not personally. But you know how you just get a feeling about someone?"

"Yeah."

"Well, he just always struck me the wrong way. But that was a long time ago."

"He was nice to J.D. and even told him about his son Steel, who's the same age as J.D."

"I could be wrong," Hawk said with a sigh. "I've been wrong before."

"How's the op going?" Alex asked, apparently wanting to move on from the topic.

"So far, so good. Quantum Glitch is holed up at a monastery, and I'm going to see if I can penetrate it and pull the little bastard out."

"Be careful, honey."

"You know me."

"That's why I said be careful."

Hawk chuckled. "Give little J.D. my love—and punch big J.D. in the arm for me and tell him to drink a glass of bourbon for me."

"He's already had two glasses of the stuff today. Now whether or not they were in your honor, I don't know. But he's definitely —shall I say—more relaxed."

"Enjoy yourselves and stay close to your phone in case we need you."

"Of course. Good luck," she said before ending the call.

Hawk pocketed his phone and looked out across the water again.

Ryder slid open the glass door and walked onto the balcony. "You ready?"

Hawk nodded. "Does a cat have climbing gears?"

"Maybe I should ask if you're ready to be all holy for a few days?"

"I went to church growing up," Hawk said. "I know how to act when I need to."

"But did you go to a Greek orthodox church?"

"I'm sure I'll learn a few new things."

"I guarantee you they won't be asking you to sing only the first, second, and fourth stanzas of *Just As I Am*."

Hawk cast a suspicious glance at Ryder. "*Just As I Am* has six verses."

Ryder winked. "I was just testing you. I'm sure you'll do fine."

"We'll see. But I'm quite certain that I'm not cut out for the monastic life."

"All you have to do is play along for a day or two until you find Quantum Glitch. Shouldn't be too difficult."

"Let's hope not."

A HALF-HOUR LATER, Hawk was sitting in a parked car outside the path leading to St. George's Monastery, which wasn't visible from the interior of the island. A well-marked trail disappeared into a cluster of trees and wound its way toward a small ridge. Below it, the monastery had been carved into the mountain, providing both privacy and seclusion. It also gave the facility security, albeit a natural form.

Hawk reviewed their protocol for getting him the tech that he needed. His bag would be thoroughly searched as a temporary guest at St. George's where all forms of technology were forbidden. According to the monastery's website—one which was monitored by a nearby orthodox church on Amorgos—all retreat guests were prohibited from bringing any items inside and would be searched. The purpose for the lack of electronic devices was to "cultivate an environment more conducive to connecting with God." While the restriction was almost guaranteed to lengthen his stay, he didn't mind. He couldn't help but admit that he was looking forward to being in a place where people were forced to talk with one another instead of staring absent-mindedly at their phones for hours on end. That's what it had been like for Hawk growing up, but he'd almost forgotten the simplicity of just sitting with another person and talking without being distracted by pings, bloops, and bings that held an unrivaled sway over most people.

"Good luck," Ryder said as Hawk opened the passenger side door.

"How about something a little more appropriate," Hawk said, "like God bless?"

"Good luck *and* God bless," Ryder said with a wry grin. "I like to cover all my bases."

Hawk slung his pack over his shoulder and strode toward the path, giving a quick glance over his shoulder as Ryder and Mia drove away. For the next few minutes, Hawk meandered along a serene path, one shaded by trees growing on both sides of it. Then he reached a suspension bridge that spanned a gorge about a hundred feet deep. Hawk scanned the area before crossing, the bridge swaying with each step. After reaching the other side, he wound his way through the path that ascended up the mountain toward the ridge and then over it. He went down a series of steps cut out of the mountain until he came to a large pair of wooden doors. He tried the handle and pushed it open, easing inside and then shutting it behind him.

"Hello?" Hawk cried.

After a brief moment, a monk approached Hawk. "Are you here for a retreat?"

Hawk nodded.

The monk glanced down at his clipboard. "Name?"

"Todd Chason," Hawk said.

"Ah, there you are," the man said as he scribbled something on the paper. "Right this way, Mr. Chason."

The monk led Hawk down a long hallway where they were joined by two other monks. They led Hawk to his room but remained to inspect his bag. Once they were satisfied that he hadn't smuggled in any contraband, they left.

The first monk stayed and then handed Hawk a slip of paper. "This is our schedule each day. Nothing is mandatory, but we think you'll get more out of your retreat if you interact with the other men here. We're all on a similar journey and think you'll benefit from listening to others and the places they've been while exploring their faith."

"Looking forward to it," Hawk said with a smile.

"Excellent. If you have any questions, I'm three doors down the hall on the right. Any time, day or night, don't hesitate to reach out and ask any questions. Priest Pappas will stop by within the hour to discuss other ways we might assist you while you're here on this retreat."

The man spun on his heels and exited the room, closing the door behind him.

Hawk sat on the bed and studied the room. The stucco walls were smooth but barren. Aside from a simple wooden bed frame and lumpy mattress, the only other items in the room were a desk and chair—and a robe on a hanger dangling from a hook on the back of the door. Hawk tossed his bag at the foot of the bed and then laid down. He wasn't supposed to connect with Ryder and Mia until later that night. And while he wanted to snoop around, he recognized that it was risky. If he got caught, the operation would be over and they might lose Quantum Glitch yet again.

The candle on the desk flickered, casting a shadow on the opposite wall in the room. Hawk had been so busy mentally mapping out the monastery that he'd almost forgotten that the place was devoid of electricity—or was it? He could've almost sworn he saw a cord running from the back of a clock in the lobby and into the wall. If there was no electricity at the monastery, a hacker couldn't have been there.

Hawk interlaced his fingers behind his head and stared at the ceiling. He thought about Alex and little J.D.—and God. It seemed like the most appropriate mental exercise to do there. But Hawk lasted all of five minutes before he grew bored and decided to explore. However, as he placed his hand on the knob, it turned and he jumped back. The door swung open and another man stepped inside.

"Mr. Chason?" the man asked.

Hawk nodded but didn't say a word.

"Andrew Pappas," the man said, offering his hand. "I'm in charge of the monastery here. Welcome to our humble abode."

Hawk shook the man's hand. "Thank you for allowing me to visit on such short notice."

"It's nothing," the man said, waving dismissively at Hawk. "We want to keep our doors open to anyone who desires to make a connection with God. And you seemed very sincere in your letter."

"I was—uh, am," Hawk stammered. "I am very sincere."

"Well, I suppose that you've been briefed on the schedule we keep around here, but you're free to approach this time however you wish. The only times we can't make special exceptions for are the meals. Those are served daily at seven a.m., noon, and six p.m., all without exception."

"I understand," Hawk said.

"Good. I hope you enjoy the rest of your time here. Just

remember to be mindful of the other guests here and the journey that they're on."

"Of course."

Pappas patted Hawk on the back. "I've got a good feeling about you." Then the priest spun and exited the room.

Hawk remained in his room until he heard the bells chime for dinner. He joined the rest of the monks in the dining hall, where a brief prayer was pronounced over the meal and then lines were formed to receive it. Beef stew and a piece of fresh baked bread served as the meal. Hawk scarfed down the food without saying a word.

One of the monks stared wide-eyed at Hawk before addressing him in an Irish accent. "Don't they feed ya where you come from, lad?"

Hawk froze and looked up, the final spoonful at his lips. He slurped it up before forcing a smile. "Me?"

"Yes, you," the monk said. "You're the only one who looks like you've got to go put out a fire after supper."

Hawk eyed the man for a moment.

"Michael McAlistair," the man said, extending his hand.

The two men shook. "Todd Chason," Hawk said before they both got up and handed their dirty dishes to the pair of monks standing behind the counter.

"First time here?" McAlistair asked.

"Was it that obvious?" Hawk said with a grin.

"Let's go talk in the courtyard."

Hawk followed McAlistair to an open-air courtyard, one where a hole had been cut in the rock, allowing natural light to pour in. But at this time of day, there was no direct sunlight.

"So, what brings you here?" McAlistair asked, gesturing toward a bench. "Doing a little soul searching?"

"I'm definitely doing some searching," Hawk said, proud that he could answer the question truthfully.

"What are you looking for exactly?"

Hawk shrugged. "Whatever I can find."

"There has to be a better reason than that."

"Honestly, I'm here to pray for all the evil in the world to end —and do whatever I can to stop it."

"Now we're getting somewhere. What kind of evil are we talking about?"

"The kind that wraps its bony fingers around your soul and refuses to let go."

McAlistair's eyes widened. "Oh, *that* kind of evil."

"It's the worst—and it needs to be defeated."

McAlistair steepled his fingers. "But does it really?"

Hawk scowled. "What do you mean?"

"What about redemption? I think it's important that even the most vile among us have a chance to be redeemed. No one is ever beyond God's grace."

"You haven't met some of the people I have. Besides, didn't God let some of those people in the Bible receive what they deserved?"

"Yes, but we must be careful in thinking we know when people don't deserve another chance. God is the God of second chances. And third. And fourth. And fifth."

"Okay, okay," Hawk said. "I get it. But there are some people who will never learn. And those are the people who met God's judgment."

"What if you had met God's judgment before you met him?"

Hawk pursed his lips and nodded slowly. "Fair point. But I still think it's important for me to introduce some of these people to their maker."

"So, you're a killer?"

"No," Hawk said. "I wouldn't characterize myself like that. I just like to make introductions."

McAlistair sighed. "Well, may God bless you during your time here this week."

"Thank you."

Hawk remained in the room until the bells tolled at 4 p.m., signaling an hour of silence and contemplation. Everyone was required to retreat to their rooms, giving Hawk a chance to do some unabated exploring. He waited ten minutes before venturing outside his room and searching the monastery.

He meandered down dark hallways, looking for any clues as to where Quantum Glitch might be holed up. He at least knew what the hacker looked like, though Hawk doubted the man would be out and about. But after a half-hour of wandering the halls of St. George's Monastery, Hawk hadn't found anything of note. He tried not to get frustrated, though he realized he'd become more familiar with the layout, which would be helpful when he resumed his search later that night.

As Hawk was walking back to his room, he heard the scuffing of feet on the stone floor. He froze, plastering himself against the wall. He didn't breathe, hoping whoever else was out would not hear him and go in a different direction.

But that was a foolish dream.

"Mr. Chason," came the familiar voice, "what are you doing out right now? This is a time of silence."

"Just wanted to walk and pray," Hawk said.

"You know that lying in the house of God will get you killed? Ever hear of a couple named Ananias and Saphira?"

"I think I remember the story."

"If you did, you wouldn't have lied to me," McAlistair said. "Now, what are you really doing out of your room?"

"What about that grace?" Hawk asked. "I think now would be a good time to believe me and give me a second, third, or fourth chance."

McAlistair's face relaxed before breaking into a broad grin. "Get on out of here right now. And I won't tell a soul what I saw."

"Thank you," Hawk said.

He turned and headed straight to his room.

Where is Quantum hiding?

SIX

AMORGOS ISLE, GREECE

LATER THAT NIGHT AFTER DINNER, HAWK JOINED THE rest of the monks in the chapel for a time of prayer and reflection. He took a seat in the back and surveyed the men, looking for Quantum Glitch. While the intel Ryder had received from Sadie was that Nikolaev had met the infamous hacker at the monastery, Hawk was beginning to wonder if the two men had left together. So far, nothing pointed to the fact that St. George's was harboring a fugitive.

This was a waste of time.

Hawk returned to his room after the service and decided to leave in the morning. He contemplated ditching the rendezvous at midnight before sticking with the plan.

Once the monastery fell quiet, he eased into the hall and slipped outside beneath the moonless sky. The waves crashed against the rocks on the cliffs below. Hawk found the set of steps leading to the top of the ridge that Mia had spotted while studying images of the monastery. He climbed them until he reached the top and waited.

Hawk found a flat area and sat down. A few minutes later,

Ryder flashed a signal from a small boat offshore, letting Hawk know they were about to send the package. Five minutes later, he heard the faint buzz of a small drone speeding toward him. The winking lights beneath the drone allowed Hawk to follow it until it reached the space just above him. Then the drone lowered slowly and released a black box. Hawk caught it and gave a thumbs-up to the drone's camera before it sped back to the boat.

Hawk had used the device designed by the Magnum Group's lead technical engineer Dr. Z several times in the past but for other purposes. It detected the smallest of electrical impulses, used to locate bombs hidden in walls or listening devices. If Quantum Glitch was hiding in the monastery, Hawk figured there was no way he'd be doing so without access to his laptop, even though using any electronic devices was against the rules.

Hawk activated the detector and then hustled down the steps back to the monastery. He stealthily re-entered the building and then began navigating the halls with the device in hand to see if there was anything behind the closed doors. He explored two floors to no avail. Room after room showed nothing but silence, not even the faintest signal that any electronics were being used anywhere.

Guess these guys are serious about the rules.

Hawk was heading back to his room when one of the doors swung open, catching him by surprise. The candles flickering on the wall illuminated the monk's face. It was McAlistair.

"So, what's your excuse this time?" McAlistair asked, his eyes narrowed.

"I wanted to get outside and connect with God in nature," Hawk said, his answer sounding more sure than when he'd been interrogated by the monk earlier that day.

"Then why are you coming from that direction?"

"I had to use the restroom. When nature calls—"

"But the restroom is over there," McAlistair said, pointing in the opposite direction from where Hawk had come.

"I knew it had to be over there," Hawk said. "I couldn't find it and—"

McAlistair's eyes darted toward Hawk's hands. "What's that?"

"It's nothing," Hawk said. "Just a little recording device so I can capture my prayers and thoughts instead of writing them down. My hands cramps up easily when I'm journaling."

"Show me how it works," McAlistair said.

"I'd rather not. My prayers are personal between me and God."

"If I don't hear them, there will be consequences."

Hawk sighed. "Look, that's not something I'm comfortable with."

"You're lying," McAlistair said. "And I don't appreciate you making a mockery of this holy institution."

"I'm not mocking it, I swear," Hawk said. "I have respect for this place and for you and what you're doing."

"But not enough respect to tell me the truth."

"I know it may look strange, but I very much want to stay."

"Are you sure?"

Hawk nodded. "Yes. I want to be here. I *need* to be here."

"Then let's find out just how badly you want to stay. Come with me."

McAlistair gestured for Hawk to follow, leading him down a hallway and then to a set of stairs that Hawk hadn't noticed before. They descended two flights before walking down another corridor. At the end, there was a wooden door with a small rectangular opening about eye level. McAlistair opened the door and indicated inside.

Hawk eased into the room. But before he knew what was happening, McAlistair yanked the door shut and locked it.

"Hey, what's going on?" Hawk shouted as he rushed to the door and peered through the slit. "What are you doing?"

"Seeing if you're telling me the truth for once. If you really want to be here, you can stay. Otherwise, you can go home."

41

Hawk sighed and slumped against the door, sliding to the cold stone floor. A few seconds passed before he heard the sound of footsteps fading down the hall. He surveyed the room, which was lit by a single candle. His new home at St. George's wasn't that different from his other room. It had a bed and a chair with a small desk. A Bible and a stack of paper rested in the center of it. The only difference was there was a lock—and it was on the outside.

He closed his eyes, growling as he replayed the events of the past few minutes in his mind. Not for a second did he think he'd become a prisoner at the monastery. And while it angered him, it also gave Hawk reason to consider that maybe there was something the monastery was hiding—and maybe that something was Quantum Glitch.

Hawk awoke with a start, the jangling of keys and a gruff voice disturbing his peaceful sleep. He was disoriented for a few seconds as his candle had burnt out. But the room was still light, this time from a different source, one that appeared to float across the room.

"Time for breakfast," said a monk flanked by two other burly men.

Hawk studied them both and knew he could dispatch all three in a matter of seconds. But this wasn't the time. The drastic decision to place him in solitary confinement seemed to suggest that there was something else that the monastery didn't want him to know about.

Why not kick me out?

Hawk wondered why they wouldn't just send him home, especially if they thought he was snooping around and wasn't a serious guest.

Why lock me up?

Then Hawk looked around his room and realized his black box was gone.

"Come on, sir. Are you going to eat or not?" the monk asked as he placed a tray on Hawk's desk.

Hawk nodded absent-mindedly. "Yeah, sorry. I was just lost in thought."

"Hopefully thoughts about what you did last night."

"Of course," Hawk said. "That's all I've been thinking about."

The monk glanced over his shoulder at the other two men. "I can take it from here."

The two men exited the room, the footsteps growing fainter with each step. The monk craned his neck toward the door and waited until no more feet scuffling along the floor could be heard.

"Are you all right?" Hawk asked.

The man closed the door behind him and nodded. "I know why you're here."

"You do? Does that have anything to do with my black box being confiscated?"

"I don't know anything about that," the monk said as he sat down on the bed. "But I know you're not here to connect with God, are you?"

"What if I told you no?"

"Then, my hunch would be correct and I'd tell you the information you came here seeking."

"Then, no. I'm not here for any spiritual reasons, though I'm not opposed to that."

"You came here looking for a hacker, didn't you?"

Hawk nodded. "Will you help me find him?"

"I know where they're hiding him—well, I know where McAlistair is hiding him."

"McAlistair?"

"Yeah, the man you're looking for is McAlistair's brother."

"So, he does believe in grace, after all. He just doles it out to who he sees fit."

"Maybe. McAlistair believes in God, but he also believes in money. And his brother donates a hefty sum each year to St. George's Monastery. It's why we don't have to do anything like brew beer or make and sell something. We're completely funded by a hacker known as Quantum Glitch."

"And how do you know this?"

"It's one of the worst kept secrets here. But we all knew this day would come. And to be honest, I'm glad you came looking for the man. It's done nothing but distract us from our true mission. Everyone has become so inwardly focused that we've lost our ability to perform our calling, which is to help the people on this island."

"So, you want me to help you by getting rid of him?"

The monk nodded and offered his hand. "My name's Judas."

Hawk's eyes widened. "I'm Todd Chason. And I don't believe I've ever met someone by that name."

"My father hated God, thought it'd be funny to name me Judas. As it turns out, God has a funny sense of humor."

"And you kept the name?"

"It reminds me every day that I could betray God if I'm not careful."

"But you're okay with betraying McAlistair?"

"One man's betrayal is another man's loyalty. Now, do you want to find Quantum Glitch?"

"Let's go," Hawk said.

They descended another set of stairs at the end of the hall before Judas pointed at the door.

"He's in there," Judas whispered. "Good luck."

Judas hustled down the hall and back up the stairs. Hawk waited until he was gone and grabbed the handle. With a deep breath, he twisted the knob and entered the room. Quantum Glitch was seated at a modern glass table against the far wall in front of a bank of monitors, his fingers flying across the keyboard. At the sound of the door opening, he spun around and locked eyes with Hawk.

"So much for no modern technology here," Hawk said.

Quantum glared at Hawk but didn't say a word. Instead, he slammed his laptop shut, slid it into a bag that he flung over his shoulder, and headed straight for the door. Hawk grinned as the slight man barreled toward him.

But just as Hawk prepared to grab the man and toss him to the floor, he reached in his bag and pulled out a can. Then he aimed it at Hawk and pushed down. A stream of mist shot toward Hawk and splattered against his face. The liquid burned, his eyes tearing up. He staggered forward, trying to wipe away the substance. And as he did, it gave Quantum the opening he needed to escape.

Hawk spun but was too late. The diminutive man zagged left and then right before zipping past him and up the stairs. Hawk staggered toward the desk, stabilizing himself by resting one hand on the back of his chair while trying to clear his vision. As he wiped away the tears streaming out of his eyes to cleanse the liquid, he noticed a flash drive on the desk and pocketed the device. After a few more seconds, he started to see more clearly, though the searing pain still throbbed in his face. He rushed into the hallway after Quantum, who had developed a big head start.

Hawk raced past other monks walking solemnly toward the chapel. He bowled over a few as he tried to maintain visual of Quantum.

The hacker raced down the steps leading out of the monastery, taking two at a time. Hawk kept running, even though he could tell he was losing ground. However, he stopped when he came to the suspension bridge. By the time he reached it, his vision had started to clear. He wiped away his tears and stared out at Quantum, who was halfway across the bridge.

Hawk took a deep breath and then sprinted toward his target.

But as Hawk reached the midway point, Quantum was already on the other side. He stopped and turned back to look at his pursuer before a smile played across his lips. Quantum reached into his bag and produced a key. He slid it into a slot and turned.

Then he hit a button. Within seconds, the taut rope holding up the suspension bridge went slack. Before Hawk realized what was happening, the bridge's planks dropped from beneath him. He spun and reached for the steel rope, still tethered to the monastery's side of the ravine. His hands burned as they slid down the only thing preventing him from plummeting into the canyon below. Finally, he slowed his momentum and stopped.

Spinning to look to the other side of the canyon, he scanned the area for Quantum, catching a glimpse of him as he darted into the trees. Hawk clambered up the rope, his heart hammering in his chest. He slowly worked his way up the rope until he reached solid ground. He looked across the ravine and into the woods. Quantum was gone.

Hawk cursed under his breath.

A man clucked his tongue. Hawk turned to see McAlistair shaking his head.

"That's not appropriate language for any man of God to be using," he said.

"And how would you know?" Hawk quipped.

McAlistair chuckled. "Oh, Mr. Chason. What a fool you are. I suggest you get on your way and never come back."

"I paid for a week."

"You didn't come here for a week of solitude. You came here for trouble. Now, there's a path about a mile east that will get you back across the canyon. Best of luck in your journey and may you find whatever it is that you're looking for."

The monk turned and walked away.

"I'm looking for your brother," Hawk growled.

McAlistair stopped and spun toward Hawk. "What did you say?"

"You heard me," Hawk said. "And I'm going to find him, too."

Hawk dug his hand into his pocket and felt the flash drive. He didn't have Quantum Glitch, but at least he had something.

SEVEN

VENICE, ITALY

Beneath a dusky sky, Robert Besserman navigated the crowded walkways connecting Italy's famous floating city. He stopped at the top of a bridge spanning a canal and watched a young couple cuddling at the front of a gondola while the gondolier propelled the boat forward with his long oar while belting out a song. The man's baritone voice echoed off the walls of the surrounding building, arresting the attention of a handful of pedestrians.

"That man should be on the stage at La Scala," said a man in a thick accent.

Besserman turned to his left to see Klaus Schreiber, the chief of German intelligence. Tieless in a gray suit, Schreiber wore a pair of sunglasses and held a smoldering pipe.

"Is the sun's glare too much for you right now?" Besserman asked.

Schreiber smiled. "I read that the moon is going to be bright tonight. One must be prepared for anything in our business."

"Anything in particular I need to be aware of?"

"There's a good pub around the corner," Schreiber said as the gondolier continued to croon. "I'll tell you all about it there over a pint."

"Please, lead the way," Besserman said.

Neither man spoke until they were comfortably seated in a booth at the back of a pub packed with customers, most of whom were enthralled with the soccer match playing on every television.

"How productive do you think this summit is going to be?" Besserman asked.

Before Schreiber could answer, a waitress sauntered over and took their drink orders. Once she left, Schreiber removed a lighter from his pocket and relit the tobacco in his pipe.

"I'm not as concerned with what's being presented as much as I am with gauging who's interested in partnering with me to stop some of these threats," he said. "And they seem to be popping up with increasing regularity, which I find extremely disturbing."

"That makes two of us."

"However, most of these threats can be handled with relative ease. You just need patience and the right people in place. But not all threats are created equal."

Besserman arched an eyebrow. "The Alliance certainly seems to be in a league of its own right now."

Schreiber sucked on his pipe before exhaling a stream of smoke out of the corner of his mouth. He nodded and looked down at the table.

"Not only are they the biggest threat, but it's one that's strengthening with each passing day that we don't take action to dismantle it. The problem at the moment for us is that Jun Fang is the one attracting all the headlines, distracting us from the network that's being constructed beneath the surface. Even if we eliminated Jun Fang today, The Alliance would remain strong, perhaps stronger than ever since we might assume that we chopped off the head of the snake. But The Alliance is more like Medusa, a head teeming with serpents. You cut off one and there are dozens more to replace it."

"Are you suggesting that Jun Fang is merely a figurehead?"

"I think Mr. Fang is being used as a distraction at best. At worst, he's trying to seize control of The Alliance. But I don't think that's even possible."

"What do you mean?"

"As you know, The Alliance has been a big mystery for a long time. From who's in charge to what the ultimate purpose of the group is, we've been in the dark for years—until now."

The waitress returned with their drinks, placing a pair of pints on the table before shuffling off to her next table.

"How'd you get this intel?" Besserman asked.

"A disgruntled member of The Alliance came to us with it."

"And how can you be sure that this informant doesn't have ulterior motives?"

Schreiber took another long drag on his pipe. "We can't be sure of much in this business, can we? But there comes a time when we have to take a chance and trust someone. Surely you understand that."

"Trust is earned," Besserman said.

"I thought it was 'trust, but verify'," Schreiber said.

"It's a good Russian proverb, but I have my own—Never trust anything a Russian says."

"Words to live by for anyone in intelligence. But unfortunately, we're not dealing with merely Russians in The Alliance. There are Germans, French, English—even Americans."

"Americans?"

Schreiber nodded. "According to our informant, most of the snakes are wealthy and very connected Europeans. And currently I'm working with financial sectors within the EU to determine how we can freeze the assets of some of these people. One of the biggest problems we have is that at least two members run some of the biggest banks in the world."

"But there are Americans involved as well?" Besserman persisted.

Schreiber reached into his pocket and produced an envelope. "Just one American that we know of."

He slid the envelope across the table to Besserman, who promptly opened it and scanned the document. When he finished, he cocked his head to one side and pursed his lips.

"So you don't actually know who this man is?"

"We have the code name he goes by."

"I saw that," Besserman said. "Remington Steele. Cute. But that doesn't help me much."

"Bobby, this organization is everything the terrorists we've been fighting for the past few decades is not. They are well funded. They are well organized. They are well connected. This isn't a bunch of angry Muslims living in the desert. In order to eliminate these people, it's going to take time and a coordinated effort on all our part. Otherwise, we might be in the middle of their sights if they manage to take control."

"We need to know their endgame."

"What difference does it make? Money? Power? Control? Revenge? Ultimately, it doesn't matter. What matters is that they could disrupt established systems that have helped the civilized people maintain peace for years."

"This is something we need to talk about at the summit," Besserman said. "We need buy-in from everyone."

"But the problem is I'm not sure we can trust everyone there. The Alliance has infiltrated so many power systems already."

"Or they're finding people already in those positions and adding them to their payroll."

Schreiber puffed on his pipe. "Also a winning strategy, especially with the seemingly endless resources they possess."

"Do you know if there are any intelligence chiefs who've been compromised?"

Schreiber shook his head. "None that I know of, but I suspect a couple. And for now, I'm avoiding them."

"Doesn't sound like you believe in 'trust, but verify' either."

Schreiber smiled and pointed at Besserman. "Your wit never disappoints, Bobby."

"We need a list of those we can trust and develop a way to

communicate within that circle so we can start to strike back against The Alliance."

"I have some ideas on that."

"Good," Besserman said before taking a sip of his beer. "And I think you've convinced me that Fang is little more than a magician's sleight of hand, something designed to get us to focus our attention on him while the real threat is realized elsewhere."

"I have a small trusted task force monitoring the people we suspect of involvement with the organization, but that's all we've been able to do at the moment. And there's nothing actionable yet."

Besserman scooped up the envelope and tapped it before sliding it into his coat pocket. "And I'll poke around and see if I can determine who this Remington Steele guy is. It's going to be much easier once we determine the identity of our enemies. It's difficult to fight ghosts."

Their conversation shifted away from work to personal matters before they parted for the evening. Schreiber left first, while Besserman remained at the table finishing his beer while the other patrons watched the soccer match. After a few minutes, the crowd roared with a goal, setting off a wild celebration that included chants and then a song.

I'll never understand the draw of that game.

Besserman paid for the drinks and then slipped back onto the Venetian walkways, mostly empty. He assumed it had something to do with everyone watching the Italian national soccer team.

As he rounded the corner to his hotel, he felt a hand grab his bicep and give it a firm tug. He spun around to see a woman in a long trench coat facing him. Samantha Williams, an Australian spy he'd once worked with several years ago, eyed him carefully.

"Sam," Besserman said, "where'd you come from?"

"Being in management has dulled your skills," she said. "I followed you for two blocks before approaching you."

"No need for the cloak and dagger bit," he said. "All you had to do was say my name."

"I had to make sure no one else was following you."

He furrowed his brow. "What's going on?"

"Do you remember the Saudi who was responsible for bombing that American base in Afghanistan?" she asked.

He nodded.

"He's here," she said.

"Where?"

"He's on a yacht moored in the harbor."

"Show me," Besserman said. "I'm going to be here for a few days. Maybe you can help me arrange for a little surprise visit."

EIGHT

MEDITERRANEAN SEA, OFF THE COAST OF GREECE

HAWK LEANED ON THE RAILING AND WATCHED THE water lap against the side of the boat. As the sun rose, it glinted off the rippling water. A lone seagull circled overhead, squawking at him. Ryder was on the deck ripping off a set of pushups, while Mia typed on her laptop. Hawk looked across the water at St. George's Monastery, which loomed over the coast and seemed to mock him. He wasn't positive but he thought he saw McAlistair standing on the veranda and looking out across the horizon.

Less than twenty-four hours earlier, Hawk had been in that monastery searching for the infamous hacker Quantum Glitch. But instead of capturing and interrogating him, Hawk was left with nothing but an encrypted flash drive and not a single lead on where the hacker might have gone.

He pushed off the rail and turned toward Mia. "Any luck yet?"

"No," she said, her voice revealing her disappointment. "I don't know what I expected. It's not like this belonged to the world's foremost cyber genius."

"I'm sure you can figure it out. It just might take more time."

Ryder huffed out a breath. "And one hundred."

He jumped off the deck, sweat glistening on his shirtless chest. Mia glanced up at him and smiled.

"Like what you see?" he asked.

She rolled her eyes. "Better than what I'm seeing on this screen, which isn't saying much since I'm only staring at aggravation and disappointment."

"What's the problem?" he asked, ignoring her indifference and taking a seat next to her.

"Most of the time, it's easy to determine what kind of encryption is placed on a file," she said. "But it seems like Quantum has an encryption for the encryption. And I have no idea what it is."

"We need to catch a break," Hawk said. "If we can't use Quantum to figure out what The Alliance is doing, we need another way in."

"That would require knowing who else is involved in the organization aside from Fang," Ryder said.

"If I could get into this damn thing, maybe I could get us some names," Mia said, her fingers clicking on the keyboard.

Hawk turned back toward the water and watched a commercial fishing boat chug eastward in the distance. "If you were Quantum and just lost your plum monastery hideout where your brother ran cover for you, where would you go?"

Mia stood up and put her hands on her hips, staring pensively back toward the rocky coastline. "What if he didn't really go anywhere?"

Deep lines etched across Hawk's forehead. "What do you mean?"

"I mean, what if he's still in the monastery?" she said. "He ran away and then McAlistair sent you on a long walk through the woods to get to the nearest bridge that spanned the ravine. What if while you were doing that, they reattached the bridge? Didn't you say that just the bottom dropped out?"

"Yeah, but—"

54

"But what?" Ryder asked. "You don't want to admit that you were bamboozled by a hacker?"

"Nobody ever would want to admit that, but that's not it. I just don't see how they could repair it so quickly."

"Maybe that's not a flaw with the bridge—that's a design. And it can be quickly reattached."

Hawk thought for a second and then spun toward Mia. "Do you still have that drone?"

She nodded. "Why?"

"I want to borrow it for a minute, if that's all right."

"Sure."

She retreated below deck only to emerge a few minutes later with a small black case. Once she placed it on a table next to her laptop and unzipped it, she dug out the small object and handed it to him.

"Whatever you do, don't lose it," she said. "This is my baby."

"I'd never do anything like that," he said.

"My history with you says that you're lying and I'm going against my better judgment, but I'm going to give you a chance to prove yourself."

"Perfect," Hawk said. "I appreciate the opportunity to affirm your decision."

"Don't lose my drone," she said with a growl.

"I wouldn't dream of it."

A few minutes later, Hawk launched the drone and flew it toward the ravine that separated the portion of the cliff containing the monastery from the mainland. Using his phone to view the drone's camera, he watched as the bridge was completely intact as if it had never been rendered useless.

Hawk cursed. "There's no way they fixed the bridge that quickly."

"I told you," Ryder said, peeking at the screen over Hawk's shoulder. "That bridge was designed to do that."

Hawk swung the drone back around and brought it back to

the boat. He noticed some movement up on the ridge and grabbed a pair of binoculars.

"What do you see?" Mia asked.

"It's Judas."

"There's a monk there named Judas?" Ryder asked.

"Yeah. He's the guy who broke me out of their solitude chamber."

"So, prison?" Mia said.

"More or less. But he was the only ally I had there."

Hawk grabbed a sheet of paper from beneath the captain's wheel and scribbled out a quick note. He used a rubber band to attach the slip of paper to a pen and then place it in the drone's grasping mechanism before quickly launching the device again.

"Hey, what are you doing?" Mia asked, looking up from her laptop.

"I've got one more flight to make," Hawk said as he sent the drone racing toward the top of the ridge.

Once the drone reached the ridge, Hawk stopped it, hovering it front of Judas. He scowled at the object for a moment and then looked around. Hawk released the pen and paper. Judas picked it up and removed the paper from the pen, quickly reading the note. He offered a faint smile and shook his head. After writing out a response, he returned the pen to the drone, which then peeled away from the ridge and returned to the boat.

"What's it say?" Ryder asked as Hawk unfurled the note.

"What'd you ask?" Mia said.

"I asked him if Quantum was back at the monastery," Hawk said.

"And?" she said.

"He said he's gone, likely for good."

"So much for that lead," Ryder said.

Then his phone buzzed with a call from Sadie Marion.

"Speak of the devil," Ryder said as he answered the call and put it on speaker phone.

"Did you find Quantum?" she asked, dispensing with pleasantries.

"Yes," Hawk said, "but he escaped. Now he's in the wind and we don't have any more leads."

"Well, if you'd like to infiltrate The Alliance, you've got a chance tomorrow night," Sadie said. "We're in Venice now. I reunited with him this morning on his yacht."

"What's going down?" Ryder asked.

"Well, I'm not a hundred percent certain about this, but I've noticed a pattern with Nikolaev. He sends me off the boat once a month, booking me a room at a nearby hotel so he can be alone."

"Sure he doesn't have another mistress?" Hawk asked.

"I'm not sure about anything, but I don't think so. I've asked some of the staff before about these meetings and told them to be honest with me. One of the chefs doesn't mince words when sharing his feelings for how Nikolaev behaves. And he told me that he locks himself in the living area and gets on a video conference. Based on his secrecy, I can only assume that's when he meets with The Alliance, because he openly conducts other types of business with me in the room."

"So you think this might be our opportunity to find out who's part of Alliance leadership?" Hawk asked.

"That's what I was thinking," she said. "I thought about sneaking back on board to find out myself, but I'm afraid he would be enraged and maybe cut me off. Not to mention I'd have to slip the security detail he sends with me."

"Don't do anything stupid," Ryder said. "We'll figure out a way to drop in on him and find out what he's doing. Just send us the location of the yacht and we'll handle it from there."

"Okay," she said. "Be careful. Nikolaev's a dangerous man."

Ryder ended the call and pocketed his phone. He was still standing up when Hawk pushed forward on the throttle. Ryder stumbled forward before grabbing the table in front of Mia to stay on his feet.

"A little warning would've been nice," Ryder shouted.

Hawk feigned like he couldn't hear, cupping his hand to his ear. "What was that?"

"I said—"

But Hawk pushed the throttle all the way forward, drowning out Ryder's voice before shouting over his shoulder at his two colleagues.

"We've got to hurry," he said. "We've got a plane to catch."

NINE

VENICE, ITALY

HAWK JAMMED HIS HANDS INTO HIS POCKETS AS HE walked along the path just along the docks outside the Punta della Dogana museum. He chewed on a toothpick, taking in the wonder of Venice through a pair of dark sunglasses as the sun faded on the horizon. Ryder and Mia trailed behind him, chatting about the pasta they'd just inhaled at a local restaurant. Hawk's mind bounced between thinking about their impending operation and his family thousands of miles away.

On the flight from Greece to Venice, he'd taken advantage of the agency's robust communication system and called Alex to check in on her. From the way she described it, she was enjoying her time in Aruba with little J.D. exploring the island, and spending as much time as possible on the beach while building sandcastles. He wished he was there with them while working hard to shrug off the guilt that crept over him like the morning dew.

But Alex had assured him that she wouldn't hold it against him, promising that they would take a nice vacation when it was over with. Hawk chuckled when she'd told him that.

"What's so funny?" she'd asked.

"You remember our honeymoon, don't you?" he'd said. "Or at least our first attempt at one?"

"I remember it being cut short."

"Exactly. We make plans, but it's like they never happen. Well, maybe they do, but never like we hope they'll happen."

"That's called life," she'd said.

Alex's response had been cold, a nugget of truth served with a side of unflinching bitterness. Everything had been that way for him and Alex ever since they got married. Even their attempts to disappear into the hinterlands of Montana had been met with mixed results. Although they'd managed to enjoy some peaceful living afforded those who retreat to the hills, they hadn't managed to escape every manner of evil. Even living in solitude hadn't enabled them to evade pervasive evil, which had even literally come knocking at their cabin door.

Hawk had been thinking that maybe once he took care of The Alliance, he could retire and let go of his compulsion to do what he could to keep Americans safe from those who threatened to destroy the country. That long list of enemies included those who lived outside the country and some who resided within it. The idea that he could reach a stopping point seemed foreign to Hawk, even if that's what he hoped for deep down. There would always be another foe, another hostile, another force resistant to peace. And Hawk knew he would have to stop them, just like he was going to stop The Alliance. Just like he was going to stop Nikolaev.

Ryder's pace quickened as soon as he noticed Sadie Marion's flirtatious. She was leaning against the dock pylon and dangling a set of keys from her fingertips. Mia offered an exaggerated eye roll as he hustled toward Sadie.

It had been years since Hawk had seen Sadie, though the two of them had crossed paths several times in the past. He hadn't remembered her being so lively.

As she approached Ryder, she throttled her enthusiasm, stopping just out of arms reach.

"We are being watched," she said through gritted teeth, just audible enough for the trio to hear her. "So, be careful. I told them that you were college friends who wanted to tour the city on your own. Then I told them that Nikolaev said you could borrow his motorboat to get a different perspective from the water."

"That was quite kind of him," Mia said.

"It was a lie," Sadie said flatly. "But I figured it might be the best way to avoid drawing suspicion from the guards watching the boat from land."

"Smart thinking," Ryder said.

She offered a weak smile and gave a disinterested shrug.

"Where's Nikolaev's yacht?" Hawk asked.

"I sent a pin with it to Ryder from my burner phone," she said. "It was docked at the Santa Marta Yacht Pier on the western end of the Dorsoduro district, but he made his captain move it, anchoring it in the open bay further offshore."

"Why'd he do that?" Hawk asked.

"No idea. His decisions don't always make sense to me, but he's one of the most paranoid people I've ever met. So, there's a strong likelihood that he's worried about *something*."

Sadie shook Ryder's hand, depressing the key into his palm.

"We appreciate this," Ryder said.

"Yeah, well, don't get yourself killed, okay?" she said before tucking her hair behind her ears and walking away.

Hawk, Ryder, and Mia piled into the boat. After familiarizing himself with the controls, Hawk backed away from the dock and began to explore Venice through the canals that sliced through the floating city. Puttering along, they all kept a sharp eye out for anyone who might be following them or watching them. After an hour, they collectively agreed that if anyone had been tailing them, they were gone.

Hawk checked his watch as twilight fell over the city. They still had another half-hour before the meeting was scheduled to begin. In discussing how they wanted to approach Nikolaev, they'd agreed to wait until he was a few minutes into the meeting before coming alongside the boat. Hawk drove past the yacht, scouting out the best angle to come at it when they boarded. If Sadie's warning was accurate and Nikolaev had some of his men on shore watching his yacht, they wanted to make sure they couldn't be seen.

Hawk estimated Nikolaev's yacht was moored at least four hundred meters off shore. If security personnel were watching for Hawk and his team, they couldn't see the entirety of the ship, which had the port side shielded from any positions on the eastern side of the Venetian Lagoon. That provided more than enough space for them to stealthily converge on the yacht.

After one more lap around the city, Hawk feigned like he was going toward the mainland. Just as he drew within a couple hundred meters of the far end of the Venetian Lagoon, he swung the boat around and set a course for the port side of Nikolaev's yacht. Hawk looked up at the starry sky dotted with wispy clouds illuminated by the glow of the city lights. He closed his eyes for a moment, drinking in the small pleasure of speeding across the water in a boat in such a beautiful place on such a pleasant night. If it hadn't been for the breeze generated by their speed, he wasn't sure he'd even need a jacket. Everything was perfect.

He hoped he would feel the same way after he'd climbed aboard Nikolaev's ship and questioned him about The Alliance.

But that hope was short-lived when he spotted a raft on the port side of the yacht.

"What the hell is going on now?" Ryder said, pointing to the suspicious activity on the boat.

Hawk cursed under his breath, realizing that his plan had been instantly thwarted with not just a wrench but a violent wrecking ball.

"So, he's called someone from his security team to join him on board," Mia said. "What's the big deal? It's not like we can't handle him."

"Of course we can, but it draws into question everything else that Sadie told us," Hawk said. "And we haven't been watching the whole time. There could be others that have boarded before that man."

"Sadie told us what she knew," Ryder said, his tone defensive. "She would never set me up."

"I'm not suggesting she did," Hawk said. "I'm just simply saying that perhaps the intel she had about what was going to take place tonight wasn't entirely accurate."

"Or the plans changed," Ryder snapped.

"Or the plans changed," Hawk agreed. "I'm not throwing her under the bus. I'm just saying that the intel is no longer reliable."

"You want to abandon the op?" Mia asked.

"No, no. We just have to proceed much more cautiously. We can't assume that there are only two people on that ship. We have to approach it as if there are a dozen or more lying in wait."

Hawk eased back on the throttle as he drew within several hundred meters of the boat. But the team's confusion grew once they noticed the shadowy figure who'd boarded moments earlier repelling down the side of the yacht back to his inflatable raft with a sense of urgency. He shook the rope free and then yanked on the pull-starter of the small outboard engine. It coughed to life before reaching a high-pitched whine seconds later as the boat sped away from Nikolaev's ship.

Hawk cut the engine as he tried to digest what he'd just seen.

"What was that all about?" Mia asked.

"Beats the hell outta me," Ryder said. "But I can almost guarantee you that it wasn't good."

"Damn right, it wasn't," Hawk said. "There aren't many reasons you'd need to leave a boat that quickly."

"I can think of two," Ryder said.

"And?" Mia prodded.

"You're either fleeing the scene of a crime or—"

Before Ryder could finish his thought, Nikolaev's yacht exploded with a chest rattling boom that sent a fireball skyward, lighting up the night. Debris scattered in every direction with a few pieces coming within a few meters of their boat.

"What was that second reason you were going to give?" Mia asked.

"Or you set a bomb," Ryder added with a sigh. "And you need to get as far away as possible."

Hawk glanced back toward the city and saw the inflatable skipping across the water likely as fast as the engine could take the little vessel. Then a thought hit Hawk.

"That wasn't Nikolaev, was it?" he asked aloud.

"Think he wanted to make himself disappear?" Ryder asked.

"Maybe he wanted to disappear with Sadie and start a new life," Mia suggested.

"Why would he do that?" Hawk said. "He has everything he wants and more right now."

Ryder shook his head. "It just doesn't make sense. I don't think that was him."

"Well, I doubt we'll ever know now because I doubt there's much left of him, if anything, to test for a DNA match."

Ryder's phone buzzed with a call from Sadie. He showed the screen to Hawk, who winced.

"Hello," Ryder said, placing the call on speaker.

"What the hell did you guys do?" she screeched, speaking rapidly without pausing for a breath. "I told you where he was so you could talk to him, not so you could kill him. He was your only link to The Alliance as I understand it and—""

"Slow down," Ryder said. "We didn't kill him. But we saw the man who did."

"What are you talking about?"

"Hawk was bringing us in before we noticed a man in an inflatable raft tether himself to the yacht and scamper up the side using a rope. Then a minute or so later, he came flying across the deck and shimmied down into his boat and raced off. Once he got clear of the blast zone, the entire boat exploded. I swear, we had nothing to do with it."

Sadie cursed under her breath. "I can't believe this. You know how long I've been working undercover on this op? I was so close to getting some names of his buyers."

"Look, I'm sorry about all this," Ryder said. "I know that's got to be disappointing. But you need to trust me when I say this —we had nothing to do with this. We wanted Nikolaev alive too."

She sighed. "Just get out of there right now. You don't want to be anywhere near this thing when it goes down. Nikolaev's wife is going to have lawyers and investigators combing through every piece of evidence she can get her hands on. And if she thinks you're to blame, you're going to find yourself in a world of trouble."

"Copy that," Hawk said as he ignited the engine. "We're outta here."

Within seconds, their boat was skipping across the calm water of the lagoon, leaving Hawk to lament what could've been—and wonder who would've wanted to kill Nikolaev.

TEN

VENICE, ITALY

SADIE AWOKE WITH A START TO THE POUNDING ON HER hotel door and angry voices demanding she open it immediately. She groaned as she sat up and flung her feet onto the cold hardwood floor.

More pounding and yelling.

Her head ached, the result of too much wine after the incident. She wanted to stay at the restaurant where she'd been dining for as long as possible, long enough to be remembered by every member of the restaurant.

Just twelve hours earlier, Sadie had been on the balcony of the Mazzo restaurant, eating a delicious plate of tortelli di zucca when she saw the fireball that lit up the Venetian Lagoon. Based on the direction of the blast, she knew almost immediately that it was Nikolaev's yacht. She stood up and walked to the railing along with most of the other customers, taking in the dramatic scene unfolding on the water. A few gasps and shrieks were audible over the murmur of disbelief. Venice had its share of crime, but such brazen acts were rare. And the locals dining at Mazzo stood mouths agape.

Such violence wasn't new to Sadie. She'd found herself in the middle of firefights and street brawls during her time with the agency. But this felt different. She was working undercover, doing her best to extract the names and contacts of some of Nikolaev's best clients. They were men—and women, too—who saw violence as the primary means to get their way. Terrorists, activists, anarchists, rebels. They were all a motley bunch, hell bent on getting their way by might. And sometimes it even worked. But the cost was always high, taking the lives of innocent people, which never endeared them to others, oftentimes the same people they were fighting for. Sadie had long since learned that people don't care about a politician's policies if it kills them or the people they love. And she had a chance to stop the blood-letting, to save innocent people while capturing the evil people and shutting them down permanently. Now it was gone.

Unfortunately, the people outside her door weren't.

"I'm coming," she snapped.

Sadie secured a bathrobe around her with a quick knot and then padded to the door. After peering through the peephole, she sighed and slid off the safety lock. With another exasperated breath, she turned the handle and yanked open the door.

"Are you Sadie Marion?" the officer asked, his English surprisingly good though tinged with an Italian accent.

"Yes," she said flatly.

"Were you a traveling companion of Alexander Nikolaev?"

"Maybe."

"Maybe? We have it on good authority that you were."

"Depends on who's asking?"

"I'm asking," the man said with a growl. "Now, answer my questions truthfully or we can do it at the police station. It's your choice."

"Yes," she huffed, "I was with Alexander."

"When was the last time you saw him?" the detective asked as he checked his notes.

"Yesterday afternoon. He said he had some business to take

67

care of on the boat and that he needed some privacy for a meeting. So, he had one of the men on his security detail take me over via the boat we use for small excursions and told me he'd come get me in the morning."

"You don't seem surprised that I'm here," the officer said.

"I know why you're here," she said. "I saw the explosion when it happened last night. I was eating alone at Mazzo on the rooftop when Nikolaev's yacht exploded."

"How did you know it was his yacht?"

She leaned against the doorjamb and looked disinterested by studying her feet. "I knew where he moored it. And there weren't any other ships around. So, when it exploded, I looked out for his boat and knew it was gone. I tried calling him, just to be sure, but he never answered. So, I assumed he was aboard when it blew up."

"And you didn't report this to the authorities?"

"Officer—" Sadie said as she scanned his chest for a nameplate. "Officer Damato. Look, I don't know if you understand how this works, but I'm not exactly supposed to be with Alexander. He's married, and happily so, at least according to his wife. So, the less I stay out of official documentation, the better. You understand my discretion, I'm sure."

"You are a permanent member of his, shall I say, *entourage*?"

"That's about as respectable as you can make it, sir."

"Okay, okay," he said, scribbling notes on his pad. "And you knew nothing of a plot to kill him?"

"Of course not, but Alexander had plenty of enemies who wanted to do all sorts of things to him, none of which were pleasant or appropriate to mention in polite company."

"I see. This morning I spoke with a member of Mr. Nikolaev's security detail. And he told me that you loaned your boat to two men and a woman. Do you know if they had anything to do with this?"

"They were my friends, just here for a visit. We happened to learn about this on social media and I offered to let them use Alexander's boat to save them some money. It wasn't sinister."

"But a boat similar to the inflatable that Mr. Nikolaev kept on board was seen speeding away from the site moments after the explosion."

"And?"

"And were those your friends?"

"They would never do such a thing. They didn't know Alexander nor were they interested in meeting him. They were just in Venice to see the sites and enjoy the food and culture. Just like me."

"We have it on good authority that someone boarded the yacht just before it blew up," the officer said.

"Then you should be able to determine who was responsible by the ship's security cameras."

Officer Damato chuckled. "You are aware that the boat was completely destroyed, are you not?"

"I saw it happen with my own eyes."

"Then perhaps you've forgotten that everything is at the bottom of the lagoon now."

"I haven't forgotten, but that doesn't mean you can't look at the security footage."

The officer's eyes widened. "And how is that possible?"

"Alexander spared no expense for anything. He was also extremely paranoid and wanted anyone who tried to kill him to be brought to justice after he was gone. So, he paid a premium to have his entire security footage—every camera, every angle—uploaded to a server on shore. But you can access it from anywhere if you have an internet connection."

Officer Damato craned his neck to look inside Sadie's room. "And do you have a computer in here that we can use to see this footage?"

"I'm not sure I should do that without the permission of Alexander's lawyer," she said.

"This is a murder investigation. If you truly care about us apprehending the person responsible for this heinous act, we need to gather as much information as possible."

"I—I don't know," Sadie stammered. "It's just that—It's just that I don't know if he'd want me to give you access to all of it. He was a very private man."

"Maybe we can reach a compromise."

"I'm listening," she said, shifting her weight from one foot to the other.

"Just give us the footage from a few moments before the explosion to the moment the ship exploded. And I promise not to ask for anymore. Deal?"

"I find your terms acceptable," she said. "But I won't show you on my computer. I'll need to use one of yours."

"There's one downstairs," Damato said. "Follow me."

As they walked to the lobby, Sadie wondered if she was doing the right thing. There was no telling who the murderer was or why he'd done it. But she knew it could invite trouble for her.

Maybe I should just run.

Her opportunity to run was the night before, moments after she'd seen the explosion. She could've disappeared into the night and nobody would've been the wiser. Nikolaev's lawyer would've done everything to prevent her from being detained and interrogated, all to preserve his client's reputation. But now there was no going back. She'd told Officer Damato what she knew. Now, she had to produce.

Damato and two other cops led her to the cramped dining hall that was comprised of about a dozen tables in the bowels of the building. After he unlocked the computer screen, she navigated to a browser and typed in the website. Then she entered a username and password, one she wasn't supposed to have but had gleaned from Nikolaev after watching him act out of his paranoia so many times. Seconds later, a screen appeared filled with small square boxes, all timestamped.

She clicked on the one that corresponded closely with the time the yacht exploded and began scrubbing forward through the files in search of another person on board aside from Nikolaev. After clicking on several different angles, she finally found one, but the intruder's face wasn't lit, making it barely visible. She switched to another camera, but this one was positioned on the corner and well lit.

When the man's face came into view, her breath hitched—and Officer Damato noticed.

"You know him?" he asked, pointing to the screen.

"No," she said, "I was just surprised when I saw someone. I didn't expect a person to be on the screen like that. Just caught me off guard."

"Okay," Damato said. "Are you sure you've never seen this man before?"

She shook her head slowly. "I wasn't always privy to Alexander's business deals. He tried to protect me from some of his clients, though I'm not sure why. Maybe he didn't want them to have any leverage on him with his wife."

Damato grunted. "At least you're honest about the reality of your whoring around."

Sadie turned and glared at the officer. "Do you want my help or not?"

"So far, you haven't really helped."

"If it wasn't for me, you wouldn't even know this footage existed. Now, I suggest you watch your mouth."

Damato shrugged and then nodded toward the screen. "Please continue."

Sadie played several more clips that corresponded with the time prior to the explosion, resulting in two more clear looks at the man who stormed the ship. She clipped all the footage and sent it to Damato's email address.

"That should give you enough to go on," she said. "But maybe he wasn't the one who set off the bomb."

"If there's one thing I've learned as a detective, it's this: if a person looks guilty, they usually are."

"Unless they're being framed."

Damato eyed her closely. "For a tramp, you seem to think you know a lot about this business."

"I watch a lot of television," she said, forcing a sarcastic smile.

"Well, thank you for your help, Detective," Damato said, mockingly. "Please give us your contact information too, just in case we have any follow-up questions."

Sadie scrawled her name and number onto a pad with the hotel's letterhead on it then pushed it forcefully against Officer Damato's chest.

"You don't have to be an asshole," she hissed.

Damato laughed before he spun on his heels and walked away.

After he left, she closed the door behind him and slunk against it to the floor. She couldn't believe her eyes. There was just no way.

She picked up her burner phone and dialed Ryder's number.

"I just spoke to the police," she said. "They just interrogated me for about a half-hour."

"About Nikolaev's death?"

"Yeah. And it wasn't pleasant."

"What'd you tell them?"

"I lied."

"You lied?" Ryder asked, surprised by her response. "About what?"

"About who the killer was."

"Wait. You know who did it?"

She drew in a long breath and then exhaled slowly. "I guess I can't say for sure, but I was able to call up the security footage that's streamed to a cloud server and played the last couple of minutes before the yacht exploded."

"And you knew who it was?"

"Yeah," she said, her voice shaky. "And there wasn't really any doubt about it."

"Who was it, Sadie?"

She swallowed hard and chewed on her lip before answering. "I saw it, but I just don't believe it."

"Who was it?" Ryder repeated again.

"It was Robert Besserman."

ELEVEN

VENICE, ITALY

BESSERMAN STROLLED THROUGH THE LOBBY, LUGGING his suitcase behind him, the wheels clicking rhythmically on the tile floor. The sun shone brightly through the skylight in the lobby as a handful of travelers funneled into the queue, all trying to beat the 11:00 a.m. checkout time. Against the far wall, a television played an Italian morning news program, covering how to defend oneself if attacked violently. The expert showed the svelte interviewer how she could block his hits and then retaliate with an incapacitating blow. Besserman figured the move might work against a street thug, but not who his CIA officers faced in the field.

After the segment ended, Besserman turned his attention back to the checkout counter. He was still behind three other guests, giving him more time than he wanted to study the people in the lobby milling around the coffee stand. While the intelligence summit had been helpful in forming meaningful connections that were sure to solidify a partnership that could eliminate The Alliance, he hadn't learned much more than he already knew about the organization. And knowledge was vital when it came to

73

snuffing out a group that had every imaginable advantage at the moment.

He stifled a yawn as he looked down at his feet.

"Too much to drink last night?" the woman in front of him asked. She'd turned around and caught the tell-tale signs.

"Not more than I could handle, but more than I should have," he said.

"That's how I usually feel," she said. "But we are in Italy, and we shouldn't be shy about indulging."

Based off the woman's accent, Besserman knew she was American, but wasn't sure exactly where she was from. Normally, he wouldn't encourage such small talk with a stranger, but she was an attractive woman, probably in her late thirties or early forties. And she had plenty of spunk based on her nervous energy. He decided to quell his boredom while waiting in line by continuing their fledgling conversation.

"So, where do you call home? Alabama or Mississippi?"

She gasped and slapped her chest. "Alabama or Mississippi? Do I not look like a respectable woman to you?"

"No, I just meant—"

She broke into a broad grin. "You should see your face. I'm just giving you a hard time and am only somewhat joking."

"So—Alabama?"

The woman waved at him dismissively. "Heavens, no. If you only had any idea how much I loathe Alabama, though mostly it has to do with their college football team. I hate them with every fiber in my being."

"I didn't peg you for a Louisiana woman, but I see how there might be a hint of Cajun accent in your voice."

The woman huffed and put her hands on her hips. "Now, are you just trying to insult me? It's a strange way to pick up a woman."

"I'm not trying—"

"Now, you just hush," she said, holding up her hand in a halting gesture. "You don't need to embarrass yourself any further. You look like you mean well, but your southern accent indicator needs some tweaking. Now, I'm from Tennessee."

"Eastern Tennessee, right?"

"Oh, dear Lord. I was trying to stop you while you were still ahead."

"Central Tennessee?" Besserman asked.

"I'm from Memphis," she said, narrowing her eyes. "Now before you make any more disparaging comments—"

"Blues and barbecue are a combination you can't go wrong with."

The woman's breath hitched. "You finally got something right. I'm so proud of you."

"If you don't risk something, you'll never gain anything."

The woman smiled and offered her hand. "I'm Georgia Anne Reynolds."

Besserman froze. He hadn't foreseen the conversation reaching the point where they actually shared their names. But maybe he should've. A kind southern woman wouldn't leave her manners behind no matter how far away she was from home. He'd become so entranced by the woman's good looks and syrupy accent that he almost offered his real name as he shook her hand. But he stopped himself, his attention captivated by the story being covered on the morning news program.

As the news anchor talked, footage from cell phones showed the fiery explosion in the Venetian Lagoon from the night before. Besserman read the caption at the bottom of the screen that was displayed in English: "Russian businessman Alexander Nikolaev is believed to be the lone victim in a bombing that destroyed his luxury yacht last night. The fiery explosion was captured by dozens of tourists enjoying the cool evening and preparing to go on a dinner cruise around the city."

But it was the next image and line that caused him to widen his eyes and ignore Georgia Anne.

"Police have just released this footage of a man who was seen on the boat just moments before it exploded. He escaped the blast on an inflatable motorboat, getting just clear before the bomb detonated. If anyone has any information on this man or his identity, they are encouraged to call the police department."

"Hey, Mister, are you all right?" Georgia Anne asked, waving a hand in front of his face.

He snapped back to reality. "Oh, yeah, I'm fine."

Then he realized he was still shaking her hand.

"I'm so sorry," he said, turning his gaze back to her. "I thought I saw someone I knew over there. I'm Thomas Knight."

Besserman wasn't sure the woman would buy it, but he had to keep her from looking at the screen while his image was still on it, frozen with a screenshot from the security camera. She glanced over her shoulder, but he gave her a gentle tug back, their hands still clasped. Then she jerked hard, wrenching her hand free.

"What's so damn interesting over there?" she said.

"It's nothing," he said as his picture flickered off the screen.

"I'm not sure that's nothing. You looked like you were transported to another dimension while you continued to mindlessly shake my hand."

"Must be my medication."

"If I had a nickel for every time I heard someone make that excuse—"

"You'd have two nickels?"

She chuckled. "No, I worked as a nurse at an assisted living facility. I hear that phrase at least twice before breakfast from patients who are trying to explain their strange behavior. By the end of the day, I've heard it so much that people say that to me in my dreams."

"Maybe it's true."

She eyed him suspiciously before casting a quick glance at the television again. Then she faced him again.

"What kind of medication are you on?" Georgia Anne asked. "I mean, at least I know my patients are actually taking something. You, on the other hand, I'm not so sure about."

"Okay, okay," Besserman said, conjuring up a warm smile.

"You busted me. I don't have any real excuse. I just zoned out while talking to a beautiful woman, which isn't something I can really explain at the moment."

She shook her head and huffed. "So, now you're switching tactics to flattery in an attempt to escape. You're not getting off the hook that easily, buddy."

Another guest in front of the woman stepped up to the counter.

"Our time is almost up, and you want to spend it playing interrogator rather than curious tourist?"

"Yes," she said. "I've watched all those *Murder She Wrote* re-runs, and if there was one thing I learned from watching Jessica Fletcher solve mystery after mystery each week, it's that there's always another explanation for how something happened."

Besserman was trying to focus, trying to dish out his charm. But he struggled, his mind whirring with questions. Chief among them—how did that look like me on Nikolaev's boat?

Another man behind the counter signaled that he was ready for the next guest.

"Looks like you'll never know," Besserman said. "This will just be one of those mysteries that never gets solved."

"Jessica Fletcher always solved the mystery."

"That was television. In the real world, many cases go unsolved."

She drew back. "Now, you're starting to sound like a cop."

"Miss, please," the hotel clerk called, trying to get Georgia Anne's attention.

Besserman nodded toward the man. "Holding up the line wouldn't be very Southern of you."

Georgia Anne playfully scrunched up her nose and then marched toward the counter, leaving Besserman in peace to mull over how his face was all over the news. And not only that, but he looked guilty as hell.

The truth was Besserman had been preparing to rent a boat to do something similar—kill Ahmad Bakir, the Saudi national responsible for a bombing at a U.S. base in Afghanistan that resulted in the deaths of a dozen U.S. servicemen. But once the explosion happened, he stopped. Police boats and fireboats flooded the lagoon, extinguishing any hope he had of eliminating a terrorist threat who'd been on the U.S. watchlist for years.

And even though Besserman had abandoned the mission, he appeared to be framed for doing the same thing to Nikolaev.

Only, he hadn't done it. He was nowhere near the yacht and hundreds of people could attest to it. His alibi would be a solid one, especially if any of the dozens of tourists in the area filming captured him with their cell phone camera footage.

But that would take a long time to uncover, not to mention the corrupt nature of the Italian judicial system. They preferred an approach more akin to guilty until proven innocent. And Besserman wasn't interested in risking anything.

As soon as he checked out of his hotel, he rushed outside to hail a taxi and head straight to the airport. He offered a sheepish wave to Georgia Anne, who was still arranging all her luggage while waiting for her ride.

On the way to the airport, Besserman called J.D. Blunt.

"What a pleasant surprise," Blunt said as he answered the phone. "I haven't heard from you in quite a while."

"I know, I know," Besserman said, doing his best to remain calm. "Guess I've just been busy."

"Of course you have. But now you're not?"

"In a way, I guess that's true, which is why I was wondering if you might be able to take me fishing tomorrow."

"In Washington?"

"No, your place."

"My place? You're not even supposed to know where I live."

"There are a lot of things I'm not supposed to know, but I do anyway."

Blunt sighed. "Well, in that case, I guess you can come, but it's going to cost you."

"Name the price."

"A good bottle of bourbon from some exotic place in the world."

Besserman smiled. "I'm sure I can arrange that."

"Good. Now, send me your arrival details when you get them," Blunt said. "I'm betting that this is an unplanned stop."

Besserman wanted to affirm Blunt's suspicions, but they'd have time to talk about it later. The CIA director just needed to get out of the country ASAP before the shit hit the proverbial fan.

TWELVE

MUNICH, GERMANY

Hawk stood waiting on the next train, hair blowing in the breeze, hands plunged deep into his pockets. The smell of cigarette smoke and vaping fumes hung thick over the platform, almost making him sick. He glanced at Mia, who stood next to him in a beige trench coat, a backpack slung over her shoulder. Ryder also accompanied them, but he intended to remain in the shadows. More than anything, he was there to offer moral support and, if necessary, a surefire shot.

Hawk hoped their visit with German car manufacturer Felix Vogel wouldn't go sideways, but he always believed it was better to be prepared than lament the lack of preparation. And Ryder was part of that prep, even though Hawk could tell he was already tired of engaging with people face-to-face. Ryder would've been happy to slink beneath the covers and not resurface for a few days given what they'd been through recently.

Unfortunately, that wasn't an option for him—or anybody else.

How they found their way to this moment was just as unexpected as learning that Director Besserman was the one responsible for Nikolaev's death. That is, if the journalists reporting the story were to be believed. Hawk hadn't spoken to Besserman but wasn't sure if what he was seeing was real or not, despite the fact that it looked every bit as authentic as anything else he'd ever seen. None of Besserman's actions could be determined definitively while he was on the luxury yacht, but it was difficult not to make, at the very least, a few presumptions.

Hawk decided to leave all that to Sadie Marion, who was the one responsible yet again for his team's presence in a foreign country—this time, Germany. Munich, to be exact.

After the fallout from Alexander Nikolaev's dramatic death, pundits the world over proffered theories as to who and why he would be targeted. His wife mourned publicly and vowed to uncover the truth behind his murder. But not even the best detectives could make a strong case for any potential killer. Nikolaev had so carefully crafted his image and his public connections that nobody could figure out where to begin unraveling the mystery of his death.

That is nobody except Sadie.

Following a visit from the detectives in Venice seeking answers, Sadie decided to launch her own investigation. It would be several days before she was recalled to Langley, allowing her to poke around and see what she could find. She decided to start by exploring all of Nikolaev's associates, particularly the ones he dealt with on a regular basis. But she wasn't searching for his potential killer as much as she was looking to unmask those affiliated with The Alliance.

Nikolaev's regularly scheduled meetings reflected his priorities. The people he was in business with managed to consume most of his meeting time. But there were a few that made Sadie scratch her head and wonder what the connection between them and Nikolaev was. If there wasn't an obvious link, she drew her own conclusions based on everything else she learned about the people. She deduced some of the regular meetings centered around political leanings, whether it was about winning approval to build a factory in certain parts of the world or donating to a candidate who was favorable to his business endeavors.

But there was one that didn't seem to fit in any discernible categories. And that was Felix Vogel.

A train whooshed through the terminal before coming to a quick stop. Passengers hustled off and on in a near quiet shuffle, the loneliness speaking loudly amid the silence. Hawk bulldozed his way through the tightly-packed car, creating an opening for Ryder and Mia to join him. Once they were inside, the doors remained open for a few more seconds before sliding shut. The train jerked forward, forcing the passengers to sway back and forth before they gained their collective balance.

A few stops later, the trio disembarked and left the train station. In the designated parking lot, they found a van that their director Morgan May had arranged for them. Venturing deep behind enemy lines required a commitment to the craft. A mere rental car would likely be flagged by the sharp security detail guarding Vogel's mansion, which is why the one Morgan directed to be left for them mimicked a license plate with a make and model that also belonged to the marketing department for Bayern Munich FC, one of the country's most storied football clubs—or soccer clubs, as Ryder called it. His insistence on calling the sport by the American name was the reason why Hawk decided to leave his partner behind. That and the fact that he wasn't fluent in German and thought it was funny to talk in English with an exaggerated German accent.

Morgan had paid a handsome sum to a person-to-person car share program that had a white van matching the description of Bayern Munich's van she'd found online. The man said it was a utility van and only had two rows of seating, something Morgan had said wasn't a problem. The Bayern Munich van she'd seen had a magnetic sticker on the side, so she'd offered to pay the owner of the van a hundred Euros if he had a similar magnetic sticker waiting for them in the back of the van.

Hans Wust, the name of the marketing representative, was

listed on the Bayern Munich FC website but there wasn't a picture of him. Morgan directed members of her technical staff to upload photos to the internet with Hawk's name beneath a picture of Hans Wust. It was performed in a rush, but it was a quick op that required expediency above all else. If it failed, they'd have to figure out a more creative way to make contact with the CEO. But if it worked, they would gain a crucial advantage in the race to pull the curtain back on The Alliance's more senior members.

Ryder climbed behind the steering wheel of the Vogel EcoVan, the signature transportation vehicle designed by Mr. Vogel himself. While the van was primarily utilitarian, Vogel's other vehicles contained leather seats and woodgrain accents throughout the interior of the cabin. While researching for his meeting with Vogel, Hawk mentioned how impressed he was with the quality of Vogel's vehicles even though he knew he shouldn't have been. BMW and Mercedes-Benz had been trailblazers when it came to crafting superior vehicles, developing brand names synonymous with luxury driving machines. If Vogel was cut from the same mold as a German car manufacturer, there was no reason for Hawk to think the CEO wasn't also capable of manufacturing that same style of vehicle. But even the EcoVan had a few bells and whistles that made it stand out from any similar vehicles he'd driven in the U.S.

Ryder let out a low whistle as he rubbed his hand along the dashboard. He patted it a few times and shook his head, the corner of his mouth creeping upward.

Hawk glanced at his watch. "How about you get a move on before we might miss Vogel?"

"Roger that, Captain," Ryder said, his voice dripping with sarcasm.

Ryder slammed his foot on the accelerator and the van's instant momentum forced all three team members back in their seats.

"What are you doing?" Hawk asked.

"Just getting the lay of the land, so to speak," Ryder said. "If I might be forced to drive this thing like my life depends on it, you bet your sweet ass I'm going to test it a little."

They roared out of the parking lot and pulled onto a main road. Hawk looked at Mia in the backseat, who was typing on her laptop in an apparent attempt to distract her from Ryder's driving. His skills behind the wheel were more akin to someone driving a derby car than a sane person traveling between two places in the city.

"It doesn't matter how fast you drive if we're not actually going to survive the trip over," Hawk said.

Ryder pursed his lips and rolled his eyes. "Don't worry, old man. I'll get us there in one piece just fine."

Hawk cast a side-eyed glance at Ryder. "Me? An old man?"

"Well, you're not old enough to be my dad, but I'm still your daddy," Ryder quipped.

Hawk pointed at the window. "Can you roll that thing down?"

Ryder furrowed his brow. "What on earth for?"

"I want to make sure your head has all the room it needs."

Ryder swatted at Hawk, who caught his hand before it make contact with his chest and bent it at an awkward angle.

"Who's your daddy now?" Hawk asked.

Ryder let out a yelp. "Do you want to make it to Vogel's place in one piece?"

Hawk released Ryder's arm and eased back in his seat with a smile on his face.

Mia leaned forward, poking her head between the two front seats. "Are you two done now? We've got some logistics to discuss."

They reviewed their plan, and less than ten minutes later, Ryder slowed to a stop about a quarter-mile down the road from the guardhouse outside Felix Vogel's mansion.

Hawk sat up and clapped his hands then rubbed them together. "Time for you to work your magic, Mia."

"Already on it," she said.

About a minute later, she announced that she had completed the task, one that consisted of her placing their appointment with Felix Vogel on his schedule. Ryder drove the rest of the way to Vogel's house and waited for the guard to question him.

"I'm sorry," the guard said in German, "but are you lost?"

"No," Hawk replied in German. "We have a meeting with Felix Vogel in fifteen minutes."

"He doesn't have anything on his schedule today."

"Might want to check again," Hawk said.

The guard sauntered back inside the hut and reviewed the computer terminal that displayed Vogel's calendar. He shrugged and sighed as he returned to the car.

"I'm sorry about that, sir. They're expecting you," the guard said sheepishly.

Ryder zoomed up the driveway to the house, skidding to a stop near the front steps.

"Keep your ear piece in," Mia said, patting him on the shoulder. "But for the love of everything that is pure and holy, don't go anywhere."

"I wouldn't dream of—" he said before stopping. "Okay, okay. I'm not gonna lie. I would dream of it. And I might still actually do it. But you know that I don't really want to, right?"

"Stay put," Hawk said in his firmest tone.

"Yes, sir, daddy," Ryder said.

Hawk and Mia climbed the steps of the Vogel mansion and then knocked on the door. A member of the staff greeted them and ushered them into the waiting area. The woman invited them to sit on a bench while they waited for Mr. Vogel.

Five minutes later, Vogel ambled into the room with a pronounced limp. He twirled a handkerchief around, stopping the motion only to dab his forehead dry before resuming. When his gaze fell on Hawk and Mia, he scowled.

"I don't remember this meeting on my schedule," he said in German.

Hawk stepped forward. "I'm sorry, sir. Would you prefer that we come back at another time?"

"No, I've already been interrupted from what I thought I would be doing at this time. No need to make you come out again. Now, what is it you're here for again? A marketing meeting with Bayern Munich FC?"

"Yes, sir," Hawk said. "We have a little presentation to show you."

Vogel held up a finger. "One moment please." Calling over his shoulder, "Franz, can you inspect my two guests?"

A beefy guard strutted into the room and took Mia's laptop before he waved a wand around Hawk and Mia. He handed the laptop back and then signaled that they were devoid of any metallic objects in their pockets before leaving the room.

Mia had taken a Bayern Munich FC pre-season video and replaced the logos on the front of the jersey with the Vogel Motor Company logo.

"Would you like to sit down?" Mia asked.

"Of course," Vogel said before gesturing toward the large table in his study.

Moments later, he was gathered around it with his skeletal advisory staff, which was comprised of two other "yes" men.

"Please explain to me what this is all about?" Vogel asked. "We've been generous supporters of the club for a long time now."

"And we think it might be time for you to take it to the next level, a chance for you to expand your brand reach. What do you say?"

Before he could respond, Mia hit play on her laptop and the video began to move. Hawk watched Vogel more closely than he did the video, seeing what might spark the CEO's imagination. Or, at the very least, garner his attention. He remained stoic, unmoved by the video's dramatic presentation that would result in the world seeing the Vogel Motor Company logo splashed across the jerseys of one of Germany's finest and most well-known clubs.

"Is that all?" Vogel asked.

Hawk shook his head and shot a quick glance at Mia. She signaled to him that she wasn't ready.

"We have some numbers for you to look at," Hawk said. "It underscores what the presentation stated at the end of this video, that for your money, there's nothing you can support to give you the kind of publicity and prestige that accompanies being the premier jersey sponsor for Bayern Munich and locking up the real estate on the front of our storied club's jersey."

Vogel glanced at the paper and then tossed it aside seconds later, exhibiting complete disinterest in everything Hawk was saying.

"Who are you really?" Vogel asked.

"What do you mean?" Hawk replied. "We're with the club."

"No, you're not. I met with Hans Wust two days ago at the Bayern Munich offices. We already arranged a deal, though it hasn't been made public yet. So, I ask again, who are you?"

Deep lines etched Hawk's forehead. "I'm afraid you've been tricked. How much money did you give those frauds?"

"I gave them what the contract stated. But it's clear to me that you are running a scam. And I hate scammers."

Vogel nodded toward two of his security staff who had quietly entered the room without Hawk noticing. While he knew Vogel had the potential to be dangerous, he didn't imagine for a fleeting second that he would be in the kind of danger he suddenly anticipated.

Telling Ryder he was left outside to help shoot our way out was a joke.

But it was no laughing matter now. Hawk and Mia both winced as the pair of guards roughly escorted them down into the basement.

"Why are you taking us into the basement?" Hawk said,

desperately trying to give Ryder some help as to where they would be.

"I'll come for you," Ryder said over the coms.

Vogel followed his guards. "After you two have had a moment to collect your thoughts, I'll be back to question you again. And this time, I want straight answers. Understand?"

Hawk and Mia nodded as they stopped just outside the doorway.

The guard trailing Hawk shoved him in the back, sending him stumbling inside a small room with a brick floor. He hit the ground hard and then quickly retreated to the cot in the corner of the room. Seconds later, Mia followed him.

As they got up off the floor, Hawk put a finger to his lips and pointed at the camera in the corner of the room, a message that Mia received. As he looked around, he knew they were in trouble and needed a way out fast.

But one wasn't readily available. And even if it was, they'd have to fight past several armed guards in the hallway.

"If they don't kill you, Ryder, I just might do it myself," Hawk said in a hushed tone over the coms.

Ryder laughed. "Don't worry, *Dad*. I'm not going to leave you."

Then one of the guards marched back into the room and snatched Hawk by his ear and looked inside. Using his index finger, he raked out the device before doing the same to Mia. Then he crushed them with his heel.

Mia looked at Hawk. "That felt like the most German thing ever."

"Let's just hope it doesn't go any more German."

THIRTEEN

ARUBA

Alex paused to look up from her computer and drink in the scene in front of her. Roiling turquoise water lapped at the sand, beginning anew its assault on the beach. Palm trees swayed in the breeze as if dancing to a rhythm only they could hear. Overhead, the sun beamed down from a cloudless sky, a perfect blue canvas marred only by circling seagulls. And then there was the object she found the most beautiful of all—little J.D. hunched over the early stages of a sandcastle with a full bucket in hand to fill the moat he'd just dug.

He looked back up toward the shore at her and waved, a thousand-watt smile to go along with his piercing blue eyes. She enjoyed watching her son delight in the moment. All around the people he loved and adored, there was unspeakable evil, angry men who wanted to seize control of the world by any means necessary. But little J.D. remained blissfully unaware. Just like she thought little boys should be.

"How's your sandcastle coming along?" Alex shouted over the wind.

"It's great," he said. "I'll show it to you when I'm finished, okay?"

"Sounds good. Have fun!"

"Oh, I am!"

Another blistering smile before returning to the task at hand.

Then Alex returned to her task, which was trying to make sense of the information she'd uncovered on the flash drive that Hawk found in Quantum Glitch's secret monastery office. She'd cracked the file but struggled to believe what she was seeing.

How is this even possible?

To Alex, it would require a diabolical mind to dream up such a program. And based on what she knew about Quantum, it wasn't exactly his style. He was more interested in "sticking it to the man" by raiding the online coffers of corporations with deep pockets and greedy shareholders. That had been in *modus operandi* for years. If he really conjured up this diabolical idea on his own, he'd definitely changed. It was something Alex struggled to believe. While Quantum had done plenty of damage, he was not evil incarnate. His name had remained on the wanted lists of countries the world over, yet Alex couldn't help but admire the hacker's sense of justice, even if she didn't agree with what he did to attain it. Even looking through his files, combing through the lines of code that affirmed his genius, Alex felt a twinge of appreciation for the man, maybe even a kinship. After all, they were in the same business, albeit playing for different teams.

Alex leaned closer to study the code, her mouth falling slack as she grasped the power contained in it. For a fellow hacker, the brilliance on her screen was their twisted version of the Sistine Chapel painting. Michaelangelo's depicted God reaching down to man; Quantum Glitch's enabled man to play God. Saints and priests wanted to harness God's power for good. Sinister hackers wanted to do whatever they wanted, whatever they deemed good.

Unbelievable.

A squawking seagull arrested her attention, sending her eyes quickly toward little J.D. He was packing down sand on one wall of his burgeoning castle. But the bird was farther down the beach, flapping furiously at a bearded man with a wide-brimmed straw hat slogging toward little J.D. along the shore. He held a drink in one hand, the kind in a clear plastic cup that he looked like he'd purchased it from a tiki bar. A sip from the straw and a dramatic wave that shooed away the bird.

The man's gait looked familiar, but she couldn't place his face. She was about to return her focus to her work, maybe even hammer out her preliminary findings and send them to her husband. But the stranger maintained a steady line, not just up the beach, but right toward the waterside cottage Blunt had reserved for her and little J.D. The man walked up the dock that stretched into the water where Blunt kept his boat and kept his gaze on her.

She reached into her purse and fingered the trigger on his Glock. The thought of having to kill a man in front of her son terrified her. But if he made even the slightest move, she wouldn't hesitate to shoot him.

"Hi, Alex," the man said, his voice seemed sure and steady.

Then he removed his sunglasses.

"Director Besserman?" she asked.

He released a curse through gritted teeth. "I really thought you wouldn't be able to tell who I was."

"I couldn't. But your smooth bass voice is unmistakable."

"So, good with the ladies, but not so good with disguises?"

"I guess," she said with a chuckle. "Are you planning on trying to pick some women up?"

Then she furrowed her brow and stared at him for a moment.

"What the hell are you doing here anyway?" she asked. "Don't you have an agency to run?"

"I could almost ask you the same question."

"I can do what I do from anywhere as long as I have a Wi-Fi connection. But I'm also not the top dog at America's foremost intelligence agency either."

"Well, the fact that you haven't heard why I'm here makes me wonder if you do have an internet connection."

"That bad, huh?" she asked.

"It's dreadful," he said. "I'm being hunted for a crime I didn't commit, for a crime I couldn't have committed, for a crime I might not ever be able to prove that I didn't commit."

"Sounds like you might want to learn how to grow a better beard and learn how to enjoy multiple glasses of tequila every day."

"Now when you put it that way, it doesn't sound so bad."

She smiled. "What are they after you for?"

"You name it, they want me for it," Besserman said before relating the story about how he was wanted in connection with the bombing of Alexander Nikolaev's yacht.

"Well, I think I can help."

"You know how they did this to me?"

Alex nodded then reached over and scooped up a stack of documents on the wicker chair next to her. "Here, have a seat. I'll explain it all to you."

"You mean this is actually possible?" Besserman asked, shaking his head in disbelief.

She nodded. "I just figured it out. Hawk was chasing Quantum Glitch and found his hideout at a monastery in Greece. His brother oversaw the place and allowed him to keep a secret office there."

"And Hawk captured him?"

"Unfortunately, he escaped, but we were able to get some vital information off Quantum, which I believe might explain your situation."

Besserman finished his drink and leaned over to look at Alex's laptop.

"You might want another one of those once I'm done," she said before tapping a few keys and opening a file.

"What are we looking at?" he asked.

"Probably won't mean a thing to you, but this is the code for a program Quantum wrote that allows you to put another person's face on someone else's body."

"So, kind of like one of those gimmicky programs where you can put Hillary Clinton's face on some guy breakdancing?"

"Sort of. The difference is two-fold. First of all, the technology is infinitely better. This isn't just pasting a 2-D image on top of a body. This is full on masking."

"I've seen this now. You can make someone look like they're singing with facial expressions and everything."

"Yes, but the facial expressions are fabricated, moved to the beat of the music. They aren't real expressions. This program, which Quantum aptly labeled Hocus Pocus, takes a person's face and puts it on another person's to the point that you can't tell if it's real or not—and it becomes part of the recorded image."

"What do you mean?"

"This program allows you to more or less paste on a person's face but does so in real time, not some post-production techno wizardry working from a file. This literally changes what you see on the screen and what's recorded."

"So, let me make sure I understand what you're saying. This Hocus Pocus program was used to alter the live security cameras on Nikolaev's yacht, making it appear as if I was the one who supposedly setting off a bomb?"

"Exactly."

"This is dangerous technology. Could you imagine being able to use this on your enemies?"

"It's terrifying," Alex said. "Never mind that most people think the truth is relative. Artificial intelligence started this whole debacle by making us question what we see with own eyes. Now, this is next level technology that can actually alter what we see in real time."

"Want to commit a crime but make it look like someone else did it? Use Hocus Pocus."

Alex nodded slowly. "The application of this program could

be a disaster for the rule of law. You could make anyone look like they're doing anything, even on live television."

"But is there a way to determine that the image has been altered?"

"I'd need to see actual footage where I know that Hocus Pocus has been used, but I'm leaning toward no. The way this program is written, it looks so seamless and embeds itself in the image's metadata that it'd be a nightmare to find."

"So what you're saying is that I'm screwed?" Besserman asked.

"The only way you'd be able to prove this was doctored was by examining the software installed on the cameras. And according to you, they don't exist anymore."

"Damn," Besserman said as he slapped his knee. "Maybe I will enter retirement early and just stay in the Caribbean and drink and fish."

"It's working for Blunt."

Besserman shook his head. "Unfortunately, I'm not ready for retirement yet. And I'm ready to fight. But we've got to have a plan first."

"We'll think of something."

Alex looked toward the water and saw little J.D. waving his arms and calling for her.

"Want to meet my son?"

"Why not," Besserman said as he got up.

They both walked toward the water's edge.

"You need to get to know him because if you somehow survive all this mess you might just be handling him."

"Really?"

"He's cut from the same cloth as Hawk."

"I'm sure he's got plenty of his mother in him."

"That too," she said with a sigh, "which is why he's a handful."

Once they reached little J.D., he scrambled to his feet and pointed at his masterpiece. The castle contained four solid walls and turrets fashioned from a molded bucket he was swinging in his right hand.

"What do you think?" he asked, jumping up and down. "Isn't it amazing?"

Alex smiled. "You did a great job. I love all the hard work you put into this."

"Thanks," he said. "I made it for you."

"That's so sweet, buddy."

Alex knelt next to the sandcastle just in time to see an approaching wave crest crashing over J.D.'s creation. Despite his sturdy structure, it was no match for the wave, the sand crumbling beneath the force of the water. She looked at her son, whose eyes welled with tears.

"It's all gone," he said. "It's no fair."

Besserman tousled J.D.'s hair. "I understand," he said. "It's the story of my life, kid. The story of my life."

FOURTEEN

MUNICH, GERMANY

Ryder took a moment to clear his head and formulate an extraction plan. The last thing he wanted to do was get into a protracted gunfight alone against an unknown number of hostiles. Without having extensive knowledge of the mansion's layout, he was already flying blind, but going in by himself would only compound the challenges he faced. But his first problem was likely his greatest—getting onto the property with a vehicle they could escape in.

For a moment he considered simply waiting near the gated entrance and sneaking into the next vehicle that stopped to be cleared at the guard gate. Yet his problem remained. He inspected his van for a moment and looked at the toolbox in the back. It was nearly empty, but he didn't need to open it, requiring it only as a prop to sell his burgeoning idea.

The fact that he couldn't communicate with Hawk and Mia anymore also complicated matters—and simplified them. He didn't need Hawk looking over his shoulder. This was *his* time to put into practice everything he'd learned and see if he was as good of a student as Hawk was a teacher. Satisfied that he had a good idea, he parked the van farther off the side of the road, veering into a small clearing and hiding the vehicle behind some bushes. Then he flung his rucksack over his shoulder and found a section of wrought-iron fence that sliced through a wooded area. He examined several security cameras and found one that had a view blocked by leaves from a drooping branch that hung over into Vogel's property.

Ryder scampered up a tree and leaped over the eight-foot tall fence. He moved quickly toward the house and found a window on the main floor that was ajar. He lifted the window and then slithered inside. The room he landed in appeared to be a guest bedroom of sorts. The bed was made and looked untouched, while the rest of the counters and drawers were devoid of any clothes. That gave him a second to catch his breath and execute the next part of his plan. He eased open the door and peeked through a slit into the hall. When he didn't see anyone in it, he eased out of the room and went a few paces before finding a bathroom.

Ryder put together a makeshift charge, affixing it to the bottom of the toilet. He put a long enough fuse on the end to give him enough time to get out of the house and halfway across the lawn before all hell would break loose. He took his time and inspected his work before flicking the lighter.

Here goes nothing.

Darting back into the hallway, Ryder walked to the bedroom and jumped through the window. Just before he leaped, he heard someone shouting for him to stop. But Ryder ignored them and counted down in his head.

Three ... two ... one ...

Boom!

The blast silenced the woman who'd been shouting at him. He hoped she wasn't dead but he wasn't trying to hurt anyone. All he wanted to do was get his friends back.

He hopped the fence with ease and scurried into the woods before watching through the thick vegetation as chaos ensued. A pair of guards ran into the yard and began combing the area for him. But he didn't move, choosing instead to stay and see how they reacted to the explosion. Surely they had to know it was intentional. But would they think an outsider did it? Or would they turn on the staff?

Ryder couldn't tell from what he was able to observe. Fifteen minutes later, he raced back to his van. He spent the next half-hour memorizing a few German phrases that he thought might be able to get him inside. Once he was confident enough to attempt to pull it off, he approached the gate.

"Do you have an appointment?" the guard asked in German.

"Ja."

"*Wie heißt du?*" the guard asked as he stared at a clipboard waiting for Ryder to give him his name.

"Peter," Ryder said. "Ich bin Klempner und wir wurden wegen eines Notfalls gerufen."

I'm a plumber and I was called about an emergency.

"*Bist du sicher?*" the guard asked.

Ryder wasn't sure what the man had said. That phrase wasn't in the imaginary conversation Ryder had in his head.

Ryder just shrugged.

"Okay, *komm rein,*" the guard said, waving him inside.

Ryder nodded at the man and eased onto the accelerator. He drove around to the back of the house where a member of Vogel's staff was waiting for him. The woman who greeted him was talking non-stop, seemingly without taking a breath. Instead of answering her, Ryder, lugging the toolbox, simply followed her.

She led him down a hallway that was coated with a thin film of water. Then she opened the door to the bathroom. The water was still gurgling from the toilet but was being held at bay by a mountain of towels, which was being managed by another staff member. Both women started talking to Ryder, who just nodded at them and shooed them out of the room with the back of his hand.

Once they were gone, he shut the door and quickly went to

work. He bent the incoming waterline into the sewage pipe, stemming the flooding. Then he eased over to the door and cracked it open, peeking into the hallway.

Satisfied that the area was clear, he crept out and began his search for stairs that led to the basement. He was grateful Hawk had enough sense to give him some sort of direction, even as limited as it was. After scanning the area, he darted toward a door and tugged it open, revealing a set of stairs. He tapped the light switch, illuminating his descent. Once he reached the ground floor, he surveyed the area and then located two hallways. He crept over to one but found it empty. Then moving stealthily toward the other, he peered around the opening and found an armed guard sitting in a chair outside the door.

Ryder dug a flash bang out of his rucksack and tossed it toward the man. Surprised by the sudden introduction of a bouncing canister, the man didn't move for a moment. And it was just long enough for him to make a costly mistake. The device exploded, causing him to become disoriented. Ryder charged down the corridor and drove his knee into the confused man's face, the crunch of soft tissue and bone echoing off the walls. Then the man fell unconscious.

Ryder tried the door and it didn't budge. He backed up and led with his shoulder against it. After two attempts, it gave way.

He reached down and grabbed the guard's gun and tossed it to Hawk.

"I hope you've got a way out of here," Hawk said.

"What's the matter?" Ryder asked. "Are you worried you didn't teach me well enough?"

"Oh, I know I taught you. I'm more concerned that you weren't paying attention."

Ryder offered a wry smile. "Now it's your turn to watch and learn."

Ryder led the way up the steps, his weapon trained in front of him. When he reached the main floor, he heard screeching and shouting coming from the direction of the hallway containing the bathroom he'd destroyed. He saw the back of a security guard's head rushing to the commotion.

"We don't have much time," Ryder said softly. "They're on to me."

He directed Hawk and Mia toward the exit and entered the courtyard at the back of the mansion and found one guard standing in front of the van and peering inside.

"Hands where I can see them," Ryder said.

The guard froze and raised his hand.

"Drop the weapon," Ryder said. "Slowly."

The man complied as Hawk walked over to the man and pistol whipped him in the head, knocking him out.

Ryder scowled. "You didn't even give me a chance to practice the German I'd learned."

"*Drop the weapon* sounded like perfect English to me," Mia said.

"Get in," Ryder said.

Before they were all seated, he eased out of the driveway and tore around the side of the house. The gate was closed and a guard stood in front of it.

Ryder laid on the horn. "Get out of the way, dude."

The guard dove to safety at the last second before the grill of the van smashed against the gate, springing it open. Ryder looked in the rearview mirror as the gate bounced off the pavement, strewn across the road.

"That was your plan," Hawk said.

"Yeah," Ryder said with a grin. "It's working out great, isn't it?"

"Hardly," Hawk said as he climbed out of his seat and moved toward the back of the van. "Keep your head down, Mia."

Seconds later, the sound of gunshots was followed by shattered tempered glass tinkling onto the floorboard of the van.

"Morgan is gonna be so pissed at you, Ryder," Mia said. "Are you sure thirty grand was in the budget for an EcoVan?"

"More like forty grand," Hawk said as he returned fire through the new opening at the back of the vehicle.

Ryder slunk down in his seat and jammed his foot onto the accelerator pedal. The van zoomed down the road, picking up steam, tires barking as Ryder attacked each new corner.

"Come on, Ryder," Hawk shouted. "They're gaining on us."

More shots pinged off the side of the van before one zipped all the way through and shattered the front windshield, distorting Ryder's view. He drew his leg back and kicked several times before the windshield peeled aside. Ryder strained to see as the wind streamed across his face and watered his eyes.

"You gonna take care of those guys or do you want me to do it or you?" Ryder shouted.

"Just keep driving," Hawk said.

Ryder watched the car behind them weave back and forth as it drew within a few feet, a decision that turned out to be fatal. Holding the van steady, Ryder gave Hawk the signal and he popped up and shot through the open window, killing the driver with two shots. The car lurched left and then right before careening over the roadway and slamming against a tree.

"Nice shot," Ryder said.

"And nice driving," Hawk replied. "I was beginning to wonder if you knew how to keep the van steady."

"And I was starting to wonder if you knew how to shoot," Ryder quipped.

"Boys, we can fight about who's better operationally later," she said. "But I thought you might want to know some good news."

Ryder hadn't paid much attention to Mia, who'd been hunched over on her laptop for the duration of the chase.

"What is it?" he asked.

"That cloning device Dr. Z gave me before we left," she said, holding up a small chip. "It actually works."

"What do you mean?" Hawk asked as he climbed back toward the front.

"I was able to clone Vogel's phone," she said, "so we can see what he was hiding."

"Great job," Hawk said. "Did you find anything?"

"Well," she said wincing, "it's not all good news."

"What do you mean?" Ryder asked.

"I found this video. You're both gonna want to see this."

Ryder pulled off a side road and then eased onto the shoulder before stopping the vehicle. Mia handed them her laptop.

"Watch this," she said before playing the footage she'd found on Vogel's phone.

When the video finished playing, Hawk and Ryder looked at each other wide-eyed.

"I told you it wasn't good," Mia said.

FIFTEEN

ARUBA

ROBERT BESSERMAN WAS ON HIS THIRD DRINK, THIS
time opting for straight bourbon. The fruity liquor drinks
weren't cutting it based on what he'd learned from Alex—and
Blunt's cabinet was predictably well stocked. He tipped his glass
back and contemplated a fourth pour before someone clearing his
throat jarred some sense into Besserman.

"Take it from me," Blunt said as he sauntered through the
door. "It's much harder to stay incognito when you're drunk."

"Yeah, but you don't *know* you're struggling to stay incognito," Besserman said. "And right now, I'd like a few minutes of
being blissfully unaware of my situation."

Blunt sighed and snagged another glass out of the cabinet and
promptly filled his glass and Besserman's with a generous pour of
bourbon.

"One more probably won't do you in," Blunt said before
holding his glass up and clinking it against Besserman's.

"You know why I'm here?" Besserman asked.

"I put two and two together. Alex texted me about her findings and then I got a call from President Bullock's chief of staff

Emma Washburn telling me what was going on. She asked me how the hell it happened."

"So, she doesn't believe I did it?"

"No. She was calling on Bullock's behalf. Everyone in Washington saw it with their own eyes apparently, and they all want to know if you snapped. Several liaisons within the CIA reported that there was an agent embedded with Nikolaev, but she hadn't gathered any real actionable intelligence, which made the messy assassination attempt seem rather odd."

"It wasn't me," Besserman said. "You've gotta believe me."

"Well, it's certainly not *like* you, but it's hard to argue against that kind of evidence."

Besserman took a long pull of his drink and smacked his lips before responding. "Alex figured it out. Just ask her."

"I read her texts. It's terrifying."

"And she knows how they did it, too."

"Who's *they*?"

"The Alliance and Jun Fang. They're the ones trying to frame me."

Blunt thought for a moment. "That's plausible, but what would be the advantage to pinning such a public crime on you?"

"Who knows? Maybe Fang was doing it because he could. And if my own government doesn't believe me, he's just created one of the most powerful pieces of technology for counterintelligence in the twenty-first century. He doesn't even have to get his hands really dirty. He can send whoever he wants after someone else, plug in his program, and *voila*—someone else committed the crime. It's gonna take the tenuous trust we have with the truth and make it unbelievable."

"Sounds like the ideal way to conduct a bloodless coup."

Besserman nodded. "All Fang needs are a few good assassins and the ability to take over some cameras."

"Or have every security camera in the world to run the specially-designed software."

Besserman polished off the rest of his glass, his mind fighting the fog of alcohol as he tried to determine the method and means Jun Fang would have to install such a program on a global scale.

"There are so many security camera models and dozens of companies that manufacture them," Besserman said. "Not to mention that there are some still in use today that are ancient when it comes to computer compatibility. That industry moves so fast with constantly upgraded features. Getting every company to install that software seems like next to impossible."

"Not if it was embedded in another program that everyone had to have."

"Unless someone is complicit at the software company, that isn't going to happen."

"I wouldn't be so sure," Blunt said.

"You know how conspiracies work," Besserman said. "They require a small number of people to coalesce around an idea and refuse to reveal the truth—all for personal gain. To do this would require so many people to conspire that it wouldn't stay a secret for long."

"What if the fellow conspirators didn't know what they were part of it?"

"That sounds ridiculous—and impossible."

"Never rule out anything when it comes to power, money, and ruthless ambition," Blunt said, "which is why you need to be extremely worried about your deputy director."

Besserman snorted. "Pickens? He's harmless."

"But he's ambitious. And it's your blood he smells in the water. He's going to send someone down here looking for you to answer for what you supposedly did."

"Steve knows I would never do anything like that."

"Doesn't matter. If he thinks allowing the accusations to stick will benefit his career, he's going to toss you under the proverbial bus."

The door swung open and Alex entered with a bag full of beach toys and a sandy little boy.

"Did you have fun playing in the sand?" Blunt asked little J.D.

"It was the best. I built this huge sandcastle, but a big wave washed it away."

"Well, you can just build another one tomorrow," Blunt said, rubbing the boy's head.

"But—"

"*Tomorrow*," Alex said. "You heard Mr. Blunt."

"I wanted to go back outside and—"

"It's almost time for dinner and you need a shower, little man."

Little J.D. sighed, resigned to his fate of cleaning up. "Yes, ma'am."

"I'll draw you some water while you go and get a towel and some fresh pajamas."

The boy scampered off, while Alex ducked into the bathroom to draw the water.

Blunt and Besserman waited until the room was clear again before resuming their conversation.

"I'm starving," Besserman said. "Where are we going to eat tonight?"

"*We* aren't going anywhere. I've got some steaks marinating on the counter and we'll stay here. The less you're out and about getting filmed by any security cameras, the better."

"Sounds good," Besserman said, pausing a moment and staring off in the distance before speaking again. "How long do you think I've got?"

"Got for what?" Alex asked as she returned to the room after getting her son squared away with his bath.

"Before they find me," Besserman replied.

"I don't know," Blunt said with a shrug. "Two, maybe three days tops. But for all we know, they could be on the way down here right now."

"I really didn't want to get you involved, but I didn't know where else I could go," Besserman said.

"You could come back to Montana with us," Alex said. "We're

leaving in the morning and it'll be difficult for anyone to find you at our place, let alone get to you."

"I don't want to impose."

"You also don't want to get arrested and let that little pencil-neck geek Pickens steal your hard-earned position atop the agency," Blunt snapped.

"Of course not," Besserman said before turning to Alex. "So, if it's not too much trouble, I think I'll accept."

"Do you have a fake passport that nobody knows about?" she asked.

He tapped his pants pocket. "Got one right here."

"Good," she said. "I'll see if I can get you a seat on our flight. And in the meantime, there's more that I learned about the program Quantum Glitch wrote and his plans for it."

"There's more?" Blunt asked.

She nodded. "I'll tell you all about it in a minute, but I need to update Hawk on what's happening. Let me call him and put him on speaker so he can hear this too."

A minute later, her husband was on the phone, listening to the latest she'd discovered while unpacking the information she'd recovered off the thumb drive at St. George's Monastery.

"While this operation might seem wild and chaotic, it's been thoughtfully constructed," she said.

"How so?" Hawk asked, his voice crackling over a poor connection.

"It actually has a name—Operation Nightfall," she said. "And if whoever is behind this continues on the timeline that I uncovered, they're going to unleash this new hellish program on the world one week from today."

"Did any of the documents you found explain how that was going to happen?" Blunt asked.

"I didn't see that covered anywhere," she said. "But I think it's pretty clear this would require a major software company—more specifically, just a single software company that is loaded onto just about every single one of those cameras—to go along with this."

"They could force this to happen any number of ways, all of which would be cruel," Hawk said. "Just look what they did to Bobby."

"Hi, Hawk," Besserman said, his tone melancholy.

"Wait," Hawk said. "Are you with Blunt and Alex?"

"I didn't know where else to go."

"And he's coming back to the ranch with us," Alex said.

"Good," Hawk said. "You should be safe there—or at least, safe for a while."

"That's what I'm counting on. And I'm hoping we can get this sorted out before anyone else finds me."

Hawk chuckled. "Well, if there's anyone equipped to keep you safe and hidden in Montana, it's Alex. You should get her to tell you about all the Russian mobsters that are buried on our property."

"I'm counting on her," Besserman said with a wink.

Alex finished sharing all the other details she'd learned about the program and how it was implemented. But her explanation was cut short by little J.D. shouting for her from the bathroom.

"Duty calls," she said. "Save the world then give my son a bath. A woman's work is never done."

"You go, honey!" Hawk said.

Blunt ended the call and turned to Besserman. "Are you sure you want to fight it this way?"

"I don't think I really have a choice, unless I want to fake my death."

"I have some experience in that department, though I wouldn't recommend it."

"No, I think I'll wait until I can prove my innocence before I fight."

"Okay," Blunt said. "I'll have your back. Just lay as low as you can for as long as you can."

"I intend to," Besserman said. "And then we're going to expose these assholes and burn them to the ground."

Blunt raised his glass, swirling the last remaining traces of the amber liquid. "Hear, hear."

SIXTEEN

VIRGINIA

MORGAN MAY LEANED FORWARD IN HER SADDLE AND stoked the neck of her American quarter horse, Magic Bullet. The chocolate horse whinnied and stamped its front foot. The wind rustled the tops of the pine trees encircling the training ring, the fresh scent drifting past Morgan.

"You like that outdoor smell, boy?" she said. "Well, me too. Now, are you ready to try this again?"

Morgan guided Magic Bullet back to one side of the dusty arena and began another attempt at a half-pass. The horse moved forward and sideways, executing the difficult movement with relative ease. After he'd gone halfway across the ring, Magic Bullet abruptly stopped and snorted.

"What is it? Is something out there?" she asked.

Morgan scanned the surrounding woods but didn't see anything. But then Magic Bullet's ears perked up.

"You hear something?" Morgan asked.

Magic Bullet craned his neck and then trotted in the opposite direction toward the fence. He stopped just shy of it and leaned forward as if still listening to something. A few seconds later,

Morgan heard it too—the sound of a vehicle rumbling up the driveway that wound through the woods to the stables.

Kensington Hills Equine Center prided itself on being secluded and far enough away from Washington that only people with money and time could place their horses there. Morgan didn't have as much of either as she'd liked, but her uncle had offered to pay for Magic Bullet's boarding costs there as part of her sixteenth birthday gift. Most girls her age would've preferred a car, but all Morgan wanted to do was ride her horse. And not being able to do so as much as she wanted was her lone regret about taking the job as the Magnum Group director. Yet when she did take advantage of the rare moment to ride, she didn't want to be bothered by anyone. The fact that cell phone coverage was spotty there proved to be a strong reason she never wanted to take Magic Bullet closer to the city. This was a place where she could escape and simply enjoy the natural surroundings without all the trappings of the nation's bustling capital.

However, someone had just allowed a convoy of television news channels to roll through the front gate without warning her. That wasn't supposed to happen. But she looked at the logo for Channel 9 Action News, an SUV wrapped with a picture of blonde bombshell Karissa Mixon leaning back-to-back with meteorologist and former Miss New York Heather Tatum. The image would be a traffic stopper if the Beltway wasn't already constantly congested.

What are they doing out here?

Morgan dug her phone out of her pocket. There were no new messages. There wasn't a signal either.

She cursed under her breath as she watched the Channel 9 SUV along with three more from other local news channels skid to a stop in a line like they were rehearsing for a synchronized parking event. One by one, reporters clambered out of their vehicles and rushed toward her, portly cameramen all struggling to keep pace with the on-air talent.

Magic Bullet snorted and then turned away from the

reporters gathering near the fence and relieved himself. Morgan chuckled to herself.

I love you, boy. Just couldn't time it any better, could you?

Karissa was the first to shout at Morgan as Magic Bullet practiced another half-pass across the ring.

"Will you confirm that you are Morgan May?" Karissa shouted.

"Will you confirm that you're a dipshit bimbo?" is what Morgan wanted to say. Instead, she just shrugged and maintained the movement with her horse.

"Come on, Morgan," one of the other reporters said. "We know it's you. We just want to get a comment from you. There's no shame in sleeping with the president. I mean, that was a pretty steamy video."

Morgan scowled, not wanting to react to the comment, but finding it harder to do the more the reporters called out after her.

"What did you think of *The Post*'s headline this morning putting you in the same category as Monica Lewinski?"

Morgan peeked over her shoulder at the reporter holding up a newspaper that said in bold letters above the fold: "From Monica to Morgan."

She broke Magic Bullet out of his trot and urged him back to the edge of the fence where the journalists had gathered. The woman was still holding up the afternoon edition of the newspaper. The subtitle under the big headline offered a better explanation of the story with a subhead of "Why Women Find Presidents Irresistible." Morgan rolled her eyes.

"What is this?" Morgan asked. "And what video are you talking about?"

"The only one all over social media this morning," Karissa said. "Surely you've seen it by now?"

"Actually, I've been minding my own business all day, trying to focus on my job, which is offering the White House the best possible advice on how to handle disputes with foreign leaders."

"We all saw the kind of advice you offer," said Brock Freeman, a reporter for *The Washington Post.* "And let me tell you, it was spicy."

She stopped and scowled at him. "What the hell are you talking about?"

"Oh, come on, Morgan," Karissa cut in. "Stop playing dumb. You're a grown woman. There's no shame in doing what you did. I'd probably do it too given the opportunity."

"Would someone please explain to me what's going on because I am absolutely clueless?"

Morgan's admission froze the pool of reporters.

"Wait, you really don't know?" Karissa asked. "We thought for sure you would know by now."

"Know what?"

"The explicit video you made of you and President Bullock," she said. "It's everywhere."

"What are you talking about?" Morgan huffed.

Karissa swiped across the screen of her phone and then handed it to Morgan. As the video began to play, her jaw fell slack and her eyes widened in disbelief.

"That's not me," Morgan said, handing the phone back to Karissa.

"That's your face—and your tattoo," Karissa said. "Are you suggesting that you don't have a small lightning bolt tattoo just above your left breast?"

"That's absolutely absurd," Morgan said.

"Then why don't you show us and end all the speculation right here?"

"I'm not going to toss aside my dignity because a pack of tabloid hacks want to drag my name through the mud off some AI-doctored tape," Morgan said. "Now get out of here before I have security escort you out."

Karissa chuckled and shook her head. "Morgan, Morgan, Morgan. Do you know who owns Kensington Hills?"

"What's that got to do with anything?" Morgan hissed.

"Because Don Rutherford, the man who owns this place, also

owns my station. And I can guarantee you that whatever little pittance you're paying to keep your little pony out here so you can pretend like you're some rich snot will pale in comparison to what our station will rake in once they see this video of you being so defiant."

"You're the asshole here, Karissa. Not me."

"I've been called worse, but let's not forget that I wasn't the one screwing the president—a president with a wife and children."

"It's not me."

"Oh, yes it is. We have had our digital forensics investigate the video. And it's not AI. It's real."

"I don't care what your little digital expert thinks. That video was doctored."

"The evidence says otherwise. Now, the longer you continue to deny this, the worse you're going to look."

"What's the timestamp on that video?"

"Last Tuesday," Karissa said. "Want to prove to us where you were?"

"I was at a Nationals-Dodgers game. I even have pictures," Morgan said.

"Oh, good. Then this ought to be easy to clear up. Let's see them."

Morgan pulled out her phone and to her horror couldn't find a single image that she'd taken. Every one of them was gone. She navigated to the deleted folder and couldn't find any pictures.

"I know they were here."

"Mmm, hmm," Karissa said. "Likely story. Just admit you're having an affair with President Bullock and move on."

"But I'm not."

Karissa laughed. "This is just getting sad and pathetic now."

Morgan wanted to go off on Karissa and the rest of the muckrakers converging on her near the fence. A few middle finger salutes and a barrage of profanities felt justified over their attempt to trash her good name. But she paused and took a deep breath, eyes closed as she weighed her next response carefully. There was still some measure of level-headedness fighting to be heard in her mind.

If you show your ass now, it'll be on the internet forever.

And then another thought.

Apparently they all think you already showed the internet your ass.

She smiled, humored by her internal dialogue.

"I'll tell you what, Karissa. Give me a week to prove to you that I'm telling the truth—proof that doesn't involve me flashing your cameras. And if I'm right, you spend one of your days off each week working for all the *rich snobs* who board their horses here."

"And if you can't prove it?"

"I'll do an interview with you and tell all."

Karissa didn't hesitate. "That's a deal."

"You're going to be sorely disappointed," Morgan said, turning Magic Bullet with the reins.

Then she stopped and spun back around.

"And why are you harassing me instead of the president right now if you really think this is true?" Morgan asked. "Awfully misogynistic of you, Karissa. You're such a disappointment to all the women out there you claim to fight for."

Morgan clucked her tongue and turned Magic Bullet toward the stables and galloped off.

Where the hell did my pictures go? And how did someone make it look like I was sleeping with President Bullock?

Questions abounded for Morgan. Her leisure time had been stolen by this manufactured incident. And she was just as intrigued by how someone did it as she was why they did it.

She wasn't sure how she was going to prove her innocence, but she closed her eyes and imagined Karissa shoveling a pile of horse manure. The thought brought a smile to her face.

As if I needed extra motivation to clear my name.

SEVENTEEN

VIRGINIA MOUNTAINS

HAWK SLUNG HIS RUCKSACK OVER HIS SHOULDER AS HE climbed out of the car he'd rented and walked toward the cabin. He stopped and closed his eyes, breathing in the fresh scent of pine trees in the crisp morning air. In the treetops above, he heard squirrels chattering and birds chirping, while a nearby stream gurgled. Despite the chaos that was ravaging both his public and private worlds, he appreciated the opportunity to escape for a minute and forget about it all in the middle of raw nature.

He opened his eyes and looked at the cabin nestled amidst a cluster of trees at the top of a small rise. The minute he stepped through that door, he knew the moment was over. There was work to be done—wrongs to right, lives to save, enemies to eliminate. And as much as he wanted to linger in the great outdoors, he knew he couldn't. He promised to find time to do it later, just as soon as he addressed the situation facing not only the intelligence community at large but also two people he reported to and respected.

Hawk took the porch steps two at a time before entering the

cabin and spotting Big Earv near the entrance to the back hall with a broad grin.

"You made it," Big Earv said. "I thought I was going to have to urge you inside with a cattle prod."

Hawk shook his head and smiled before embracing his colleague. "I just needed a minute to clear my head."

"You good now?"

"I won't be good until we've shut down The Alliance."

"You and me both, brother. Now, let me show you our bunk room."

Hawk followed Big Earv until he stopped outside one of the rooms and gestured inside. Of the four bunk beds, the two on the bottom appeared to be claimed, leaving Hawk with his choice of either of the upper beds.

"Which one is you and which one is Ryder?" Hawk asked.

"Right here," Big Earv said, pointing to the nearest one.

"You snore, right?"

"Sometimes."

Hawk flung his bag onto the other bunk bed. "No offense."

"None taken, though I'm not sure how much better it's going to be sleeping above Ryder. He may not snore, but he's a restless sleeper."

Hawk cracked a faint smile. "You are offended."

"Nah. I did miss you though."

An ear-piercing whistle came from the front of the cabin, making Hawk wince in pain.

"Does she have to do that?" Big Earv said.

"You missed Mia, didn't you?"

Big Earv sighed. "Maybe, but I didn't miss *that*."

The rest of the Magnum Group team congregated around the large dining room table. Morgan sat at the head of the table, while Ryder, Mia, and Rebecca Fornier were already seated. Dr. Z, the team's lab guru, joined remotely via a flat screen on the far end behind Morgan.

Hawk and Big Earv took a seat at the table across from each other as Morgan opened the meeting.

"Before we begin, I want to go on the record with all of you that I absolutely did not sleep with President Bullock nor have I or ever will have an affair with him," Morgan said.

"You didn't need to say that," Mia said.

"Probably not, but I needed to tell someone and have them believe me," Morgan said, her face grim.

Hawk studied her for a moment. Over the past few years working with her, he'd found the Magnum Group's director to be a strong personality, unflinching in the face of opposition and defiant power brokers, both within the U.S. and abroad. Her leadership had been challenged, even threatened, by certain lawmakers who didn't like her because of how she handled foreign agents and various terrorists. And despite bold opposition, she never seemed rattled.

But this was different.

Jun Fang had commissioned a program to be developed that could be used to destroy personal lives, let alone the fledgling trust that remained—if at all—with government officials and intelligence agencies. If this was unleashed on the world, there'd be no stopping what he could do, how Fang could not only craft narratives but fabricate them out of thin air and foist them as fact upon a global population forever unsure of what they saw as being authentic and not a high tech parlor trick.

And Morgan had been placed in Fang's sights, a target to destroy, a character to assassinate. Fang could do it all without ever saying a word. In a world before such diabolical inventions, to assassinate someone else's character required mudslinging and private investigators willing to dig through a target's closet in search of proverbial skeletons. Now, not even a word was required. A few clicks on a keyboard and an email with a video attached would suffice.

Hawk knew Morgan didn't deserve it. But the pain and anguish perched on her face like an unsightly wart. She didn't even try to hide it. However, Hawk didn't doubt for a second that she had the resolve to fight it, no matter how long it took.

"As my uncle used to say, 'If you don't have character, you don't have anything'," she said. "But we can worry about my character another day. We need to stop Jun Fang from unleashing this horror on the rest of the world."

"We know where he is, right?" Hawk asked.

"We have an idea of where he might be," Morgan said. "But none of that really matters."

"Why not?" Hawk asked. "We should put all our effort and resources into capturing him."

"Exactly," Ryder said. "He'll fold like a cheap suit if we corner him. And if he doesn't, we'll light his ass up."

Morgan scanned the room. "Look, I appreciate the enthusiasm for capturing Fang. And to be frank, it's not like we haven't been trying to capture him for a while now. But if we go after him now, he's got his get out of jail card."

"How's he going to do that?" Ryder asked.

"He can manipulate any video to make any high-ranking official look like they're doing something they shouldn't be," she said. "Then, the charges are dropped and he walks. It's that simple."

"Then we should definitely eliminate him," Ryder said.

Morgan shook her head and let out a big breath through puffed cheeks. "Okay, look. As much as I want to do that—and probably just like everyone in this room wants Fang gone—it's not just Fang that we have to worry about. He might appear to be in charge of The Alliance, but if we eliminate him, another person steps in to take his place. Our priority needs to be ensuring that Fang's software doesn't get implemented widely. That's where we need to put our focus for this meeting. Revenge can wait for what he's done to me and President Bullock. There are some things more important right now."

"So, we need to gain some leverage on Fang, correct?" Hawk asked.

Morgan nodded. "If we can hold something over him, then

we might be able to broker a truce or, better yet, force him to hand over the software."

"I doubt he'll do that," Big Earv said. "That's his problem-solver hack."

"I just want to know why he went after you," Mia asked. "Of all the women he could've humiliated in Washington, he picked you."

"Well, I'd like to think that Fang views me and this organization as his biggest threat," Morgan said. "But speculating on his motivation for targeting me isn't going to solve our biggest problem right now."

Mia smiled. "Then maybe I can help."

"You have something?"

"Alex broke down the file for me, but I've been able to further break down the code and figure out not only how it worked but how to implement it ourselves. If we want to go after Fang, maybe we can beat him at his own game. Maybe make him look like he did something illegal that he never actually did."

"No," Rebecca said, interjecting into the discussion for the first time. "There are other ways to do this. You guys understand force, but there are other means to accomplish your goals."

Morgan arched an eyebrow. "Such as?"

"So far, Fang's method of attack has been very direct. He's specifically targeted his enemies. And based off the briefing I read on the past operating methods of The Alliance, that's a little odd. I can't help but wonder if he's only recently assumed command or removed some of his best staffers."

"They also could've left after what Fang was accused of," Big Earv said.

"True," Rebecca said, nodding at Big Earv. "That also might explain it. But whoever was there before understood the value of forcing people to *volunteer* their services, so to speak. If we want Fang to do something for us, the best way to do that is by putting someone he cares about in our crosshairs."

"And I know just the person," Morgan said with a smile.

Mia grinned. "Are you thinking what I'm thinking?"

Morgan nodded and then turned to Rebecca. "How would you like to kick off this operation?"

"What do you have in mind?" Rebecca asked.

"For starters, a job tailor-made for your special set of skills."

EIGHTEEN

ARUBA

J.D. Blunt, unlit cigar dangling from his lips, wiped his hands on his bloodied apron and snatched another rainbow runner out of his cooler, dropping the dead fish on the table. He smiled with satisfaction as he glanced over at his pan of fish he'd already cleaned. While he considered a bad day fishing better than a good day doing pretty much anything else, Blunt felt giddy after a good day fishing. And this day had been better than most. He felt as if his boat *Mas Borbon* was like the Caribbean's equivalent of the Pied Piper. Everywhere he went, fish seemed to be following him.

He brought down his cleaver with a forceful whack, severing the fish's head from the rest of its body. A grunt morphed into a delighted chuckle as Blunt picked up another blade and dug the tip into the fish and raked it along the bottom, splaying it. He was so focused on his task that he didn't hear the convoy of SUVs skid to a stop on the street running parallel to the beach. However, the familiar thud of a half-dozen car doors slamming almost all at once perked up his ears.

He cursed his decision to stay at the rental house rather than returning to his floating home at sea. With Besserman having stayed at the house, he knew the agency would eventually track him there. It was just a matter of time—and that time had arrived.

Reaching behind his back, he felt for his gun before instantly remembering he'd left it in his boat. He angled toward *Mas Borbon*, hoping he could get there before whoever had just arrived reached the back of the beach house. The heavy sand weight from a recent high tide slowed down his efforts to reach the vessel.

"I hope you don't think you're going somewhere," came a familiar voice.

Blunt turned slowly to see the CIA Deputy Director Steve Pickens marching toward him. Four other agents flanked him, pistols all drawn and trained in front of them.

Blunt sighed and then rubbed his face with his hand. He removed the baseball cap he'd been wearing and scratched his head.

"A little bit of an overkill, don't ya think?" Blunt said with a scowl.

"When it comes to hunting down trained killers, you can never be too careful," Pickens fired back.

"Look, if you didn't want me fishing for rainbow runners, you could've just told me. No need to come down here as if I murdered the president."

"Not funny," Pickens said with a snarl. "And besides, nobody said you ever murdered the president. Or anyone else, for that matter."

"Deflect all you want, Pickens," Blunt said. "But your goons are all still pointing their guns at me. I can promise you that the only life I've ever wanted since arriving down here was that of hapless fishing. Whatever it is that you're doing down here, I don't want any part of it."

"Where's Robert Besserman?" Pickens snapped.

"Who?"

"Oh, come on, J.D. We don't have time for games."

"Apparently you do," Blunt said as he dug the cleaver into the chopping table and wiped fish guts off his hands with his apron. "You're down here acting as if I'm hiding the CIA director. So, first off, I'm not. And secondly, who cares if I did? He's the damn director of the CIA. If you still haven't figured out why I tried to get as far away from Washington as possible, you've got brain rot. This is all so absurd."

"Have you seen the video?" one of Pickens' lackeys asked. "He climbed on a boat and raced away before it exploded."

"I haven't seen it, but that doesn't sound like it proves a damn thing," Blunt said. "Plus, I don't need to see it to know it didn't happen. The director is an honorable man who is entrenched in the day-to-day minutiae of running the agency and doesn't have time to run around setting off bombs in foreign countries. I swear, you guys must plug your ears when you talk so you don't realize how stupid you sound."

Pickens gestured for the CIA officers accompanying him to lower their weapons.

"There are at least three other foreign intelligence agencies pursuing Besserman, expressing a strong desire to bring him to justice for what he did," he said. "Now, I know you have a good relationship with the director, but I'm also guessing you'd rather us catch him than the Russians or the Italians or the Albanians."

Blunt removed the cigar from his mouth and scrunched up his nose, as if in disbelief. "The Albanians? What the hell do the Albanians—ah, never mind."

"I know it's jarring when one of your friends goes rogue, but you can't provide safe harbor without expecting severe repercussions," Pickens said. "Now, where is he?"

"I already told you—I don't know," Blunt said, speaking in a slow and deliberate tone. "If you'd like to search my boat, knock yourself out."

Pickens nodded at his agents, who scurried over to *Mas Borbon* and scoured the vessel for any signs of Besserman.

"You're wasting your time," Blunt said. "In fact, you could've saved yourself a trip, not to mention thousands of dollars of taxpayers' money, and just given me a call. I could've told you over the phone that he's not here."

"But he *was* here, wasn't he?"

"Steve, I hope you understand that what you're doing is not only wrong, but it's also criminal. Even if he was sitting in my kitchen, you couldn't forcibly take him back to your country without help from Aruban government. And I'm willing to bet that you don't have permission to conduct any extraction operations."

"Maybe you've forgotten that Prime Minister Etienne is a close friend of mine from our days together at UCLA," Pickens said. "I don't think I'll have any trouble getting him to sign off on the extradition of a foreign terrorist."

"If I didn't know any better, I'd think you were just a dumb ass," Blunt said. "But I do know better. And I know exactly what this is all about. You're just trying to make a play to become the director, even though deep down you know it's all bullshit."

"Wait a minute, J.D. I thought you didn't know what was going on."

"Get outta here, Steve. And take your thugs with you. You're never gonna get appointed to that position, no matter how badly you want it."

"We'll see about that."

Pickens whistled at his team, directing two of them to search the beach house. Then he turned his gaze back toward Blunt.

"Now, where's Alex?" Pickens asked.

"Alex? What the hell do you want with her?"

"Just answer the question," Pickens snarled.

"Well, gee, Steve. I don't know. Have you tried her ranch in Montana? She lives in the good ole USA, last time I checked."

"We already checked her ranch. She wasn't there. But we also received some reliable intel that she was here in the country and visiting you."

Blunt bit down on his cigar and slowly shook his head. "Maybe there's a problem with your intel. Ever consider that?"

Blunt picked up his cleaver and hacked off the head of another rainbow runner, ignoring Pickens and his team. A few minutes later, they drove off, tires screeching as they peeled away.

"Amateurs," Blunt said to himself with a snort.

He retreated into the house, washed his hands, and then called Alex.

"Be careful," he said. "Pickens and the CIA are looking for you."

"Don't worry," she said. "They're messing with the wrong woman."

Blunt chuckled again before ending the call and resuming his chore of cleaning fish. He planned to fry up a feast of fish. And drink some bourbon too—lots of bourbon.

NINETEEN

WASHINGTON, D.C.

PRESIDENT BULLOCK PINCHED HIS NOSE AS HE SCANNED the notes resting on the lectern. He took a deep breath, settling his nerves as he looked across the White House press room. Bullock's communications team shoehorned reporters of all types along with television cameramen into the tight space, fulfilling as many requests as possible for the president's highly-anticipated press conference.

Bullock chewed on his lip a moment as he considered the right tone to deliver his opening remarks. In the hours leading up to the event, he'd contemplated everything from a disinterested monotone to an angry tirade—and just about everything in between. He couldn't even believe he had to address the most ridiculous rumor to surface about him since he'd been in office. But the video that was circulating on social media demanded he say something. Yet it wasn't for a lack of trying. He'd had his office respond initially by dismissing the video as one generated by artificial intelligence or simply a deep fake. However, that tactic failed when news organizations began delving deep into their vast roster of experts, many of which were happy to get the airtime to discuss

127

arguably the greatest scandal in American politics in the twenty-first century. And that was quite an achievement given what it was competing against.

As Bullock paused to look at his notes one final time, he closed his eyes and said a prayer. He needed to strike the perfect tone or else his legacy would forever be tainted. While he wanted to vehemently deny what the world had now seen depicted in the obviously doctored video, he also didn't want to be forever mocked like a previous president had been—and forever would be —for denying the event ever occurred. That president's entire legacy was forgotten once he denied it and the truth came out shortly thereafter. While there was a stark difference to Bullock, there wouldn't be to the American public. The report just reinforced what most Americans already thought about the office of the president—that it was a position for an entitled elitist who excelled at leveraging his power for personal gain. Bullock aimed to restore dignity to the White House, especially after all that had happened under the watch of previous corrupt leaders. Yet he looked the same as his predecessors to everyone else.

Bullock cleared his throat, took a sip of water from a bottle left for him on the lectern, and started with his opening remarks.

"As you know, we live at an interesting moment in history," he began. "It's a time when we don't know what's real and what's not, even when we see it with our own two eyes. So, it comes as no surprise that someone would make an attempt to smear me in this way. And the sad part of it all is that I have to take up all our precious time to address these accusations."

He put his hands in his pockets and rocked back and forth on his heels for a moment before continuing.

"I happen to be a very happily married husband who cherishes his wife and would never do anything like this to her," Bullock said. "I wouldn't do it because it would hurt Cori. And I wouldn't do it because it's wrong and goes against what I believe. We share both mutual admiration and respect for one another and wouldn't even consider doing this.

"Now, I don't know who is responsible for this, but I have created a special task force to investigate not only who was behind this but also how it could happen. I'm also asking Congress to pass a law against the creation of such videos or amend current ones so this type of video falls under the category of slander. Just like you can't say things that are untrue about another person with the express intent of hurting them, you shouldn't be able to fabricate videos that do the same thing."

He nodded at his press secretary, who flipped on his mic and turned to the pack of journalists. "At this time, President Bullock will field a few of your questions regarding the recent release of the video. Let's start with Karissa Mixon."

"Thank you," she said as she stood and snatched a microphone offered to her by one of the aides. "Good afternoon, Mr. President. Now, you have denied that this interaction ever occurred, but you have never denied knowing Morgan May. Can you tell us a little bit more about her and her role with the White House?"

"She's not a public official," Bullock said. "She operates a think tank that weighs in on issues related to national security and the like. Her company is public and you can look it up."

"But she hasn't been to her office for the past few days. Would you have any idea as to why she would be avoiding going to work?"

Bullock forced a smile. "I'd try to avoid work too if I knew you guys were going to harass me the moment I tried to get into my office."

The aide tried to take the microphone from Karissa, but she refused to hand it over.

"Just a moment," she said, wagging her finger at the young woman. "I have two more questions, questions that the American people want and need answers to."

"It's all right," Bullock said to the aide. "Let her continue. She's fine."

"Thank you, Mr. President," Karissa said. "Now, in some of

your previous denials regarding this affair and even today, you've alluded to the fact that this video was generated by a computer. Can you elaborate on the technology that your team has uncovered that makes this type of deception possible—and even believable?"

"We're still working on that. As soon as we have more, believe me, my office will be getting that information to you. It needs to stop as soon as possible before others get hurt."

Karissa looked down at the notes in her hand, running her finger down a list before stopping and then glancing up at Bullock with a wary look.

"Sir, you've also claimed that you have proof that you were in a private meeting the night this event allegedly occurred at a downtown restaurant," she said.

"That's correct."

"Then how do you explain the video we found of you leaving the dinner early and the presidential limo entering a parking garage adjacent to the condominium where the alleged tryst between you and Morgan May was filmed?"

Bullock grimaced. "We had a security event that forced us to divert from our regular path, and the Secret Service team decided it would be best to get off the road and seek shelter somewhere. We were only there for fifteen minutes, and I believe the video was longer than that if I'm not mistaken."

"The video was only eight minutes, sir."

"Well, I'm sure my office can provide you with the documentation that a safety threat forced us to take shelter in a parking garage."

"Those answers all seem quite convenient," Karissa challenged as she handed the mic back to the aide and then sat down.

"The truth always seems convenient when you want it to be a lie," Bullock said, feeling his face flush red with anger. "Next question, please."

A reporter raised her hand and took the mic from the White House communications team. "Mr. President, if there was a private meeting, can you provide us with the names of the people who were at that meeting so they can corroborate you were there?"

"I'm sorry, but that meeting was private and I can't divulge the names," Bullock said.

"What if they wanted to speak up on their own?" the reporter asked.

"Like I said, it was a private meeting. The participants and the matters discussed will remain confidential."

Another man stood up and took the mic. "Mr. President, how well do you know Morgan May? How often do you work with her?"

"I already told Ms. Mixon that she consults with my office on various issues."

"But how well do *you* know her?" the reporter asked, a deviant smile playing across his lips.

"Thank you for coming," Bullock said before he scooped up all his notes and stormed off the stage.

Reporters shouted at him as he strode toward the door, but he ignored them all. He clenched his fists, crinkling the papers in his hands. He'd blown it and he knew it. It didn't matter what he said, he'd already been deemed guilty by the press.

Then he turned down the hallway and found his wife there, arms folded across her chest, foot thumping the floor.

For a moment he considered returning to the press room.

I can't win today.

TWENTY

LONDON

Jun Fang straightened the collar on his dark Henry Poole suit jacket and inspected it for lint before he got out of his limo. He usually preferred to drive himself, but his return to London demanded style and panache. His media relations team had arranged for a brief news conference at Heathrow Airport, marking his first return to JF Industries since the scandal of his adoption business began. And Fang wanted to look sharp for the cameras.

A pack of photographers had followed him to JF Industries, all shoving their camera lenses through the gaps in the black iron fencing around the property's perimeter.

Mei Ling Wu, who wore a gold sequined dress that hugged every contour of her body, patted him on the knee before taking his face in her hands and forcing him to look at her. He looked her up and down and grinned.

"You stand proud," she said. "You did nothing wrong. Let them know you know you're innocent and have been vindicated."

"I don't know any other way to act," he said before kissing her.

Fang's lawyer, sitting opposite the couple, cleared his throat. "You need to get going. You have some paperwork to sign in order to make official your return to the company."

"Of course," Fang said as he pulled back from Wu, his gaze still locked on her face.

Fang opened the door where he was greeted by the CFO and COO of JF Industries as well as his two members of his communications team that had followed him from the airport.

"That was a jolly good chat with the press," said Elizabeth Arnold, the director of communications. "If social media is any indication of how well your initial return to London went over with people, this is going to be a smooth transition back."

Fang turned and waved to the cameras, offering a broad grin as he did. Then he spun and walked toward the entrance to his headquarters.

"What exactly are people saying, Elizabeth?" he asked.

"They're saying that you were unjustly targeted by the authorities and that the notion you were siphoning off kids to be killers always sounded ridiculous."

He nodded. "It did sound ridiculous, didn't it?"

"Of course," she said with a laugh. "It's not like you're some secret spy or anything. Your company has provided some of the most innovative products the world has ever seen. It's not like you have time to do something like that. And even if you did—"

"God, enough with the ass kissing, Elizabeth," said Vincent Reid, the COO. "Might as well make your pucker-face permanent."

"Don't be so hard on her, Vince," Fang said. "I know everyone is excited to see me back and doesn't know how they're supposed to act. Just a few weeks ago, you all thought I was an evil psychopath. But today? Now I'm deemed a productive member of society. It's enough to make anyone's head swim."

Fang entered the front doors to a standing ovation from the employees lining both sides of the hallway.

"We never doubted you," said one woman.

"We knew it was all a lie," another man shouted.

"Welcome back, Mr. Fang," said another.

Fang, smiling and waving, turned and looked at his COO. "And who's responsible for this, Vince?"

"I thought it'd be a nice way to set the mood today."

"Talk about ass kissing," Fang said with a shrug before turning his attention back to the employees who'd gathered.

Fang stopped in the middle of the hallway and addressed the crowd, turning from one side to the other as he spoke.

"Thank you so much. This means a lot to me. To know that you all still believed in me and remained at this great company lets me know that you're all committed to the work, no matter what challenges come our way. And if there's one thing I know about the great people who run this place, it's that you know how to embrace a challenge and turn it into the best damn product in the world. And as I return to my role at the head of this company, that's what I'm expecting from each and every one of you. Now, let's go have a great day!"

The employees clapped and then dispersed, some lingering to shake Fang's hand. After a couple of minutes, he retreated to his office with Wu and Elizabeth.

"I've got everything set up for you already, sir," Elizabeth said after shutting the door behind her. "I brought in some lights like you requested and have a microphone with the backdrop. Everything is set up and ready to go. When you want to go live, just click on this button here and it'll give you a ten-second countdown. And when you want to show the video, just click here."

"Perfect, Elizabeth," Wu said. "I think we can handle it from here."

"If anything else pops up, you know where to find me," Elizabeth said before leaving.

Wu crossed the room to Fang and put her arms on his shoulders, interlacing her fingers. "Now, where were we?"

Fang kissed her and then drew back. "We can pick up where

we left off later, but we've got some work to do first. You ready to help with that?"

"Of course, dear. Just tell me what you want me to do."

Fang gave her brief instructions before they both walked over to the mirror hanging on the back of the door. After inspecting themselves, they moved into position. Wu pressed the button to start the recording and rushed back into place, her heels skittering against the floor.

"Good morning—or good afternoon or good evening," Fang said. "I hope wherever you are and whenever you are that your life is going good. As you might have heard already, mine is going better than good at the moment after the authorities dropped all charges that had been levied against me. I've always maintained my innocence, but being able to fight the baseless charges filed against me without being confined to prison was important, which was why the last time you saw me on social media I did some shocking things."

Fang moved closer to the camera, his face solemn.

"And for those of you who were traumatized by my last appearance on a social media live stream, I apologize for the shocking incident. My twin brother, God rest his soul, was dying of a painful form of cancer and didn't want to suffer any longer. He wanted his last act to be one that helped secure my freedom. And thanks to his selflessness, his act provided me with just that —an opportunity to prove my innocence and get my life back."

Fang stepped back from the camera, providing a fuller view of his body.

"Now, you might be asking yourself why any of that matters to you, but the truth is if I'm able to do what I do best, you just might be able to have a better quality of life. And that's why I wanted to mark my return to JF Industries by showing you our latest innovation that is destined to transform the world. I want you to meet our newest product, PowerBox."

Fang played a video that detailed how PowerBox would revolutionize the way cities are developed by changing the way they were powered. His new device used an advanced technology to better capture solar rays before converting it into usable power, eliminating the need for a power grid, making communities less vulnerable to terrorist attacks and providing the security of stable power. As the footage rolled, a man showed how PowerBox was installed in homes in a small village in Kenya that previously didn't have access to power. After six months, the entire village was thriving, both as a community and economically. Children had access to education through computers connected to the internet. Families had new sources to create income and develop wealth by selling some of the village's tribal hand-crafted flutes that had become an internet sensation due to attention on social media. Then there was a half-minute of slow-motion footage of people smiling and laughing, interspersed with images of PowerBox devices attached to the outside of primitive houses.

"And if you think that's cool," Fang said as he returned to the screen in a live shot, "we're just getting started. The extraordinarily talented and incredibly beautiful Mei Ling Wu has joined me today to talk about the future of JF Industries moving forward."

Wu affirmed her support of the new ventures before taking a moment to encourage others to seek opportunities to do the kind of good that Fang was doing.

"This is what the world needs right now," she said, tilting her head and eyeing the camera cautiously. "We need good people coming together to do good things for one another. Instead of fighting over silly things that don't matter, we need to come together to make our lives better."

She tucked her long dark hair behind her ears and stepped closer to the camera.

"And if anything I've said has struck a nerve with you, I want to invite you to join me in Washington, D.C. next week for the IFF conference. At the Influence, Fortune, and Fame event, I will be speaking on how to leverage social media for good and how you can use your talents and skills to do the same. And I hope to see many of you there."

Fang spoke briefly to reiterate what he was doing with PowerBox devices and when they'd be available to the public before closing out the live stream.

Within seconds, Elizabeth burst into the room, her eyes wide and a big smile on her face. "That was incredible, you two. You almost broke the internet with that live stream."

Fang scowled. "Broke the internet? I don't believe that's possible."

"Well, believe it," she said. "There were outages reported everywhere because of the stress placed on many service providers. That's quite likely to happen when you get two hundred *million* viewers logging in to watch."

Wu looked bug-eyed at Elizabeth. "Are you serious? *Two hundred million* viewers?"

"Yes," Elizabeth said, a smile still plastered on her face. "It makes your live stream the most-watched event online in the history of the internet."

"Great," Fang said. "Now I'm going to be hearing from the PowerBox engineers."

"You sure will. One of the sales guys texted me and said it'll take them a week to reply to all the inquiries."

"Might get a similar complaint from the IFF conference organizers, too," Wu said.

"I saw a post on social media that IFF leadership has created a second session for the conference to occur earlier that morning."

"This is great," Wu said, turning and taking Fang's hands. "Do you know what this means?"

"Of course," Fang said with a sly grin. "It means I'm back."

TWENTY-ONE

BRIDGER, MONTANA

ROBERT BESSERMAN SAT ON THE BACK PORCH OF THE guest cottage Alex and Hawk had built for the parade of guests who frequented their isolated property. Whether it was Morgan visiting to ride horses in the Montana mountains or Big Earv coming out for a big game hunting trip—or any other of their colleagues seeking to escape city life—they had decided to build a small guest house on the back of their property to accommodate friends and family. Besserman sat on a small bench on the back porch that offered a breath-taking view of the surrounding peaks while he tied his shoes.

The branches of a nearby cottonwood tree swayed in the wind, clattering together. A tumbleweed bounded along the ground, seemingly urged forward by a streak of dust. Overhead, an osprey circled as it sought an early-morning snack. It wasn't the same type of serenity Besserman had experienced while drinking a glass of bourbon on the beach, but it was still peaceful in other ways.

He literally couldn't see anyone, easily spotting more wildlife than humans.

The osprey broke out of his circular pattern, diving toward the creek. The bird swept low, its talons protracting as if ready to pounce. Then it barely dipped its claws into the water before soaring skyward clutching a wriggling fish. Plucked from its habitat, the fish thrashed in the osprey's talons yet didn't seem to even concern the bird. It screeched, the sound echoing off the nearby rock walls before disappearing around a bend.

Besserman thought the scene reminded him of himself—a fish ripped from its comfort zone through no fault of its own and wholly unable to do anything about it. First the sand castle, now the fish. He stood and stretched out his calf muscles, hoping he didn't see anyone get shot or run over.

I'm supposed to be running the CIA but I'm hiding out in the hinterlands of Montana. Can it get much worse than this?

Besserman knew it could. At least for the moment he was still free.

After filling up a water bottle, Besserman struck out on the trail that led from the cottage into a wooded section of the substantial acreage owned by Hawk and Alex. According to Alex, the three-mile loop wound through a canyon and along a creek, dipping into a ravine and then back up to a plateau that looked out across the surrounding mountains. She told him that was Hawk's favorite hike when he needed to process tough decisions, guaranteed not to see another human.

As Besserman ventured down the trail, he immediately pushed aside the thoughts of his looming battle in Washington. He knew he couldn't hide out forever, but he decided to pretend like he was there on his own volition as opposed to being forced there. Instead of thinking about what awaited him, he thought about the chipmunks he saw darting back and forth across the trail and where tumbleweeds came from and how come the big sky country wasn't more populated. Anything to avoid dwelling on his current state of affairs.

Besserman paused to watch an osprey. He removed the binoculars from his pocket and followed the bird across the sky. Then chattering from a nearby treetop made him turn and investigate the source—a red squirrel, who stared angrily while twitching his tail.

"You don't like me?" Besserman said to the squirrel before resuming his walk. "Take a number."

When he reached the creek, he sat on a large rock and watched the water bubble and gurgle, battling its way past sticks and stones and other debris. He picked up a handful of rocks and tossed them into the water, enjoying each satisfying *thunk* as they broke the surface. He wiped his hands off on his pants and resumed his uneventful hike.

But as he rounded the bend, he looked off in the distance and caught a glint of sunlight reflecting off something. And immediately Besserman didn't think it looked natural. He took a step back in an attempt to see it again. But it wasn't there. If it had been a fixed object, he would've been able to see it again. It wasn't there.

He furrowed his brow and continued walking only to catch a glimpse of it a second time. Instead of ignoring it, Besserman removed his binoculars and peered in the direction of where he'd seen the glint. There was nothing there. Just deadwood from a fallen tree.

I'm getting paranoid.

Besserman continued his hike, meandering up the trail that looped past Hawk and Alex's house. Alex was feeding the horses in the barn while little J.D. was ducking behind a hay bale, aiming his wooden gun and making shooting noises with his mouth.

"Did you get the bad guys?" Besserman asked.

"There's so many of them," J.D. said before rolling along the ground and opening fire on his imaginary enemies. "I need backup."

Besserman hustled over to his spot and pretended to shoot a finger gun at the ghost army storming toward them.

"Nice shot," J.D. said. "I think we got them all."

Besserman laughed and eased to his feet. "We make a pretty good team, don't we?"

J.D. smiled and nodded. Then his expression turned serious.

"Get down," J.D. said.

Besserman ducked and J.D. trained his gun in the direction just beyond him, making more firing noises with his mouth.

"You were almost a goner," J.D. said. "That guy snuck up on us, but I think we got 'em all now."

"Thanks," Besserman said, offering his hand for a high-five.

J.D. slapped Besserman's palm before running off to fight more imaginary enemies.

Besserman poked his head into the barn to let Alex know he'd made it back.

"How was it?" she asked, jamming a pitchfork into a busted bale and tossing the hay into a trough.

"It was great," Besserman said. "Just what I needed."

"I knew you'd like it. There are a few other good hikes on our property as well. If you want to go on another one, just let me know."

"I'll definitely do that," he said, pausing for a moment. "But there was something odd that happened on my hike though."

"What was it?"

"Well, I think it was odd, but maybe it's just that I'm very paranoid right now."

"Hard not to be after all you've been through. But what happened?"

"I was coming out of the ravine and I saw sunlight glint off something in the distance. I thought maybe it was some stationary object, so I backed up to the spot where I noticed it but couldn't see it. Then I pulled out my binoculars and didn't see anything. Whatever it was, it was gone. So, I don't know. Think it was a car?"

Alex rubbed the back of her neck and scrunched up her nose. "I don't know. You'd have to show me the direction where you saw it glinting."

"It was kind of to the northeast of here."

"Interesting. Can you point to the general area where you think you saw something?"

"Yeah, right over there," he said, pointing toward the top of a ridge. "Want to use my binoculars?"

She shook her head. "I want something a little stronger and a little more focused."

Alex ducked into the house, leaving Besserman on the porch by himself.

"She's going to get her gun," little J.D. said.

"Her gun? You've seen her shoot it?"

The boy nodded. "Daddy always says never get on Mommy's bad side."

Besserman chuckled as he watched J.D. make truck noises and pretend like he was driving away very quickly. The CIA director was still smiling when Alex returned with a Mauser M18 rifle.

"What's so funny?" she asked. "Did J.D. tell you a joke?"

"Not intentionally."

Alex jammed the butt of the M18 against her shoulder before peering through the scope. "He'll do that from time to time. It's not always funny when he tries those shenanigans around bedtime."

"So he's like his father?"

Alex pulled back from the scope and gave Besserman a sideways glance. "Hawk would say he's like me."

Besserman looked sheepishly at his feet. "So you're both a pair of smart asses. Got it."

Alex returned her attention to the scope and studied the area, the barrel sweeping back and forth.

Then a growl and a curse. She looked over her shoulder, presumably to make sure J.D. didn't hear it.

"What is it?" Besserman asked.

She cursed again.

"This was plan A," Besserman said. "Do we need a plan B?"

Alex shook her head. "I refuse to be a prisoner in my own home."

"What is it?" Besserman asked.

She handed him the rifle and pointed in the general direction she was looking when she'd become angry.

Besserman cursed too.

TWENTY-TWO

WASHINGTON, D.C.

THE MAGNUM GROUP'S PLAN TO SET UP MEI LING WU required a few favors to be called in, first and foremost getting the IFF conference director Pamela Sanders to allow Rebecca Fornier to show the star guest speaker around Washington. Rebecca pulled up to Wu's hotel in a black Bugatti Divo rented from an exotic car dealer. While a 24-hour rental of a vehicle stretched the budget, it kept Wu's security team in a trailing SUV and also ensured that she would document every second of her excursion, leveraging the opportunity to look filthy rich on social media.

Wu strutted out to the Divo wearing a Thom Browne gray merino wool dress with a white spread collar and black pumps. Rebecca thought the outfit wasn't flattering to Wu's voluptuous figure, but it was sure to attract attention from the fashion writers, which was what Wu was obviously most concerned with. She spun and waved at the cluster of photographers on the sidewalk before slipping into the passenger seat. The door shut automatically and then Wu turned to Rebecca.

"Make sure you speak to Nelson after we're done," Wu said. "I'll make sure you get a substantial tip for arranging this car."

Rebecca wanted to make small talk with Wu, but she put her head down and started scrolling through her phone.

"Anything in particular you'd like to see in Washington today?" Rebecca asked.

Wu didn't look up. "Whatever backdrops will get me the most likes, though I don't expect you to know that off the top of your head."

"The Smithsonian has a collection of some of the world's most interesting art as well as artifacts, both ancient and modern. It's hard to go wrong there."

"Then I guess that's where we'll go," Wu said, offering a smile that looked more like a pain expression than genuine joy.

She put her head back down and swiped away on her phone.

Rebecca hadn't officially been on the Magnum Group team for long and she wasn't sure how she felt about what she was going to do to Wu. But less than ten minutes into meeting her, Rebecca knew she wouldn't have a single regret. Wu may have been a rising star internationally due to her good looks, but she seemed to excel at being insufferable.

As Rebecca drove past several iconic symbols in Washington, Wu begged her to stop in order to capture the moment.

"My followers will just love this," Wu said, almost verbatim at very location.

Rebecca found herself serving as not only Wu's driver but also her photographer, snapping photos in front of the Washington Monument, the Lincoln Memorial, and the Capitol Building. Eventually, they wound their way to the Smithsonian's National Museum of Natural History, pulling up to the front where a group of photographers descended upon her as she made a dramatic exit from the vehicle.

Rebecca remained in the background as Wu lapped up the attention, posing next to the car and then strutting toward the entrance. It wasn't until she entered the building that she even looked for Rebecca.

One pool reporter and photographer were allowed to

accompany the social media influencer during his tour of the museum. As they drifted from one room to the next, Wu looked for the most exotic object in the room and lingered by it until the photographer snapped a picture. At one point, her tour intersected with a group of elementary school students on a field trip, which Wu took advantage of, stopping to interact with them. The photographer rushed over to capture the interaction where Wu knelt in front of a couple of girls and told them they could be anything they wanted to be in the future and to work hard to make good grades. Rebecca wanted to roll her eyes but refrained for fear of her reaction getting caught on camera.

Rebecca handed a note to the reporter that said Wu's team wanted to get her on camera answering a particular question. The reporter nodded, signaling she was fine with granting the request. It was benign in nature—and maybe even one that would create a viral clip for social media, depending how she answered. But Rebecca still felt a twinge of guilt for setting up Wu.

As they climbed to the second floor, they entered the room containing the Hope Diamond, a 45-carat diamond extracted from India in the 17th century. The rare jewel had a storied history as one of the world's most desired diamonds by both collectors and thieves alike. Situated in a special case that allowed museum patrons to view the Hope Diamond from four sides, it sparkled beneath the special lighting from the enclosed case as Rebecca circled it.

Museum handlers prevented other patrons from looking at the diamond until the current group gathered around the display case moved on. Once they moved on, the tour guide gestured toward the jewel, signaling for Wu to step forward and take a look. Wu's eyes widened as she looked at it, her mouth falling slack.

"Isn't it beautiful?" Wu asked, her hand reaching for her neck, as if she was imagining what it would feel like to have it there. "I've never seen anything like it."

Wu's joy seemed genuine, her pretentious attitude gone. She smiled at Rebecca.

"Have you seen this thing?" Wu asked.

Rebecca nodded. "It's something else, isn't it?"

"I mean, yeah. It's amazing. Who wouldn't want that in their jewelry collection?"

Rebecca smiled. She didn't even need the reporter to ask any questions if that exchange had been captured. It might as well have been a brazen prediction of what she would later do.

"What do you think of the Hope Diamond?" the reporter asked, following instructions, as if it wasn't already obvious.

Wu repeated her previous statement to Rebecca before gushing about it. "That diamond has to be one of the most beautiful things I've ever seen. Just look at how it sparkles and shines."

The photographer who'd been capturing the museum tour moved in for a closeup of the jewel before shooting through the case and getting a shot of Wu staring at the object. Her eyes shone bright, her smile broad. Then she mouthed a "wow," one that was long and drawn out.

She'll be proud to post that one on social media.

The photographer clicked away until he was satisfied that he had several good images. He even alerted her to the fact that he was done. But her awe was real as she lingered for a moment, staring at the rock.

After they finished the tour, Rebecca drove Wu back to her hotel. The model shook Rebecca's hand, pressing a folded-up bill into her palm. Rebecca didn't look at the money until Wu was inside the hotel. It was a five-dollar bill. Not that she expected a tip for the tour, but it was almost an insult. She would've rather received nothing.

Despite Wu's rude disposition, Rebecca couldn't help but feel like they were doing her wrong.

"How'd it go?" Hawk asked over the coms.

Rebecca looked into her purse and dug out a small black box. "The cloning device worked. I've got her phone."

"And everything else?"

Rebecca sighed as she eased into gear and pulled away from the hotel. "Do we really have to do this? I mean, she doesn't really deserve to be treated like we're going to treat her, does she?"

"Of course not," Hawk said. "But that's the point. We're doing this to get at Fang, okay? Just remember that. This isn't about Mei Ling Wu, though I hear she's insufferable and it might be fun to watch her squirm. But this is all about Fang and stopping Operation Nightfall. If we don't do this, he's going to do far worse to far more innocent people."

"But here's the thing. I think she's completely innocent in all of this."

"Nobody's ever *completely* innocent. Besides, if you remember that the entire reason that Besserman is holed up to avoid getting arrested for a crime he didn't commit, you've got a short memory. This is for Bobby, too. Remember?"

"I know," she said. "There's just something that doesn't feel right about all this."

"You can work out the ethics and morality of what we're doing later. But in the meantime, we need to shut down Fang before he gets to be more powerful."

Mia's voice piped in over the coms. "Great work, Rebecca. I just checked the download. We've got everything we need off Wu's phone."

"And?"

"And what?"

"And does it look like she's some hardened criminal mastermind who's part of all this?"

"Not at first glance, but I just started digging," Mia said. "You just keep up the good work, okay?"

"Yeah, yeah," Rebecca said, still unable to shake off the guilt that was gnawing at her.

But she told herself that it didn't matter and to stay focused.

"The only thing that matters is stopping Fang," she said aloud to herself, almost as if she was trying to convince herself it was true.

It was. And she knew it. But the image of Wu staring giddily at the Hope Diamond was forever seared into her brain.

She would do her job when the time came, but she wasn't sure she'd be happy about it.

TWENTY-THREE

BRIDGER, MONTANA

Alex went to her room and retrieved her camera and telephoto lens. It had been a while since she'd been on a surveillance op, but she was proud of the way she'd mastered capturing images from such a long distance. She grabbed a tripod as well before returning to the living room.

"Whoa," Besserman said. "That's quite a camera you've got there."

"Sometimes size does matter," she said.

"I see that. So, we're just gonna take pictures of these guys?"

Alex placed the camera on the table and ejected the memory card, replacing it with a clean one. "I could just pull out the M18 and start taking shots. Doesn't matter to me either way. I mean if the director of the CIA says it's all right, it'd save us a lot of time."

"No," Besserman said with a sigh. "We can't do that. We're on American soil, remember?"

"Yeah, I know. Due process and all that other fun legal stuff. If we were in Yemen, I wouldn't have hesitated to take aim and pull the trigger."

J.D. thundered into the house and ran straight to the kitchen. He opened a drawer in the fridge and pulled out a cheese stick.

"Make sure you throw away your trash," she shouted.

"I always throw away my trash."

"Young man," Alex said, stopping to give him a piercing stare.

"Okay. Don't worry, Mommy. I'll throw it away."

"Right now."

Little J.D. unwrapped his cheese stick and tossed the plastic wrapping into the trash can before darting back outside.

"Thanks, J.D.," she called after him in a sing-song voice.

Besserman shifted his weight from one foot to the other. "Have you got a plan? Or are you just winging it here?"

"Hawk always says the best plans come to us when we're in the middle of the action."

"Really?"

Alex cracked a smile. "Of course not. We've always got a plan. Doesn't mean it won't fall apart, but we at least start with one."

"And what one are you starting with here?"

"I want to find out if that little party up there on the ridge is legit first. And then there are a few different ways we can handle this."

"Okay. Just let me know what I can do to help."

"Once I take a few pictures, you can help me identify who these guys are."

Alex slid open the glass doors leading to the deck from the upstairs bonus room and set up the tripod. After a couple of minutes, she had zoomed in on the men gathered around the trucks marked as Montana State Police. There was also a sign warning motorists to slow down and prepare for a search.

"Now I've never seen anything like that before," she said.

"What is it?" Besserman asked as he joined her on the deck.

"It's a roadblock. Now, I can understand if there's one on the main highway. But on a county-maintained gravel road that only ranchers use? Seems a little suspect to me."

She framed the men's faces as best as she could, trying to get each one looking straight at the camera. The more direct the image was, the better chances she'd have of a match in the facial recognition database.

As she continued taking pictures, she dialed the phone number for the Montana State Police. A cheerful woman answered the phone and asked Alex about the nature of her call.

"I was wondering if you're currently conducting a roadblock on Pryor Mountain Road near Bridger," Alex said.

The woman laughed. "A roadblock? Up there? Absolutely not. Currently, the MSP isn't conducting any roadblocks anywhere, so I don't know what you're seeing ma'am, but it's not our guys."

"Okay, thanks. Maybe they're local."

Alex ended the call.

"Maybe they're local?" Besserman asked. "There's nothing local about those vehicles."

"I didn't want her to think I was a lunatic," Alex said. "Besides, I just wanted to make sure we were covering our bases."

"So, they're frauds," he said. "Why don't we just call the cops on them?"

"They'd vanish before the county sheriff could get here, guaranteed."

"Maybe we could make sure they couldn't leave," Besserman suggested.

"Look, I appreciate the ideas, but you have to realize that we're in the middle of nowhere and whoever that is up there can go off-road in that truck. And the last thing I want is to remain here as a sitting duck. If we call the cops, nothing's gonna happen to them except that they'll be pissed off and maybe get aggressive about coming after us. Now, I think we could handle them, but I try to do my best to avoid an ambush in my own home. It's happened before and it wasn't pretty. Plus, I don't want J.D. being put in harm's way. Understand?"

"Copy that. So, what is the plan?"

"Let's see if we can figure out who these assholes are first."

Alex began transferring the pictures she took from the camera into her laptop and then feeding them into facial recognition databases. However, Besserman stopped her after the third image.

"I know who this is," Besserman said, pointing at the screen.

"Really?"

"Yeah, that's Steve Wingate. I'd know that ugly mug anywhere."

Alex stared at Wingate's pockmarked face that had small scar across his cheek. "Friend of yours?"

Besserman snorted. "This guy has been a pain in the agency's ass for a while now. He's a mercenary and constantly winds up butting heads with us on certain ops."

"So, this is definitely not any government sanctioned roadblock?"

"Not a chance with that guy. Every federal and local law enforcement agency is required to do a background check before hiring anyone. No way anyone would touch him."

Alex arched an eyebrow. "He's not wanted right now?"

"He's more of a nuisance than a raging criminal. He blocks our investigations but does so legally. However, he does have a lengthy rap sheet from previous altercations with various agencies, U.S. marshals, local deputies—you name it. But he's well-connected from his time in the military, so he lands a lot of private contract jobs."

"So, he's just going to harass me but not take any action? All bark, no bite?"

"I wouldn't bet the farm on it, but that's been his M.O. for a while now."

"Okay," she said. "There's no other reason for him to be here, except he's looking for you."

"And probably legally."

"So, I'm gonna go have a little chat with him, show him that he's wasting his time."

"I don't know, Alex. You need to be careful around him."

"If he's getting paid to bring you in, and he learns that you're not here, he's gonna go elsewhere, right?"

"Most likely."

"So, I just need to convince him that you're not here."

She walked over to a picture in the bonus room and tugged on one side. A set of hinges allowed the picture to open like a door, revealing a safe hidden behind it. She entered the code and a latch clicked, releasing the lock. She pulled out a pair of pistols, a Glock 17 and a Beretta PX4 Storm, and two boxes of ammunition.

"Damn, Alex. Do you live a double life as an assassin?"

"Always be prepared."

She shoved the ammo into her jacket pocket and headed downstairs.

"Keep an eye on me, will ya? The M18 has a powerful scope. You should be able to see what's happening with me."

"You need me to do anything?"

"If I look like I'm in trouble, start shooting."

"And what's trouble look like for you? I feel like I need a definition."

"If you see a gun that's not mine, I'm in trouble."

"Copy that."

"Think you can handle that thing?" she asked, nodding toward the rifle.

"I like to show up each new class of recruits at the range."

"Do you hit the target?"

"I'm a formidable shot."

She smiled. "Let's hope we don't have to find out if you're lying or not."

"Now, what about little J.D.?"

"He'll be fine. I leave him here to play while I go to the store all the time. And if things get dicey, you can always call his aunt and uncle. Their number's on the fridge."

"Good luck, and be careful."

"Of course," she said. "I'll send this Wingate character on his merry way and we'll keep working on how to prove you're innocent."

She climbed into the driver's seat of her Subaru, stopping briefly to tell little J.D. that she was running to the store and would be right back. He skipped off in search of another mountain of hay bales to conquer. Alex smiled and adjusted the rearview mirror before heading up the half-mile-long driveway toward Pryor Mountain Road.

After turning north on the road that led to Bridger, she drove about a quarter of a mile, a contrail dust left in her wake. Then she slowed down as she reached the roadblock. The men, who were all wearing Montana State Police uniforms, spread out, each taking up different positions as she approached. Wingate held out his hand, signaling for her to stop. Alex put the car in park but left it running. She rolled down the window and put her hand on the side of the door.

"What's the problem, officer?" she asked. "Got another coyote on the loose?"

Wingate flashed a warm smile and tipped his hat. "Ma'am. Unfortunately, it's something far more severe."

"More severe than a coyote?"

"Yes ma'am. We've got a killer on the loose and we are trying to cut him off."

"A killer? All the way up here in Bridger? What is the world coming to?"

"I wish I had better news for you, but right now we're just trying to secure an area and create a net around him."

One of the other men peeked through the window in her car.

"Is that really necessary?" she huffed.

"Just making sure you don't have any hitchhikers."

"Hitchhikers? I just left my house. I think I'd know if someone was trying to hitch a ride."

"If it's all the same to you," Wingate said, "I'd like to check, both for your peace of mind and for mine."

She sighed. "I don't like this. This feels like an invasion of privacy."

"Can I see your driver's license and registration, ma'am?" Wingate asked.

"What do you need that for?"

"Just fork it over, lady. I'd like to get this over with sooner than you do, trust me."

She handed him her license.

"Okay, thank you. Now, Mrs.—Hawk. Alex Hawk. Can you help me out here and please open up your trunk?"

"I don't think that's necessary."

"And why is that?"

"If you're looking for someone who's jumped into my trunk, unless he's done it while I was driving up the road, he's not in there. And I can promise you, nobody did that. So, I'd like to be on my way now so I can get groceries and have dinner ready in time for my husband when he gets home."

"Now I know you're lying, Mrs. Hawk," Wingate said before drawing his weapon. "Please step out of your vehicle right now."

Alex closed her eyes and took a deep breath. She left the car running as she climbed out and raised her hands in the air.

TWENTY-FOUR

WASHINGTON, D.C.

HAWK JAMMED HIS HANDS DEEP INTO HIS POCKETS AND bopped to the music playing through his headphones. He wore a pair of dark sunglasses with a backpack, doing his best to look like a meandering college student walking home from class near Georgetown. At the corner, he took a sharp left and wound back down the sidewalk until he came to an alley with rear garages to the townhomes facing the main street. Trash cans were wedged into tight spots in narrow spaces between the houses that were mere feet away from each other. There was no grass to cut or yards to manicure. It was concrete jungle living at its finest nestled in the heart of Washington.

Once Hawk was in position, he activated his coms. "How's my little survey guy?"

"I'm gonna choke you with my butterfly net," Ryder growled.

Hawk laughed. "I think the mechanical monarch on your shoulder is a nice touch. Where'd you get that anyway?"

"You know I'm gonna kill you in your sleep with butterflies— lots of them. They'll be swarming all over you and you'll be begging for help. And I'll just sit back and watch them gnaw away at you until you're nothing but skin and bones."

"Man, that escalated quickly. I was just giving you a hard time."

"I'm approaching the house, so I'd appreciate it if you'd keep the comments to yourself. *Comprende, amigo*?"

"*Si, señorita.*"

"*¡Muerte a ti!*"

Hawk listened over the coms as Ryder took deliberate steps up the walkway, each footfall scuffing against the pavement.

While Hawk and Ryder were accustomed to ops that required ingenuity as well as sharp-shooting skills, this one was a little different. If the situation had been different, a simple snatch-and-grab robbery would've worked. But this particular mission required the utmost discretion. If they were going to pull it off, no one could even know what happened, most of all, Smithsonian Natural Museum of History curator Kimberly Jordan.

According to the briefing Morgan May cobbled together, Jordan had only been on the job a couple of years. The frumpy history lover had pivoted in college when she realized her history degree didn't promise much in the way of a salary. So, she started volunteering at the Smithsonian and changed her major to archeology, putting herself on a track to possibly become a curator. And it didn't take long for her talent to shine. Six months after graduation, the Smithsonian gave her a full-time position as a curator. And in two years' time, she climbed the federal ladder and earned the title of senior curator.

Jordan was the best mark because of all the access she held, but she wasn't an easy one. Her townhome consisted of a motion-detection security system and a fierce Rottweiler named Gunther. She also competed in local Krav Maga competitions and had a bookshelf full of trophies commemorating first-place finishes. Despite how the briefing portrayed her, Jordan was an enigma, all the way down to her blue hair teeming with conservative roots.

Cracking the Kimberly Jordan code wouldn't be easy, but the best idea Hawk crafted was the one they decided to try first.

Ryder, his blond hair with lime green highlights, wore a knit polo shirt with a butterfly embroidered over his left breast and clutched a clipboard against his chest. Though Hawk couldn't see Ryder, he could imagine the mechanical butterfly opening its wings and closing them with a slight whir that was sure to drive Ryder insane.

"Chin up and smile," Hawk said over the coms. "And for the love of all things good and true, don't remove the butterfly."

"I'm gonna rip this damn thing off my shoulder and shove it up your ass," Ryder said before Hawk heard a muted doorbell chime over the coms.

"Good luck."

Seconds later the door creaked as it opened.

"Good afternoon," Ryder said. "I was wondering if I could speak with you for a moment to discuss the Butterfly Migration Conservation Society."

"I don't know," came the voice of Kimberly Jordan. "It's been a long day."

Ryder cleared his throat, the signal for Hawk to proceed into the back of her house. With the front door open, the alert that a door or window had been opened was temporarily disabled. Hawk turned the handle to the right and it clicked open. He slipped inside and could see Kimberly with her back to him, facing Ryder.

Hawk scanned the townhome, a quaint one that looked like it hadn't been updated since the mid-1980s. Flower print wallpaper, all white appliances, gaudy fixtures that looked like they were installed by the original builders. His shoes caught before giving way on the slick sheen of the linoleum, a sun-aged cream color with sunflower patterns in grids marked by trellises. Even Kimberly's furniture looked like it came from decades ago. Hawk thought to himself that he wouldn't be surprised if she had a waterbed in the master bedroom that she bought off layaway from a Sears.

"Come on," Ryder insisted. "It's for the butterflies."

A second later, Hawk watched as Kimberly tilted her head to one side and let out a tenderhearted expression of emotion.

"Awww," she said. "Look at that little butterfly on your shoulder. How did you do that?"

Hawk grinned. *He's got her now.*

Feeling more relaxed, Hawk went deeper into the kitchen, getting a closer look at the kitchen table and counters. He needed to find her purse, grab her Smithsonian security card, give it to Mia, and return it to Kimberly's purse before she noticed.

"I'm in position," Mia said over the coms before ringing the bell on her bike in the back alley. "Ready whenever you are."

"Great," Hawk said. "Just got to find her purse now."

"Probably by the door," Mia said. "That's where most single women leave their purses."

Hawk peeked around the corner and noticed Kimberly's purse sitting in a chair by the door.

"You should be the one in here doing this," Hawk said.

"Is it there?" she asked.

"Of course."

"I knew it. You're right, Hawk. I should be in there."

Hawk moved toward the door and then saw a new problem— Gunther. The Rottweiler was right next to Kimberly, who was holding the screen door open but hadn't committed to going all the way outside onto the stoop. And if Hawk went much closer, Gunther would surely hear him—and the op would be blown.

"Okay, Ryder," Hawk whispered in the coms. "I need a big favor. See if you can get Kimberly to step all the way onto the porch with the door closed behind her—and with that big dog too."

Hawk looked to Ryder's hand for confirmation. He gave a quick signal that he understood and coaxed Kimberly outside.

"I have this petition to get more government funding for

butterfly migration that I'm hoping you'll sign," Ryder said. "You might be able to see it better out here in daylight."

Kimberly stepped forward and let go of the screen door. But Gunther took a couple of steps back and was shut in the house when the door latched behind Kimberly. Hawk eyed the purse—and then the dog.

Gunther growled at Hawk, which immediately arrested Kimberly's attention.

"Oh, Gunther. I'm sorry, boy. I didn't mean to shut you inside like that."

She reopened the door and gestured for him to come outside before the dog complied.

As soon as the door latched again, Hawk rushed over to the purse and went through it. He found Kimberly's security badge and then hustled to the backdoor, shoving the card through the doggie door to Mia.

"Keep her out there, Ryder," Hawk whispered over the coms. "I'll let you know when we're ready for you."

Hawk watched Mia on the back porch through the window. She shoved the card into her machine and it whirred to life.

"How long is this gonna take?" Hawk asked her.

"I told you it takes about sixty seconds. Just be patient."

Hawk watched nervously as Kimberly continued chatting with Ryder on the front porch. When Mia was done, she handed the card back. Hawk hurried back to Kimberly's purse and returned the security card to the spot where he'd found it.

"All clear, Ryder," Hawk said as he moved to the back door where he waited for Kimberly to come back inside so he could open the back without triggering the security sensor.

He listened as Kimberly said she wanted to add her phone number to the survey just in case Ryder had any follow-up questions. Hawk rolled his eyes.

"Enough with the flirting," Hawk whispered.

Craning his neck to see into the front of the house, Hawk watched for the door to open. As soon as it did, Hawk opened the back door and darted outside. However, Gunther hadn't forgotten about him. He barreled through the doggie door and bounded into the alley behind the townhomes.

Hawk hustled away as Gunther stopped and bared his teeth with an angry growl.

"I'm so sorry," Kimberly said as she rushed after her dog. "He's just been cooped up all day."

Hawk offered an acknowledging wave without looking back, continuing to hustle forward. Mia had long since left with the security card, leaving Hawk alone to walk back to their van two blocks away. He glanced back over his shoulder to see Kimberly leading Gunther back inside. The dog turned back around and barked sharply before she ushered him inside.

"Nice work, Ryder," Hawk said over the coms. "I thought you were going to take her to dinner."

"Whatever it takes for the mission," Ryder said. "Was Mia able to duplicate the card?"

"Yes," Mia said over the coms. "All we have to do is verify that it works."

"And then finish the assignment with the most difficult task of all—steal the world's most secure diamond."

TWENTY-FIVE

BRIDGER, MONTANA

ALEX FELT THE COLD STEEL FROM THE TWO WEAPONS hidden beneath her shirt pressing against her back. She hoped that Besserman was still watching what was unfolding. She knew she couldn't take all of four of them, but with a little help and the element of surprise, she figured it was possible.

With her hands raised high, she walked toward the back of her Subaru.

"Is this how you normally perform a search?" Alex asked. "I mean, I don't ever remember having a gun pulled on me when a cop wanted to search my car."

"Is this a common occurrence for you, ma'am?" Steven Wingate asked as he lowered his weapon.

"Not really, but it's happened before. I just don't appreciate the threat."

"We're just doing our job," another one of the mercenaries said. "We just need to make sure that you're not smuggling anyone out of here."

"I told you nobody's in the trunk," she said with sigh. "You're just wasting your time."

"Due diligence is never a waste of time," Wingate said.

"Is that what they taught you at state trooper school? Because I feel like they would teach you how to identify threats first and foremost."

"Everyone's a threat under the right circumstances."

Alex lowered her hands and crossed her arms. "Do I really look like a threat? I'm a soccer mom living in the middle of forgotten Montana without any weapons and surrounded by four armed men. Use your brain, officer."

"We'll wait until we've fully inspected your vehicle to make that determination."

"Whatever. What do you want me to do?"

"Pop the trunk," Wingate said, backing up behind the Subaru and training his weapon on the back.

"You can see there's no one inside," she said, leaning toward the window and tapping it.

"Just open the trunk, Miss. Okay?"

"Fine," Alex said as she glanced back toward the house and made an exaggerated expression with her face, one she hoped Besserman understood.

Two of the other officers moved behind the car as well, awaiting the trunk to mechanically lift. Alex walked back to the driver's side where the door was still open and depressed a button to the left of the steering wheel. A series of beeps preceded the tailgate rising. With all eyes focused on the back, Alex glanced at the back deck of her house where Besserman was watching the action unfold.

"Now," she mouthed to him.

Before the trunk reached its apex, a rifle shot cracked through the air and Wingate collapsed. Alex drew her weapons and double tapped the man nearest the driver's side before wheeling around and firing at the two remaining men behind the car. She hit the first one in the chest, knocking him to the ground. But the other one fired and took cover behind the vehicle.

Alex jumped behind the steering wheel and jammed the car

into reverse before stomping on the gas. The Subaru lurched backward, clipping the man and knocking him into the ditch. With the man exposed, she put the car in park and dashed to the backend. She crouched low and peeked around the corner before firing on the man. He ducked down beneath a boulder in the ditch, poking his head up to shoot intermittently. A couple of his shots shattered the car windows, sending a spray of tempered glass over Alex's head and cascading onto the ground. She duck walked to the front, changing her angle of attack. Her new position rendered the man exposed and she took aim, catching him off guard. The first bullet hit him in the chest before the second tore through his forehead.

Alex looked over the men and fired a bullet into each one to ensure they were all dead. Then she called Besserman on his cell.

"Why the hell are you behind a computer?" he asked as he answered his phone.

"Because unlike Hawk, I don't enjoy this part of the job. Now, tell little J.D. that you're gonna be gone for a few minutes and grab the keys to the Mule off the key chain by the holder and get up here to help me clean this mess up."

"I'll be right there."

While she waited for Besserman to arrive, Alex collected the men's cell phones.

"Dead men tell no tales, but they still can access a cell phone," she said to herself with a chuckle.

One by one, she held up their phones in front of their faces to activate them. She quickly scrolled through them, looking for incriminating information and a way to figure out who ordered them to come after her. She scribbled down the number of the person Wingate was communicating with and pocketed the slip of paper.

Besserman roared up on the ATV, the engine clattering as he brought the vehicle to a stop.

"Nice work," he said as he walked over to look at the bodies. "Are you sure you don't want to be in the field?"

"I've got a son who needs me," she said, dragging one of the bodies over toward the MSP cruiser.

Besserman opened the back door and heaved the man inside with Alex.

"That was just impressive, that's all."

"Well, it took you long enough to take the shot."

"Wingate was a little jittery, and moving around like he was amped up on something. But I must confess that it felt good to watch him go down like that."

"In the end, you got the job done, which is all that matters. And if you need me to vouch for you at Langley, I'll be happy to do so."

"I think my target shooting with all the new recruits speaks for itself," Besserman said as he grabbed the arms of the next dead mercenary and dragged it over to the ATV with Alex.

The body toppled onto the floorboard in the backseat, the man's shirt blooming with a red stain in the center of his chest.

"You recognize any of these other bastards?" Alex asked.

"This guy looks familiar," Besserman said. "I also heard your laptop beep just before all the action. So, maybe you've got something from your facial recognition search."

Alex pulled out her phone and used her camera function to snap headshots of all the men. "Just in case we need a better image."

They piled Wingate's body in last, placing him in the front seat on top of another man.

"What's the plan for these bodies?" he asked. "I'm assuming you have one."

"Yeah, there's a desolate canyon just over this ridge," she said. "I figured they can take a fun ride off the edge, full of flames and everything."

"I like it," Besserman said.

"It'll be days before anyone notices, though I'm counting on whoever was running them to collect the bodies at some point," she said, pulling out her knife.

She slashed a slit in the man's midsection and stuffed a tracker inside.

"If they bother to come back for the bodies, we'll know how to find them," she said.

Besserman sighed.

"What's the matter?" she asked.

"You're better than most of my trained assets," Besserman said.

"I already told you, I'm not going into the field. My son needs me more than you do."

"I know, I know. I'm just lamenting out loud."

"If you need my help training some of your recruits, you know I'll help you do that. But my place is here on the ranch—as long as the dolts don't keep coming out here and ruining my day."

"Don't say it unless you mean it because I will take you up on that," he said.

She tossed the keys to the police cruiser to Besserman. "Now, for lesson one. How to dispose of dead bodies when there's no swamp around."

He cocked his head to one side. "Exactly how many dead bodies have you fed to alligators?"

"More than I care to remember. Come on. Let's get a move on."

Alex climbed into the ATV and started up the ridge, gesturing for Besserman to follow her. They drove along for a few minutes before Alex stopped. She directed Besserman to stop before opening the doors and taking pictures of the bodies splayed across both the front and back seats with Wingate's phone. She composed a text with the image.

> Didn't quite get the job done. I recommend against sending any more.

She pressed the send button and then placed the phone in Wingate's hand. Then she turned to Besserman.

"Time to send these guys out in style, a la Thelma and Louise."

"You think they deserve that?" he asked.

"They deserve what they already got. This is for my entertainment at this point—that and to make sure there's no real evidence to collect."

She grabbed a fuel can from the back of the ATV and doused the car. Then she picked up a large rock and placed it on the gas pedal with the car in neutral facing the edge of cliff. With the flick of match, she tossed it inside and tugged the gear shift into drive.

By the time the cruiser reached the edge, the engine was roaring as the interior of the car was engulfed in flames. Alex and Besserman followed the vehicle to the edge and watched the fireball rocket toward the bottom of the ravine. The metal crunched against the canyon floor before it was overshadowed by an explosion. The cruiser, roiled in flames, was barely recognizable as a vehicle.

"Let's go," Alex said as she walked back to the ATV.

"What now?" Besserman asked.

"You need to find a new hideout."

TWENTY-SIX

WASHINGTON, D.C.

REBECCA FORNIER LEANED FORWARD, RESTING ON HER knuckles as she inspected the schematics for the Smithsonian's Museum of Natural History. She made note of where the potential problems might arise in her mission to snatch one of the world's most iconic diamonds. Her first big challenge was getting access to the diamond. Her second was a clean getaway. But that wasn't the only thing about this operation that made her nervous.

It was one thing to lead Mei Ling Wu around the Smithsonian with pre-arranged questions with other assets. It was another to trust a team of people to avoid landing in prison. If Rebecca got caught, she knew the CIA wouldn't help her, despite the fact that, in essence, she was working for them. One wrong move could mean years behind bars for Rebecca, a fact she was all too aware of.

Mia eased next to Rebecca and put an arm around her. "It's gonna be all right. We've dotted every i and crossed every t. We're going to make this work one way or another."

Rebecca gathered her hair and tied it up in a ponytail. "It's the *another* way that I'm most concerned about. If this doesn't work—"

"It's gonna work. You'll see."

"The cool thing is you don't have to worry about your face being captured," Mia said. "All you need to do is have one clip where your face is clear and we'll take care of the rest."

"Are you sure you're comfortable with this?"

"We've made more than two dozen test runs, all flawlessly executed. And we've run them all with the same system that the Smithsonian uses. Then we ran two tests after tapping into their own system, producing the results we were looking for. It's not gonna be a problem. And if it is, Hawk and Ryder will take care of you."

Rebecca's phone buzzed with a text message from Besserman wishing her good luck.

She chewed on her lip as she scanned the schematics once more.

"You good?" Hawk asked as he reached for the paper. "Because it's time."

"I think so," she said as she looked up.

"Think so?" Ryder asked.

She nodded emphatically. "I'm ready."

"Then let's do this," Hawk said.

They piled into a white work van and drove toward the Smithsonian's Museum of Natural History. Hawk parked the vehicle a couple of blocks away at the corner of 9th and D streets before the team went to work.

Ryder and Hawk paired up to gain access to the museum's security system, posing as utility workers. They set up a small gate around a manhole and navigated the space beneath the museum until they found the access point to the museum's basement. Ryder identified the utility cable and splintered off the network, setting up a router point for Mia.

"How are we looking?" Hawk asked over the coms.

"Coming on line right *now*," Mia said, pounding the last key emphatically.

"All right, Rebecca," Hawk said, turning to the newest member of the team. "Sounds like you're up."

Rebecca took a deep breath, double-checked all her equipment in her bag, and got out of the van. She walked along the sidewalk and crossed over one of the more desolate streets in the area before winding her way to a back entrance into the museum.

"Here goes nothing," she said softly before sliding the security card.

The red light on the keypad blinked, giving way to a green light, followed by a slight clicking noise in the door. Rebecca tugged it open and entered the building.

"I'm inside, guys," she said over the coms.

"Just remember to activate that light to hide your face once you're certain your face has been captured by the security cameras," Mia said.

"Copy that," she said.

Rebecca glanced around the room, which looked different when it was empty. The dissonant noises that rose up toward the rotunda were gone. Only the faint sound of footsteps coming toward her down the hall.

She walked over toward a camera and then looked around for a moment.

"Got it," Mia said.

Rebecca hit a button on the visor she was wearing, lighting up the LEDs that turned her face into one giant white blur.

"Keep walking, Rebecca," Mia said, waiting a few more seconds before continuing. "Now stop. Give me fifteen seconds to freeze all the cameras."

But the footsteps stopped sounding so faint, growing louder with each passing second.

"Can you hurry up?" Rebecca said. "I think someone is coming."

"Almost there," Mia said. "Ten more seconds."

"Mia," Rebecca said, the urgency in her voice communicating everything that needed to be said.

"Just get out of sight," Mia said. "The cameras will be frozen in three ... two ... one ..."

Rebecca dove behind a large donation box near the ticket kiosk. It was large enough for an adult or two children to hide inside it. She curled up on the floor, shrinking behind the box and hoping the security guard waving his flashlight in her direction didn't see her. The light swept just over her head before she heard the guard mutter aloud to himself.

"What have we got here?" he said.

His footsteps echoed in the room, each one becoming more thunderous than the last. Rebecca listened and then scrambled to the opposite side he was approaching, doing her best to keep from being seen.

She peered around the corner to see him stoop and pick up a twenty-dollar bill. He looked around and then looked at the camera.

Holding up the money, he said, "You didn't see this, Jamie."

With a wide grin, the guard tucked the bill into his coat pocket and continued to make his rounds. He stopped and made one last sweep of the lobby with his light before moving into one of the exhibit areas.

Rebecca exhaled and then flicked the LED light back on. She scrambled to her feet and raced upstairs. She approached the room containing the Hope Diamond and walked up to the display case. It was even more spectacular at night, especially without anyone else around.

She opened her backpack and retrieved all the tools she figured she would need to extract the diamond.

"You ready?" Hawk asked over the coms.

Rebecca inspected the hand saw with the carbide-tipped blade. "Let's do this."

MICHAEL FRANKLIN PUT his shoulder into the door leading to the security office and gave it a nudge. The door sprang open, allowing Franklin to lumber inside. He found Emilio Sanchez sitting in front of a bank of security camera monitors, his eyes flashing between the magazine in his lap and the images on the screen.

While Franklin had come to Washington with dreams of becoming an FBI agent, he'd struggled with the aptitude test during training. His shooting skills and fitness were off the charts, but he couldn't figure out basic problems he'd likely face in the field. He was offered a desk position, but that felt like a slap in the face after all he'd trained for. After spending two years at the Metro Police Department, he was fired for an incident where he let his anger get the best of him and pummeled a suspect who was high on crack. His superior officer offered to write a recommendation for him to serve as a security guard, one on the night shift where he wouldn't have to deal with any people. And that's how his decade-long tenure at the Smithsonian came to be. He'd come to terms with it, but secretly he held out hope one day that he'd have a chance to get with the bureau.

Sanchez used his straw to search for the final sip of diet soda lingering at the bottom of his 44-ounce plastic cup. The gargled slurping noise annoyed Franklin.

"You know that stuff's gonna kill ya, right?" Franklin asked as he walked in the room and slapped Sanchez's feet, which were resting on the desk in front of him.

Sanchez struggled to regain his balance in the chair, which rolled backward as he flailed around.

"If somebody decided to back a truck into the loading dock, I don't know if you'd make it down there in time before they cleaned out the first exhibit," Franklin said, continuing to berate his colleague.

"Oh, come on, Mikey. It's just a soda, man."

"And it's rotting your brain."

"Maybe. But my rotten brain is still working better than your dumb ass that flunked out of the bureau."

Franklin clenched his fists, knuckles whitening as he grit his teeth and glared at Sanchez.

"Hey, man, I'm sorry," Sanchez said. "I thought we were just joking around with each other. Take it easy."

"Here," Franklin said, reaching into his pocket and producing the twenty-dollar bill. "You can have the money I found as long as it goes toward the first month's payment of you signing up for a health club."

"Wait," Sanchez said, holding the money up to the light. "You found this?"

"Yeah, you dope. I held it up to the camera and told you not to tell anyone."

"When?"

"Fifteen minutes ago. What were you doing? Sleeping?"

"No, I didn't see anything. What room were you in?"

"The main lobby," Franklin said with a sigh. "I swear, I don't know how some people stay employed in this business."

"I was watching the whole time."

"Well, I call bullshit because I stood in front of the camera for about thirty seconds and had an entire conversation."

"You know I can't hear you, right?" Sanchez said. "Yeah, but you're a damn lip reader, if anything."

Sanchez shrugged. "I never saw you. I think you're lying."

Franklin growled and yanked back the open chair next to Sanchez and sat down. "Go back about fifteen minutes on this camera right here."

"Okay, whatever you say."

Sanchez scrubbed back fifteen minutes on the footage from the camera Franklin indicated and played it at double speed. Both men watched as nothing happened.

"That's odd," Franklin said.

"See, I told you," Sanchez said, picking up his cup and shaking the ice. "I was watching."

"Something's wrong," Franklin said. "Check Mammals Hall. I circled through there before coming in here."

"Like five minutes ago?"

"Maybe ten. I don't know. You shouldn't need to go back more than that."

Sanchez repeated the procedure, synchronizing all the cameras in Mammals Hall and tiling them on the largest screen. They both watched as there was no movement in the exhibit.

"Are you sure that's where you went last?" Sanchez asked.

"Yeah," Franklin said. "I'm positive."

"Come on, Mikey. Are you sure?"

"Shit. Something's not right."

"Yeah, that noggin of yours."

Franklin ignored the comment as he pushed his chair back from the desk and spun around before he darted toward the door.

Then an alarm whooped. Franklin stopped and looked back at Sanchez.

"What is it?" Franklin asked.

"It's the Hope Diamond."

REBECCA'S APPROACH to stealing the Hope Diamond was different than most of her previous heists. Instead of trying to get the jewel out without detection, the entire plan was to trigger a silent alarm, which would set off a chain of events that would allow her to quickly grab the diamond and go.

At least, that was the plan.

Once she started to attack the glass with the carbide-tipped saw, the vibrations set off a protocol that dropped the jewel into a small case beneath the display. And there were only three people who could access the case, one of them being Kimberly Jordan.

As soon as the diamond retracted from the case and sank

beneath it, Rebecca swiped Kimberly's security card on the panel near the bottom of the display. A small door opened up and she inserted her card into a slot that opened a small door.

Rebecca was so focused on easing the diamond out and into a safe pouch that she didn't immediately hear the pounding footsteps racing toward her. But when she finally recognized it, she knew she was in trouble. She scooped up her supplies and shoved them into her pack as she started to run toward the exit.

"I'm gonna need some help here," she said.

"What happened?" Alex asked. "I got a notification that the alarm is going off."

"That's right," Rebecca said. "The vibrations from the saw were just supposed to trigger a lockdown, not an alarm. At least, that's what I was told about the custom-built display case. But I hear at least two guards running toward me."

"Can you make it outside?" Hawk asked.

"I think so," she said. "But once I get out there, they'll probably be able to run me down if I have to go the full distance to the van."

"I got you," Hawk said. "Just make it to the side exit like we talked about and I'll give you a hand."

HAWK HURRIEDLY PULLED on a ratty trench coat and a beanie before jumping out of the van. He raced toward the museum, stopping to grab a handful of dirt and smear it on his face. Hidden beneath the shadows of the trees lining the walkway leading to the museum, he sprinted toward the building.

"How's it looking, Rebecca?" Hawk asked.

"Almost there, but it's gonna be tight," she said, panting.

"Just stick to the escape route and trust the plan."

"Roger that."

When Hawk saw the side exit door fling open, Rebecca

followed, head back, feet and arms pumping. She zipped right past him, and he wasn't even sure she recognized him.

Seconds later, he saw a fit security guard barreling through the door in pursuit.

It's showtime.

Hawk began to sway from side to side as he neared the building. The guard was focused on Rebecca and didn't appear to acknowledge Hawk. But Hawk's herky-jerky movements caught the guard's attention right before Hawk took out the man in full stride, sending him tumbling to the ground and rolling to a nearby park bench.

The guard winced as he tried to get up.

"What the hell, man?" the guard shouted as he staggered to his feet before collapsing onto the bench. He sighed as he looked down the sidewalk and watched Rebecca disappear from view.

"Do you know what you just did?" the guard asked.

Hawk ignored the man, resuming his swaying gait. With a grunt, Hawk raised his hand and walked in circles.

The guard let out a string of curses, some of them directed at Hawk.

"What happened?" asked another guard as he trundled over to his colleague on the bench.

"That asshole knocked me down," the guard said, gesturing toward Hawk.

Hawk pointed at his chest, feigning surprise without a word.

"Yeah, you, asshole."

Hawk mumbled something before he walked in the opposite direction of the museum. Eventually, he crossed the street and didn't break character until he climbed in the van.

"Did you get it?" Hawk asked.

Rebecca held it up with a wide grin on her face. "Thanks to you. All of you, really."

"Nice team effort," Hawk said, patting Ryder and Mia on the back. "Did the software work?"

"Worked like a charm," Mia said. "I replaced the looped video I'd uploaded to the security system with the real footage—without Rebecca's face of course."

"And?" Hawk asked.

"It looks just like Mei Ling Wu," Mia said.

"Perfect. Now, let's get the hell outta here and go celebrate."

TWENTY-SEVEN

WASHINGTON, D.C.

PRESIDENT BULLOCK RECLINED ON THE LEATHER couch in his living room, feet propped up on an ottoman, a book on the history of Middle Eastern policy spread out in his lap. His wife Cori marched into the room with a fistful of wildflowers in one hand and a small cup of water in the other. She threaded the stems into the opening of the vase and then poured water inside. For a moment, she fussed over the flowers, spreading them out into an arrangement she was satisfied with before walking toward the door.

"Dolly Madison would be proud," Bullock said.

Cori stopped and slowly turned around. "Excuse me."

"I said, Dolly Madison would be proud. She made that vase. I asked to have it brought into our living quarters just for you."

"That was a nice gesture, but don't think for a second that it absolves you."

Bullock removed his glasses and rubbed his eyes. "Okay, here we go again."

Cori sat down on a chair opposite her husband and leaned

179

forward, resting her arms on her knees and clasping her hands together.

"I don't really want another lecture from you," Bullock said, his tone measured, "especially when I didn't do anything wrong."

"Do you just think I'm stupid and that I don't notice what's going on with you?" Cori fired back. "All day long, you are around some of the world's most amazing people, while your staff trots me out for grip-and-grins with the Arlington Garden Club. You meet rock stars, pop stars, political stars, sports stars, and even people who discover stars or even explore them. And there I am, stuck in the shadows. The little ole First Lady, dutifully doing her job."

"Come on, dear. This isn't fair, and you know it. We discussed all these things before I ran—before we ran. I remember having a long conversation one night about how if I was going to run for president, we were going to do it together. And I explained to you that sometimes, I would be on the stage alone, but that you'd always be with me in everything I did. In all my decision making, in all my suggested policies, in all my meetings— even when you couldn't be with me in person, you would still be there because of the man you've helped me become. This isn't platitudes either. That's how I felt then and how I still feel today, even with everything that's going on."

"*Everything that's going on?* You make that sound like some benign euphemism."

Bullock sighed. "There's a lot going on, Cori. We've got some serious threats against this country. And we've got some major tension between powerful countries as well, starting with how the Russians are blaming the CIA director for the murder of one of their most prominent citizens. So, yeah, there's a lot going on besides the fake tape that you are believing is true."

"Come on now. You don't expect me to believe that it was all some AI stunt. I've seen Morgan May. And she's beautiful."

"So are you. What's your point?"

"You're around these beautiful women all the time—and

you're around them with every opportunity to *exercise your authority*, so to speak."

"I still find you insanely attractive, but that's not what keeps me faithful to you. It's everything else about you—your compassion for others, your strength in the midst of chaos, your calming presence when stress threatens to overwhelm me. I could go on, but you have to know that I don't want to be with any other woman but you."

She waved dismissively at him.

"Honey, I'm serious," he continued. "Please don't ignore what I'm saying."

"It'd be a lot easier to believe you if I hadn't seen those pictures. But you're just like every politician. You talk a good game but when it comes down to it, you're only out for yourself."

"That's not fair, and you know it. In fact, you know that's not true either."

"Do I? I don't know you anymore. And to be completely frank, I don't know much of anything anymore—except that you are a liar."

Bullock stood and walked behind the couch, leaning forward on the back of it.

"I don't know how else to convince you, but those videos are not real. I wasn't in those places at the time I was supposed to be there. And I wasn't with Morgan May either."

"Of course you'd say that."

"I'm saying it because it's true. And now you're asking me to prove something that never happened. And you want me to do it by disproving something that never happened. Do you have any idea how difficult that is? If I say it didn't happen—because it didn't—you want me to prove it. I wasn't there. But my cell phone, which could show where I was for a private meeting at that time with the Secretary of State, can't be tracked for security purposes. Nobody that was with me could have their phone tracked. So, all I can do is tell you that I had a private meeting with someone that isn't recorded anywhere beforehand because that would be a security threat."

"And was it recorded afterward?"

"Well, there was no reason to, especially since our meeting was entirely confidential."

"So, you had a secret meeting that you can't prove you were attending at the exact same time the video occurred? Am I getting this right?"

"I've already told you all this, but, yes, that's exactly right."

"Well, stop treating me like I'm some low-information dumbass voter you're trying to persuade to cast a ballot for you. Because I'm much smarter than that."

Bullock snorted and shook his head. "I feel like this is impossible for me to show you the truth."

"Lucky for you, I already know it. I went out and hired a digital forensics expert, someone who could tell me the *actual* truth, not some political speak that consists of massaging words to convey a message without technically lying."

"And what did this digital forensics expert say?"

"He told me that you're lying. He said there was no indication that AI was involved in the making of that video. He said the metadata that included the geolocation was accurate, even to the point that he went to the location and found it—and found it just like it was in the video of you and Morgan May."

"Cori, there's new technology that I guarantee you your digital forensics expert guy has never seen and knows nothing about."

"Again, how convenient for you," she said, her tone sharp.

"I'm serious. I could get you security clearance so you could get read in on this."

"Please, spare me. I'm not interested in going along with your games so you can convince me of your lies."

"I swear it's true. There's a new technology that's being used, and it's making everyone doubt what they're seeing."

Cori rolled her eyes and huffed. "I'm tired of being insulted. I'm also tired of being made to look like a fool."

"I wouldn't lie to you."

"Okay, Mr. President, what's the name of this new technology so I can go look it up myself?"

"I—I—I don't know. It's *that* new."

"Sorry, hon, but I'm not buying it. Go peddle your lies to someone else. Maybe the blonde bimbo in the video will believe your story."

Cori got up and stormed out of the room.

Bullock growled as he paced the floor, his anger growing over his wife's refusal to believe him. On one hand, he couldn't really blame her; but on the other, he thought he had earned the right to be trusted after years and years of being a faithful and loving husband. But she wasn't having it.

Bullock grabbed the vase and hurled it across the room, shattering as it hit the wall.

Sorry, Dolly.

TWENTY-EIGHT

WASHINGTON, D.C.

FROM THE BATHROOM OF HER ROOM AT THE WALDORF Astoria overlooking Pennsylvania Avenue, Mei Ling Wu studied her face in the mirror. She inspected every last square inch before deciding she needed to remove a few straggling hairs in her eyebrows. With careful precision, she honed in on the rogue strands and plucked them out. After scrutinizing her appearance one final time, she walked over to the windows and thrust open the drapes.

The sun was peeking over the surrounding buildings while commuters honked their horns as traffic crawled through downtown. She was thankful that she wasn't stuck in a car somewhere fighting to get to a boring job on time. No, she was free to live her life however she saw fit, a perk that she relished even more than the obscene amount of money she made every month from her position as a social media influencer. Being tethered to a desk felt like the worst punishment possible, though one she understood people not as talented or as beautiful as her were destined to endure.

"You are beautiful, Mei Ling," she said to herself as she glanced at the mirror over the bed. "Absolutely gorgeous."

She looked across the room and saw Jun Fang's clothes strewn along the floor. Rushing over to them, she gathered them up and stuffed them in one of the drawers. He'd apparently gotten up much earlier to conduct business elsewhere but didn't wake her.

A knock at the door jolted her. She wrapped herself up in a plush robe she retrieved from the bathroom and shuffled to the door.

"Coming," she said before glancing at her watch.

It's a little early to try to get me to check out.

She peered through the peephole and then opened the door as wide as the security chain would allow her.

"I'm sorry, but I didn't order anything," she said to the man standing outside with a cart.

"It's your complimentary in-room breakfast," the man said. "It's all part of your package during your stay."

"Oh, well, in that case, come on in," Wu said, sliding the chain free and opening the door.

"Where would you like this?"

"Over there," Wu said, pointing toward the small round table in the corner.

"Of course," the man said.

He pushed the cart to the corner and removed the lid off the steel tray, showing her the food.

"Poached eggs with an English muffin and hollandaise sauce, garnished with fresh fruit and a pot of coffee," he said before replacing the lid.

"Excellent," she said before thumbing a twenty-dollar bill out of her purse and handing it to him. "Thank you so much."

"Also, I heard that your drop drawer was giving you problems."

"I don't think so, but if you'd like to check."

"If you don't mind. It'll only take a second."

"Sure."

The man eased open the drawer and fiddled with it for a second before closing it.

"Seems fine to me," he said.

"Thank you for checking."

Wu closed the door behind the man and continued preparing for her morning. She set up the ring light she used for close-up social media videos, softening the often harsh lighting certain environments cursed her with. If she could enhance how people saw her, all the better. It was something she liked to talk about from the stage at conferences. If she could do anything, she wanted to inspire others to be the best version of themselves—and that included looking their best, too.

Wu adjusted her strapless dress and fluffed her hair before going live. She began almost all her days like this, sitting in front of a camera and interacting with all her followers. She would dish on her latest adventures or recap her previous night on the town, all while answering questions from viewers hungry for her secrets to living such a carefree and interesting life. Almost all her interactions were positive, and she didn't hesitate to block any trolls who peppered the comment section with negativity or hateful remarks. However, those were usually few and far between. And that's why when she went live, she was surprised by the unusually high number of ugly comments flooding the stream before she even said a word.

What is going on?

"Good morning," Wu said, saying the phrase in ten different languages before continuing in English. "Or maybe it's a bad morning for many of you. Seems like more than a handful of you woke up on the wrong side of the bed today. And to that, I can only say, being your best you means focusing on yourself and becoming a better version of the person you want to be.'"

But instead of the comments being filled with heart emojis and viewers agreeing with her, it was more hate. The posts scrolled through so quickly that she couldn't even read more than a few words of them before they rolled off the page.

She sighed and shook her head before adjusting the settings on the live view.

"Now, I don't know what's gotten into most of you today, but I'm going to turn the comments off for a minute so I can address all the negativity today," Wu said. "Being negative isn't the way I suggest you behave. It's quite the opposite."

Wu leaned closer to the camera.

"Now, I'm going to turn the comments back on, and I want to see if everyone can be nicer now."

She tapped a button on the screen, allowing comments from viewers again.

"Now, let's start over. Anyone want to guess what I did last night?" she asked.

Wu scowled as she read the posts.

You don't need to tell us. We all saw.

We know. And so does every other media outlet.

Good luck in prison.

I always hated your streams. You're such a phony.

A millionaire from social media? Guess again. Your secret's out of the bag. We all know you're a thief.

WU COCKED her head to one side as she scanned the incoming comments. "I don't know what to say. But it seems like some of you aren't in a good place right now. More than anything, I have no idea what you're talking about because last night I was at a dance club for a private event. I'll post a few photos when I get a chance, but this is absurd."

More negative comments filled up Wu's page. After a few more seconds, she decided she'd had enough and needed to figure out what everyone was talking about.

"Everyone have a lovely day," she said before logging off.

Then Wu navigated to another social media site that had video of her running from a security guard.

What the hell is this?

Then she saw a screenshot from security cameras at the Smithsonian's Museum of Natural History with her staring lustily at the Hope Diamond as she inspected it with eyes as big as saucers. She knew it wasn't her, but she couldn't deny that it looked just like her. Suddenly, she couldn't blame the viewers. Nobody in their right mind would think the woman in the picture was anyone but her.

Wu scrambled for her phone and called her lawyer. The phone rang several times before going to voicemail. Then she dialed his number again.

"Oh, come on. Answer the phone."

Another call, this time straight to voicemail.

She sighed as she collapsed onto her bed. While she knew she couldn't hide from her problems, she just wanted to curl up under the covers and go to sleep. Maybe when she woke up, it'd all just be a dream and she could go about her day in peace. But deep down, she knew it was real, undeniable if everything she saw on every news site she navigated to online featured her prominently next to a picture of the Hope Diamond.

"The Queen of Hope Allegedly Steals the Hope Diamond," read one headline.

At least they got my brand right.

Then she read the first of several ominous texts, all of which notified her that her deal promoting certain products was ending, effective immediately. In a matter of minutes, she went from spreading her joy and positivity to trying to shake a soul-crushing depression that had settled over her.

It wasn't her, that much she was sure of. But why did it look like her? And how come nobody was answering her calls?

A few seconds later, another knock at the door. She remained on the bed, staring straight up at the vaulted ceilings and wondering what fate awaited her in the hallway.

"Who is it?" she asked.

"FBI," shouted a man. "We need to speak with you, Ms. Wu."

She opened the door and a team of agents spilled into the room, searching through every drawer and under the bed and every bathroom cabinet—all before she could protest.

"What's going on here?" she asked. "You don't have a right to come in here like this."

"Actually they do," said a hotel manager, tapping a document in his hand. "There's probable cause based on video evidence."

"What are you talking about?" she asked.

"We know you have to have seen it by now," said one of FBI agents, who offered his hand. "Agent Carlson, ma'am. I'm sure you've seen the footage by now."

"Yeah, but that wasn't me."

"Then explain this," said another agent, whose gloved hand held up a blue diamond.

"How did that get there?" Wu asked. "Because I certainly didn't squirrel it away in my hotel dresser."

"I've got the entire search on video," the agent said, handing it to Carlson.

"Sorry, ma'am, but I'm gonna need you to turn around so I can put these handcuffs on you."

"Are you suggesting that I stole that diamond?" Wu asked, her eyes narrowing. "This is outrageous."

"Please, ma'am," Carlson said. "Don't make this any more difficult than it needs to be."

Wu growled as she complied, while another agent read off her rights.

"You're all going to regret this," Wu said. "In fact, I can prove that you're wrong right now. Last night, I was out with friends. I can show you the pictures, which would prove where I was."

As FBI agents continued to catalog evidence, one woman standing near the dresser looked at Wu's phone.

"Ma'am, did you realize that your phone was still streaming?"

Wu cursed under her breath.

"Would you like for me to end it?" the woman asked.

"Yes, please," Wu growled as she was led out into the hall. "Just check my phone for the pics from last night."

The agent swiped through Wu's photos and looked at the dates.

"See?" Wu said, expecting the agent to acquiesce and release her. "Tell Agent Carlson here."

"Sir, there are no pictures from last night," the woman said. "The oldest photo in her folder is from her visit to the Smithsonian."

"Interesting," Carlson said before nodding to the agents to take Wu downstairs.

"You're making a big mistake," Wu shouted, struggling against her bindings and the two agents ushering her toward the elevator.

The elevator doors peeled open and Jun Fang walked out. His jaw dropped as he stared at the shocking scene.

"Honey, what's this all about?" he asked.

"Talk to the FBI agents," she said. "They'll tell you everything."

Before he could protest, she was taken onto the elevator. The door slid shut, making Wu feel like she had just been shoved into a coffin and the lid slammed tight.

TWENTY-NINE

VIRGINIA HIDEOUT

WITH THE FIRST MAJOR PHASE OF THE PLAN completed, the Magnum Group team reconvened at a cabin in the Virginia woods over an hour outside of Washington. Hawk volunteered to run the meeting since Morgan decided to stay away. With national press members turning over every rock in search of her, she exercised wisdom in avoiding any potential problem that might arise should she be caught with the rest of her team. Instead of being there in person, she texted that she would join via teleconference.

Alex was the first to call in, participating from Montana, while the rest of the team filed into the conference room.

"It's good to hear your voice, honey," Hawk said as Alex's face materialized on the screen. "And see you, too."

"It's been a rough few days," she said. "Did you hear about the accident out here?"

Hawk smiled wryly. "I've only heard what you've heard, I'm sure."

"Well, I wish that was the end of it, but I feel like it's only the beginning, though I've made it clear that I don't know where the CIA director went."

"And neither do we," Morgan May said as she joined the meeting virtually. "And it's best we keep it that way. Considering all that we have going on right now, if we have one less thing to worry about, that's probably best."

"Agreed," Hawk said. "It's pretty much a nightmare right now."

Mia, who clicked away on her keyboard, paused for a moment and nodded, almost absent-mindedly. "Sure is. Morgan, you're being accused of sleeping with the president, Besserman is wanted for murder, and Mei Ling Wu has been arrested for stealing the Hope Diamond."

"One out of three isn't bad," Hawk said. "Those numbers in baseball will get you enshrined in the Hall of Fame."

"Well, this isn't baseball, Hawk," Morgan said. "This is intelligence work where nothing less than a hundred percent success rate is acceptable."

"I know. One mistake and thousands of innocent people could lose their lives," he said.

"Or in this case, thousands of people could be manipulated by a monster to do whatever the hell he wanted them to do," Morgan said. "And we cannot allow that to happen. I'm living proof why we must stop it."

Ryder cleared his throat before he spoke. "I think we're in a good spot right now. We just need to apply a little pressure and watch Fang snap like a twig."

"I agree," Hawk said. "We've engineered the right environment, forcing him to taste his own medicine. He'll have to back down now. Once I confront him—"

The computer screen beeped as Morgan unmuted her microphone.

"I'm not sure confronting Fang is the right thing to do," she said. "You'll only make him more desperate by revealing to him what you're doing—and what you've got."

Hawk shook his head. "No, I'm not about to tell him our plan. But he does need to know that he's going to be subject to the same constraints we are when it comes to this software. If he wants to back us into a corner, we'll back him into one as well. Fighting fire with fire is the best way to cut him down."

Morgan beeped back in.

"Look, I want to go on record that I think holding this over Fang is a terrible idea. I'd rather us just have a press conference where we—or someone within the intelligence community— hosts a demonstration of how this software works."

"Yeah, and then everyone and their brother will be claiming that any video evidence that they committed a crime should be thrown out," Hawk said. "It'd be a disaster for the court system in this country—and probably the world over."

"Yes," Alex agreed. "I think this is one of those times where if we don't provide the right context for how this program was conceived and how it works, we're going to have the knowledge of its existence leveraged by attorneys for real criminals to walk free."

Morgan sighed. "I'm not sure that's most important right now. Our own president is being dogged by this faux scandal and it's hindering his ability to lead."

"I know it's got to be an awful feeling," Hawk said. "But Bullock isn't going to lose his job over this, at least, not yet anyway. However, we need to stay focused on the ultimate goal here, which is making sure that The Alliance doesn't inject this software into nearly every camera in the world. If so, nobody will be safe."

Mia nodded her head in agreement. "And that's exactly what they want."

"All right," Morgan said. "I know you're right. Having every journalist write about you and pick through your friends on social media in search of someone who will affirm that you're a tramp is my personal hell right now. But I suppose pressing forward with the original plan is what's best. So, any ideas on how you're going to make that happen?"

"I've got a few," Hawk said. "And by this time tomorrow night, if we play our cards right, Mr. Fang will be telling the world all about his software and how he's going to destroy it so people aren't unjustly accused ever again."

"Let's hope you're right," Morgan said. "And good luck, team."

Morgan signed off, leaving the rest of the Magnum Group team to discuss the specifics of how they were going to confront Fang, who was hanging around Washington and had reportedly volunteered to stand in for Wu at the IFF conference. When they finished, Hawk slapped the table, unable to restrain his excitement.

"We're gonna pin Fang to the wall tomorrow and he won't have any other choice," he said.

THIRTY

TANGIER, MOROCCO

BESSERMAN MANAGED TO FLY COMMERCIALLY UNDER fake passports he'd accrued for other missions, documents that weren't in any official records at the agency. It was the only way he could get out of the country without alerting Deputy Director Steve Pickens. After Pickens sent agents to Aruba and the hinterlands of Montana in search of Besserman, the director recognized he needed to disappear completely. And his quest to do so took him to Tangier, Morocco, a place nobody would've expected him to go.

Besserman stayed in disguise as he hailed a taxi and went straight from the airport to a train station. Once there, he visited a locker stashed with money and weapons, both ample enough for him to stay off the radar until the truth came out about Fang's deceptive software.

Slinging the backpack over his shoulder, Besserman returned to the taxi stand in front of the station and found the next waiting driver. Once inside, Besserman gave the man the neighborhood but not the address, wanting to be cautious.

And five minutes into the drive, Besserman was glad he did.

He spotted a pair of headlights that swerved in and out of traffic to keep up with him. Besserman wasn't sure if the person following him knew who he was or simply saw him as a mark. Either way, Besserman felt uncomfortable.

"Change of plans," he said to the driver. "Take me to Petit Socco."

"Petit Socco? Are you sure? Most of the shops are closing soon. And it's a long way from that neighborhood."

"Petit Socco," Besserman repeated.

"Okay."

At the next traffic light, the driver hung a left and zipped along several tight surface streets. Besserman glanced out the back and noticed the other car continuing to keep pace.

As they approached the market, Besserman handed the man a hundred-dollar bill and told him to keep the change and to be discreet. Then Besserman secured his backpack and darted out of the car, slamming the door behind him.

He worked his way down an alley, searching for a good intersection. At the next one, he spotted an even tighter alley with plenty of objects to hide behind, including a stack of sacks that appeared to contain flour. He looked over his shoulder and didn't see anyone behind him before ducking down the alleyway.

Once he reached the sacks, he sat down beside them, using the stack to shield him from any cursory searches of the alley.

As Besserman caught his breath, his heart hammered in his chest. For the first time in a long time, he felt truly alone. At least in the last two locations, he had someone to hide him. But not in Tangier. He only had a house—and with someone tailing him, he had to consider the possibility that it was compromised.

With his back to the wall and his knees tucked against his chest, he considered his other possible options, starting with the notion that the person pursuing him was an ally who was afraid to make contact any other way. He didn't want to rule it out, but given his situation, Besserman didn't figure that to be as likely as the reality that he was being hunted by someone Pickens hired off the books.

Besserman closed his eyes and rested. Though his adrenaline was still pumping, he needed to calm down to think. His fight-or-flight response was strong—and it heavily favored a speedy exit from his situation.

A gust of wind tousled Besserman's hair and carried with it the scent of freshly baked bread and strong coffee. He thought he caught a hint of sweet pastries tagging along as well. And though he could likely get both at a small street side cafe just around the corner, the bakery might as well have been a thousand miles away. Besserman couldn't stroll into the open without risking exposure to whoever was following him.

A couple of minutes later, a woman dawdled through the door opposite the flour sacks and sat down on a plastic bucket. Without acknowledging him, she lit a small pipe and puffed on it several times before taking it out of her mouth and releasing a plume of smoke.

"*Est-ce que tu te caches de quelqu'un?*" she said.

The use of French caught Besserman by surprise. If she was going to say anything to him, she figured it would be in Arabic. But her question also caught him off guard.

Are you hiding from someone?

"Is it that obvious?" Besserman responded in French.

"There are more comfortable places to take a break. And you don't look like any courier I've ever seen around here before."

He nodded. "I am hiding from someone."

"You owe him money?"

"I don't know who he is or what he wants."

"Then what are you running from? It's always better to get answers first."

"I wish I could, trust me."

"If you don't know your enemy, how will you defeat him?"

Besserman heard deliberate footsteps coming down the alley.

He peeked around the edge and saw a man with a cap pulled low across his brow heading toward him.

"That's an excellent question," the man said in English as he stopped in front of Besserman, a gun discreetly pointed at him. "If you don't know who your enemy is, Director, how will you defeat him?"

Besserman glared at the man while trying to stealthily grab his weapon. The man clucked his tongue and shook his index finger.

"On your feet," the man said.

The woman with the pipe eased to her feet as well and backed through the door, closing it behind her and latching it shut.

Besserman stood and placed his hands in the air.

"Now, it's just you and me," the man said.

Besserman recognized the man's voice, but not his face. He wasn't sure why it was so familiar, but he couldn't place it.

"You and I are going back to Washington together," the man said. "And then you're going to have to answer for your crimes."

"My crimes?" Besserman asked. "I've committed no crimes."

"Fortunately, you aren't the one who decides what's a crime and what isn't. Now, let's go."

Besserman took a deep breath and moved slowly toward the direction the hostile indicated with his weapon and away from the open market. The man yanked Besserman's backpack off his shoulder and carried it with his free hand, using it to shield his gun from plain view.

Just minutes ago, Besserman had thought exposing himself in the market would put him at risk. But he wished he was out there now, confident that he'd at least have a chance to escape if he was.

However, that opportunity was gone, his hindsight leaving him with nothing but regret.

But Besserman couldn't give up. As long as they were still outside with the chance of others seeing them, he had a chance.

Once they reached the next intersection of alleys, the man nudged Besserman left and they walked into a wider corridor, albeit a darker one. Besserman wanted to test the man and see what he would do for non-compliance. After striding a few more steps, Besserman stopped cold. The man bumped into him.

"What the hell are you doing?" the man said through a clenched jaw. "Keep moving."

Besserman took note of how the man handled the situation and waited another ten seconds before doing it again.

For a second time, the captor bumped into Besserman. But this time, Besserman drove his elbow back and up into the man's jaw, snapping his head back. Besserman wheeled around and kicked the stunned man in his arm, jarring his weapon loose as well as the backpack. Next, Besserman slung the man against the wall, which enraged him instead of knocking him out. He charged Besserman, putting a shoulder into him and pushing him against the opposite wall.

Besserman's back slammed against the stucco, scraping through his shirt and breaking the skin. The man delivered a one-two combination to the director's mouth. He twisted free, spinning to the opposite side of the alley, the metallic taste of blood strong in his mouth. He spat and refocused.

Besserman gestured for the man to come at him. And the man complied. But instead of trying to block the oncoming blow, Besserman waited until the last second before dropping to the ground and sweeping his left leg, toppling the man. Then Besserman snatched up his pack and sprinted away.

As he ran, he unzipped his pack and dug inside for his gun. He slipped his K-bar knife up his sleeve first before freezing when a bullet pinged off the wall.

"Not another step," the man said.

Besserman fingered the trigger on his gun, which was still in his pack. He shoved the weapon down the front of his pants. He was far enough away in a dimly lit spot that he was certain the man wouldn't see the weapon until they were much closer. Then Besserman turned around slowly, his hands again raised in the air.

"Now, slowly, come this way."

"Why didn't you take the shot?" Besserman asked as he

started walking. "You only get paid if you bring me back alive, right?"

"Shut up," the man said. "Keep this up and I might just kill you for the hell of it."

Besserman took a few steps toward the man before stopping and bending over.

"What are you doing?" the man barked. "I told you to come here."

"I need to tie my shoes. Chill."

As Besserman reached for his gun, he felt cold steel jammed against his head.

"Nice try," the man said. "Now, nice and easy. Put it right there."

Besserman stood and held the gun tenuously in his left hand and tossed it aside. The man watched the gun clatter to the ground, giving Besserman all the opening he needed.

Jerking his arm forward, the knife slid out far enough for him to wrap his hand around the hilt and then slam the blade into the man's midsection and drive it upward.

The abductor cried out in pain, dropping his weapon as he collapsed to the ground. Besserman continued his assault by kicking the man in the face. He listlessly rolled aside, one hand depressed against the wound, blood blooming across his tattered shirt, the other hand groping along the cobblestone path for the weapon.

"Looking for this?" Besserman asked before kicking the gun aside.

"I would tell you to pass along a message for me," Besserman said, "but I'd rather just send one myself."

He fired two shots into the side of the man's head, the suppressor keeping the shot quieter than the shell casings when they clinked off the ground.

Besserman scooped up the evidence, then placed the man's gun in his lifeless hand after removing two bullets. It wasn't the

OPERATION NIGHTFALL

best set up he'd ever done, but it was the best he could do under the circumstances.

He dug through the man's pockets and grabbed his cell phone before slipping off unnoticed into the night.

When Besserman rounded the corner, he entered a coffee shop still open and teeming with young people. He found a booth near the back and looked at the man's cell phone. The last message was from a number without a name, but Besserman recognized it—Steve Pickens.

Besserman powered off the phone and then grabbed his phone and called Morgan May.

"We've got to end this as soon as possible," he said once she answered. "Pickens sent one of his goons after me. I want my life back now."

"You and me both," Morgan said. "And I'm working on it right now. Just try to be patient and stay low for another couple days. We'll get you home soon enough."

Besserman ordered a cup of coffee to go and meandered back into the market. He dumped the dead man's cell phone into a trash can and tugged his cap low, trudging down the street and disappearing into the darkness.

201

THIRTY-ONE

WASHINGTON, D.C.

FANG STEPPED OUT OF HIS LIMO AND ENTERED THE
courthouse through the back entrance, one devoid of the throng
of reporters hoping to catch a glimpse of him camped out on the
front steps. A guard ushered him through the metal detectors,
requiring him to empty his pockets before he did. While he
walked through it, the machine beeped.

"Are your pockets completely emptied?" asked a bored guard
positioned next to the conveyor belt.

Fang shoved his hands into his pockets and pulled out a
money clip with a large stack of cash.

"Ah," Fang said, making a show of the money as if he'd
forgotten it was in there. "I'm always forgetting about this."

He dropped the thick stack of cash into a small bowl, which
moved through the machine, and repeated the procedure.

Once Fang crossed through the metal detector without incident, a guard on the other side waved a wand around the contours
of his body before indicating the back of the conveyor belt.

"You can retrieve your personal items over there," the man
said.

Fang found the bowl and scooped out his money clip and cash. He also found a folded up piece of paper with his name scrawled on the outside.

"I didn't put this in here," Fang said to himself as he pulled out the paper.

He looked around for a moment but didn't see anyone nearby that looked like they could've dropped the note in the bowl.

Fang held up the note. "Did you put this in here?" he asked the man operating the scanner.

The man scowled and shook his head, returning his focus to the monitor in front of him.

Fang unfolded the paper and scanned it before shoving it back into his pocket and walking toward the courtroom. Right outside the doors, he found the lawyer he'd hired, Chase Hunter.

Hunter, his hair slicked straight back, wore a navy suit with brown shoes and a red tie and was clutching a briefcase against his chest. He offered a warm smile once he made eye contact with Fang.

"Mr. Fang, it's truly an honor to meet you," Hunter said.

Fang shook the man's hand but wasn't interested in indulging the man's ass kissing.

"Let's get this over with," Fang said.

They both entered the courtroom and waited for the judge to call Mei Ling Wu's case. After a few minutes, he began the hearing. And despite Hunter's request for bail to be set so Fang could pay it and have Wu released, the judge denied it, ruling that Wu was a major flight risk and ordered her to remain in jail until the next hearing the following week.

Fang wanted to scream at the judge, upset that he couldn't buy his way out of a problem. Then he thought perhaps he could, but he just needed to find the right people to wave the money in front of. That's how he'd elevated his business to the next level— offer enough incentives to the people with power and you eventually get a return on your investment. But that didn't seem to be an option this time. Even with an expensive attorney, Wu remained imprisoned.

How could this have happened?

He was sleeping in the bed next to her when the heist took place. Then he considered that maybe he didn't know his girl-friend as well as he thought he did. Maybe she was a thief.

Has she stolen any money from me?

Fang couldn't be sure of anything anymore, though he realized that part of that was his own doing. He wanted a world where truth was indiscernible to most—as long as he was the one helping everyone else realize what the truth really was. It was the power he craved, the power he couldn't wait to wield on his enemies as well as anyone else who got in his way.

Fang dressed down Hunter in the back of the courtroom before entering the hallway. Journalists, relegated to a roped-off section at the far end of the corridor, shouted for Fang to answer questions about Wu. He paused only to smile and wave, ignoring their questions.

Once outside, he strode toward his limo. The driver hustled out of the front to open the door for Fang. Head down, he grunted as he ducked into the vehicle. When he looked up, he was staring down the barrel of a gun.

Fang scowled at the man. "Who let you in here, Mr. Hawk?"

Hawk studied Fang for a moment before responding. "We meet again, though under vastly different circumstances."

"Aren't you just going to put a bullet in me and get it over with?"

"As much as I'd like to, I have a different agenda this time."

"Whatever it is, just know that you're being recorded right now," Fang said, nodding toward the camera at the far end of the limo.

Hawk smiled as he held up a section of wire. "Actually, we're not. But that's irrelevant right now because I don't intend on doing anything to you—yet. Now, did you get my proposal?"

"That was from you?"

"So, that's a yes?"

Fang shifted in his seat. "I read it."

"And are you ready to make a deal?"

Fang shook his head and laughed. "You probably thought you were clever, didn't you? You thought you'd take something that I valued and put it at risk. But that's the difference between me and you, Mr. Hawk. There's nothing I value more than myself and my ambition."

"I wonder what Ms. Wu would think if she heard you say that."

"She probably thinks the same thing. We're just using each other, like most people do in relationships. I'm just bold enough to admit it."

"Must be some kind of ambition."

"If you only knew," Fang said as he leaned back in his seat. "Now, would you mind putting that thing down and getting out of my car? I've got a busy day ahead of me."

"I think I'll stay for a few more minutes. I've got some questions that need answers."

"I'm not sure what I can say that you don't already know. So, if you're not going to pull the trigger, just get out so we can both get on with our lives."

Hawk adjusted the watch on his wrist and locked eyes with Fang. "Why such allegiance to The Alliance? You know they're going to dump you as soon as you've outlived your usefulness."

"You really don't know much about what's going on, do you?"

"I know The Alliance is behind so much of what's going on right now—and that you want to take control of it."

"Who says I haven't already done that?"

"I still have good intel that says you haven't."

"Ah, *good intel*. Nice line, Mr. Hawk. The truth is you have no idea what's going on and you're grasping at straws."

"Maybe I should just shoot you and get it over with."

"If you kill me, your big problem isn't going away."

R.J. PATTERSON

"What do you think my problem is?"

"You think it's me and Operation Nightfall, but The Alliance as an organization poses the kind of threat that will make you spend a lifetime hunting them. You'll be like a man trying to rid the beach of sand. You've already lost and you don't even know it."

"Perhaps I have, but I'm not going to stop fighting."

"Oh, yes, you will. Just wait."

Reporters closed in on the vehicle, tapping on the windows to try and get Fang's attention.

"If I roll down this window, people will take pictures of me and you—and you'll forever be tied to me. Questions about our meeting will haunt you to your grave."

Fang noticed Hawk's trigger finger twitching. "Yes, shoot me and see where that gets you. If you think things are bad now, just wait. It can get much worse."

Hawk lowered his gun and pushed the intercom, directing the driver. "Let's go."

The limo lurched forward as it left the back alley and pulled onto Main Street.

"Mr. Hawk, what's important for you to remember is that my mission is bigger than myself. It's what propels me forward, guiding all of my decisions. So, if you think you've got me figured out, you're wrong, as you discovered today with your amateurish play. As soon as I saw Mei Ling carted off by the FBI, I knew where this was going—which was nowhere. If you think I have a greater allegiance to anything other than The Alliance, you're wrong."

They rode in silence for a few minutes before Fang told the driver to stop.

"I think you've spent more than enough time in my limo, Mr. Hawk," Fang said as the car came to a halt at a traffic light. "Time for you to get out."

Hawk sighed, his demeanor resigned to defeat.

"But good talk. I'm sure we'll see each other again soon, but

206

likely under different circumstances because before you know it, I'm going to be controlling more than you ever imagined. And I won't have to spend a dime to do so."

Hawk climbed out of the vehicle and slammed the door.

Fang grinned. For once he told the truth and it felt good. At least, most of it was true.

He pushed the intercom. "Take me back to the Waldorf Astoria."

The day was young and he still had plenty of work to do.

THIRTY-TWO

VIRGINIA HIDEOUT

Slumped in a chair at the head of the conference room table, Hawk cradled a cup of coffee and stared down at the steaming black elixir. He wished he could inject it into his veins. The relentless pace of trying to stay two steps ahead of Fang was wearing on him. And when that was coupled with the realization that they were facing a soulless enemy, Hawk was beginning to wonder how much more he could take.

He swiped open his phone and navigated to a folder with family pictures. One of Alex and little J.D. both flexing while standing on top of hay bales brought a smile to his face. It also made him wish he was home in Montana. After a brief moment of lamenting his situation, he reminded himself that he was doing what he did for all the other moms and dads out there who wanted to be with their children and the kids who wanted to be with their parents. Never was that purpose more real than it was as The Alliance was on the cusp of implementing a software program that could control people in the cruelest way possible—with lies that couldn't be refuted.

Alex and Morgan joined via teleconference, while the team

208

settled into their seats around the table, the sense of angst visible on all their faces.

"I don't think I've ever seen a bunch of people who all need a stiff drink more than this crew," Ryder said with a chuckle. "You all look like death warmed over."

"Maybe it's because the reaper is knocking on the door—and we all know it," Morgan said.

"Come on," Ryder said. "It's not that bad. Besides, you can't make me the harbinger of hope here. If I'm the one trying to keep everybody's spirits up, we're in serious trouble."

"Well, we are in serious trouble," Hawk said. "We just executed a plan flawlessly to gain leverage on Fang, and the heartless bastard threw it right back in our faces. I'm not sure what we have now."

"It doesn't seem like much," Alex said. "And it certainly doesn't seem like we have many allies anywhere, especially with Besserman still on the run."

A dreadful silence settled over the room.

Dr. Z beeped in from the Magnum Group headquarters in Los Angeles. "Sorry I'm late. What'd I miss?"

Nobody said a word.

"Well, don't all talk at once," he said.

"Not much to say, Doc," Morgan said. "We're in a pretty tough spot and it doesn't look like it's getting any better."

Hawk had another thought but wasn't sure he wanted to share it based on the mood. But he wanted to keep the team talking instead of letting them wallow in their depressing reality.

"We're facing a dangerous foe," Hawk said. "The Alliance remains shrouded in mystery as well as layers of people. And the one man we've been able to identify appears beholden to an ideology so much so that he doesn't care what happens to him as long as he implements it."

"That seems like a curious shift," Morgan began, "especially since for so long he seemed intent on taking control of The Alliance, not just serving its purposes."

"If he's to be taken at his word, Fang has had a change of heart, though why he's done that isn't clear," Hawk said.

Alex rocked in her chair as she spoke up.

"We can sit here and try to psychoanalyze Fang, or we can try to solve the biggest problem we're facing right now," she said.

"Which is what, exactly?" Mia asked.

"Figuring the vehicle by which The Alliance and Fang are trying to get their software onto almost every security camera in the world. Seems to me that if we want to ultimately stop this from ever happening—not just now, but ever—we need a multi-pronged attack."

Morgan huffed. "If I'm going to help, I need to get my life back ASAP. I need this lie that's been shared with the American people to be exposed for what it is."

"I agree," Alex said. "But we can't let that be our focus right now or else we'll lose everything. We have to figure out a way to stop the software before it's installed everywhere, all while rendering it useless by developing a way to detect its existence in computing software systems. Right now, it's like a ghost and we wouldn't have any way to know if it was embedded anywhere without figuring out a way to do that."

"I can work on that," Mia said. "Now that I have the code they're using, I can create a program that will search for any of the lines of code they're using. It may take some time, but I can do it."

"That would be helpful," Alex said. "That leaves us with figuring out how Fang plans to put this on all these computers and stopping him before it happens."

"Nearly every security camera in the world uses the Nexus platform," Mia said.

Dr. Z unmuted his microphone. "This is true. I've created ways to piggyback onto security cameras by using Nexus. And unless the camera is ancient, it uses Nexus as its main operating system."

"Is that the only way to seize control of these cameras?" Morgan asked.

"I think so," Mia said.

"I agree," Dr. Z said. "But the other caveat here is that Nexus would have to force an update to get this on every camera. And that's not likely."

"Why not?" Morgan asked.

"Because it's so costly for the company," Dr. Z said. "Unless they absolutely have to, they won't."

"But what could force their hand?" Hawk asked.

"A virus, maybe one they couldn't explain or figure out a way to extract without reinstalling the entire operating system," Mia said.

"And this would be *forced* on everyone?" Morgan asked.

"Not exactly forced," Dr. Z said. "At least, not in the literal sense. It would be virtually forced if the virus made the cameras inoperable. That would mean without the new operating system, all those expensive cameras would be useless."

Hawk took a sip of his coffee, the positive headway perking him up more than the caffeine.

"In my conversation with Fang, he's acting like this Operation Nightfall is going to happen very soon. So, how's The Alliance going to do all this if the Nexus system is still operating without any issues?"

"I think I might have your answer," Mia said, her fingers clicking on her keyboard. "I've been reading about some issues all day with transportation software glitching, leading to flight delays and some near misses between planes taking off and landing at a handful of airports across the country."

She shared the webpage containing the article up on the screen for the rest of the room and the other online participants to read.

"That doesn't look good," Morgan said.

"No, it's not," Mia said. "And from what I've been able to gather on this story, it hasn't been fixed permanently. There have been some temporary repairs to the software, but the glitch hasn't been completely eliminated."

"And what's being done to correct this?" Hawk asked.

"Well—surprise, surprise—FAA officials said they believe that the problem has something to do with the Nexus operating system and that Nexus is already working on creating a patch for it."

"So, they'll be rolling out a download that everyone will get, right?" Morgan asked.

"I don't know if everyone will get it or only those who are affected by it—but it does seem that way," Mia said.

"At least we know how The Alliance is planning on implementing this," Morgan said. "That's a step in the right direction. But there's still much more work to be done—and it needs to be done quickly if we're going to stop this for good."

Rebecca sighed and cursed under her breath.

"What's wrong?" Hawk asked.

"I just got a notification on my phone," she said. "Mei Ling Wu was just granted bail and released."

Morgan growled in frustration. "*Sonofabitch*. He figured out a way to get to the judge. I can't believe it."

"Believe it," Hawk said. "Fang is going to fight."

Then Big Earv, who'd been silent for the duration of the meeting, cursed and indicated their bank of security cameras and the red flashing light. "Security breach."

Hawk spun to look at their security monitors and saw two SUVs speeding along the driveway toward them.

"Everyone out," Hawk said.

Hawk and Big Earv directed the team members through the back door and into the surrounding woods. Then Hawk rushed back inside to make the place look benign. He shuttered the blinds and then searched for a random video of background conversation from a coffee shop on YouTube and set it to play on a loop. Anything to buy them time.

Hawk checked his gun and joined the others as he heard the sound of car doors slamming and voices shouting commands.

THIRTY-THREE

WASHINGTON, D.C.

PRESIDENT BULLOCK INVITED HIS ADVISORY TEAM TO A special meeting to discuss how to handle the fallout from the accusations levied against him. Chief of Staff Emma Washburn showed up early, lugging an armful of documents. Bullock glanced at his watch as she dumped her papers on the table and collapsed into one of the chairs.

"A little early, aren't we?" Bullock asked.

Emma blew a dangling tendril of her blonde hair out of her face and sat up before gathering the loose strands and tucking them behind her ears.

"I'm sorry, Chuck," she said. "I just needed to talk to you before everyone else got here."

"Something on your mind?"

"Yeah, this whole thing with Morgan May is really bothering me."

Bullock leaned back in his chair and gestured toward her. "Please, go ahead. You know I value what you have to say, so let's hear what's bothering you."

"I—I—" Emma looked down at the table, unable or

unwilling to look at him. "I just don't know if I can work for you anymore."

"And it has to do with this situation with Morgan?"

"Yeah," she said. "I don't mind a lot of things about working in the political sphere. But there's one thing I do know, and that's this—I don't want to work for a philandering leader."

Bullock studied her closely, nodding to acknowledge her comment.

"You know that I think you've got some of the best policies any U.S. president has had in the past two decades, but I think integrity matters. Ethics matter. Faithfulness to your wife matters. And it's becoming more difficult for me to put my heart and soul into this job knowing what kind of man I'm working for."

Bullock cocked his head to one side and pursed his lips. "Can I ask you a question, Emma?"

"Sure," she said, looking up at him for the first time since she entered the room.

"How long have you known me?"

"I don't know. Fifteen years or so."

"Seventeen years," he said. "I calculated it the other day. And during the past seventeen years have you ever felt like I was doing something immoral or unethical?"

She closed her eyes and slowly shook her head. "Not that I recall."

"Okay, so you created a perception of who I am based off of years of observed history. You've seen my character, character that's been consistent whether I'm at a fundraiser event or behind closed doors with only one or two people in the room. Right?"

She nodded.

"And during that time, did I ever do anything that made you feel uncomfortable or say something that was inappropriate or suggestive toward you or anyone else?"

"No."

"Then why do you think my character has suddenly changed?"

"I don't know. It's just—I *saw* it. I saw you and Morgan. And it made me think that maybe I didn't really know you."

"You mean to tell me that not for one second did you think it was an AI generated image of me?"

"At first I did, but then every AI expert affirmed that it was you, according to metadata and the geolocation embedded in the original video. I mean, it's easy to fake some things, but not that."

"Well, I need you to look at me and trust me when I say this, okay," he said.

Emma locked eyes with Bullock.

"That wasn't me. In fact, that wasn't Morgan either. Everyone I know told me it wasn't AI either, but I know it wasn't me because I was somewhere else when that video was allegedly filmed."

"Where were you?"

"Like I said at the press conference, I was at a private dinner."

"Then why can't you get those people to come out and affirm that you were with them and expose this lie?"

Bullock bit his lip and winced. "Unfortunately, I can't."

"And why not?"

"It's complicated."

"Well, complicated is making you look guilty right now. So, whatever it is that you're trying to hide, it can't be worse than what that video looked like. Because I'm having a hard time right now with everything."

"Emma, just stop and think about it. You know who I was with that night."

Emma chewed on her lip a moment before the realization hit her. "No. Not him."

Bullock nodded. "Yes. Him."

"Just call him," she said. "See if he'll vouch for you."

"I doubt he will," Bullock said. "If he admitted that he was with me, reaching across the aisle to not only talk with me but support me financially through very generous campaign donations, it'd ruin him. You know how people are these days. If he broke ranks from his party's position, he'd be a pariah. Not to mention, people on our side of the aisle would call him a snake in the grass."

"I don't care. You have to ask. Pitch it to him like this is his chance to fight against the establishment for once."

Bullock shook his head and looked down. "I don't know. He made me swear not to tell anyone. And I don't see anything that would make him change his position. I know he'd like to help me out if there wasn't any backlash on him, but I don't think he'll view me as worthy of risking his entire career on."

"There's only one way to find out," she said, picking up his cell phone and dangling it in front of him. "Call him."

Bullock scratched his neck, contorting his face as he did. Even the decision to call Kip Hughes, a political strategist who spent most of his time on television and a substantial amount of it skewering Bullock's policies, was a difficult one, fraught with risks. Through countless conversations, Bullock viewed Hughes as a friend. And it was still rocky at best. But turning him into an enemy? That was the last thing the president wanted. He needed Hughes, someone to slip behind enemy lines and share an idea that both parties could agree on for the betterment of the country. But if Hughes truly viewed the president as the opposition, it would come at a great cost to Bullock, both personally and politically.

"I can't," he said.

"Do it," Emma said, her eyes bulging. "You can't afford not to, unless, of course, the video's real."

"Come on, Emma. I told you it's not real."

"Then at least try. Ask Kip. If he tells you no, he tells you no. He can't get mad at you for at least asking. After all, what good are his political connections to you if you're not in office anymore?"

"Okay, fine. I'll call him. Stop harassing me."

"I mean, call him now."

Bullock growled and reached for his phone. He scrolled to

Kip's number and initiated the call. The two men exchanged pleasantries before the president got straight to the point.

"So, I hate to ask you this, Kip, but I feel like I'd regret not doing so."

"What is it, Chuck? Just spit it out."

"You know this whole debacle going on right now is completely fabricated."

"I suspected as much."

"Well, Cori's mad as hell at me because she's called in an AI forensics expert who's telling her that the video is real. But I happen to know that this is a new technology that's close to being launched worldwide, if our sources are to be believed."

"And?".

"And Cori suggested she might leave me."

"Give her time. I'm sure she'll come around."

"Maybe, but then there's the political fallout this is having on my administration. All the good things we're doing are being swept aside."

"This sounds like you think I can help you."

"You can—if you're willing."

"What do you mean?"

"The night that this alleged tryst happened between me and Morgan May is the night you and I were meeting."

"No, absolutely not," Hughes said. "Not a chance. I told you not to breathe a word of our meeting to anyone. It'll undo me."

"I understand, but I'm already being undone. If you would be willing to admit that you were meeting with me privately, it might help people realize what's going on."

Hughes snorted. "You think people would actually believe that you and me could get together cordially to discuss policy initiatives?"

"It might actually lead to something really good if Americans knew that people on the opposite sides of the aisle could have these types of conversations."

"I agree, but I'm not willing to be the guinea pig for this. And don't even dare float my name to the media that I was in a meeting with you. I'd flat out deny it."

"But surely you can see I'm in a bind."

"Yeah, but you'd put me in a bigger one. You know I love you, Chuck, but if you did this to me, I'd make you an enemy. And I promise, you don't want me as an enemy. I know where all the bodies are buried, the ones that will get you significant jail time."

Then the line went dead.

Bullock placed his phone on the desk.

"Did he just hang up on you?" Emma asked.

Bullock nodded. "He refused to help and threatened me if I leaked his name to the press and suggested we were meeting privately."

"Some kind of ally he is," Emma said.

"Yeah, some kind of ally."

Bullock sank back into his chair and sighed. He needed some help but he'd run out of ideas and people to turn to. He clenched his fist and slammed it on the desk.

"I want Jun Fang dead," he growled.

THIRTY-FOUR

VIRGINIA HIDEOUT

OVERHEAD, A FULL MOON SHONE BRIGHTLY AS A SLIGHT breeze rustled the leaves of nearby trees. Hawk spied between a few low-hanging branches at the squad that was spreading out around the building. He noted that the unit appeared to be a serious one based off their discreet communication through hand signals and advanced weaponry. Night vision goggles strapped across the foreheads of each team member, automatic rifles, and enough ammo to fend off a small militia. Whoever they were, they were professionals.

Mia handed out coms units as the Magnum Group team members spread out around the compound. Hawk took command, explaining the terms of engagement. With the hideout compromised, there was no need to salvage it. If this group knew about it now, there were no assurances that they were the only ones privy to its location. And that made things a little easier for Hawk.

"We can light up the building if we have to," Hawk said. "But what we can't afford is a protracted gunfight. These guys are loaded for bear."

Hawk counted eight hostiles, making the Magnum Group slightly outnumbered. But he figured they could gain the upper hand quickly with the right moves.

"How do you want to play this?" Ryder asked.

"I'm thinking the South African Special," Hawk said.

"So, we trap them inside?"

"If we're lucky. But we need some help. We can't just stay outside and shoot at them. They can just stay holed up and wait us out. Then we're screwed."

Big Earv worked over a toothpick and stroked his chin. "You ever go coon huntin'?"

"Oh, no," Ryder said with a sigh. "Here we go again."

"Listen, city slicker. Some of my college football teammates were country, so much so that our six-eight, three-hundred-and-sixty-pound lineman was nicknamed Country Biscuit."

"Get to the point," Hawk said.

"A bunch of us went coon huntin' and the dogs treed a coon who would not come out of that tree. So, another kid on our team—a little punt returner named Jack Rabbit Johnson—was with us and he was given the dubious honor of scaling the hollowed-out tree and dumping a flare inside. That thing burned for about a minute before the coon came flying out of there like somebody had stuck it with a cattle prod."

"So you're suggesting we smoke out these bastards?" Hawk asked.

Big Earv nodded. "All we need is some smoke."

"I've got a few flares in our SUV, but I need to get back over there to them."

"And then what?" Ryder asked.

"I'll light them and throw them inside to force the men out," Hawk said. "You take the back porch and I'll take the front."

"They won't be stupid," Ryder said. "They're not all going to rush out at once."

"Of course not, but I've got some other tools to help with that," Hawk said with a wink.

He explained the plan to everyone else, pairing Big Earv and Mia, while Ryder and Rebecca partnered up. Hawk, who was going on a solo mission to retrieve the flares from the SUV, considered another option to force the hostiles out, if it came to that. Normally, he'd be very curious about who they were and who'd sent them, but he didn't have time to think about that, nor did it matter. He just wanted them all eliminated so he could get his team to safety.

Hawk waited until nearly all the hostiles entered the building before making a run for the flares. Two men remained outside keeping watch, one at the front door and one at the back.

Hawk crouched low as he hustled toward his SUV. Stealthily opening the trunk, he found the emergency kit containing four flares. He also snagged his K-bar knife and a bottle of bourbon he'd picked up for J.D. Blunt while in Italy.

Sorry, old man. Maybe I'll get you another bottle a different time.

Hawk saw an opportunity as the guard patrolling the front porch wasn't handling his assignment with the necessary caution. And Hawk intended to make the man pay for it.

With the hostiles inside, Hawk knew it wouldn't be long before they discovered no one was there and recognized he had to act quickly.

"I've got the flares," Hawk whispered over the coms. "Ryder, I need you to wait to take out the guard in the back on my mark."

"Copy that."

Despite having his suppressor, Hawk preferred to avoid gunfire if he could, keeping the sound outside the cabin to a minimum. The longer he could keep the hostiles in the dark about the reality of their situation, the better.

As soon as the guard on the front porch turned his back to walk away from the door, Hawk rushed over to him, crouching low as he went. When the man spun around to return, Hawk allowed the man to pass before leaping onto the porch. He started to turn to address the noise but stopped short as Hawk slid his blade through the man's back and through his heart. The guard gurgled before collapsing. Hawk caught him before he hit the deck and carried his body off the deck and onto the ground.

"One down, seven to go," Hawk whispered over the coms. "Ryder, you're up."

A few seconds later, Hawk heard the suppressed shot of a rifle followed by the sound of a body crumpling against the wooden deck.

"Nice shot," Hawk said.

He opened the front door and fired three flares in succession, creating further chaos among the six remaining combatants. They shouted and screamed, demanding to know what was going on outside. Hawk could hear their panicked exchanges coming from the cabin as well as from dead man's ear piece a few feet away.

Hawk sprinted away from the cabin and readied himself for a fight, taking up a spot fifty meters away at the edge of the tree line. Red smoke rolled through the cabin, creating a haunting image. Then a burst of fire.

"What the hell was that?" Hawk asked.

"Caught one of the assholes trying to sneak out a window on the side," Big Earv said.

"Good shooting," Hawk said.

Five to go.

One hostile poked his head out of the front door and scanned the area. "Ringo, you out here? Ringo!"

Hawk lined up his target—the hostile's head—and squeezed the trigger. The man fell face forward onto the porch, leaving the door cracked. Another hostile pushed the dead man's body all the way out of the door before shutting the door.

"Down to four," Hawk said.

"I like these odds," Ryder said.

"Don't get cocky. We've still got a long way to go."

There was no movement for a couple of minutes, making Hawk antsy.

"What can you guys see from your position?" he asked.

"Nothing," Ryder said.

"Looks like they might be trying to wait us out," Big Earv added.

"Then we have to smoke them out," Hawk said.

"You already tried that," Big Earv said. "They're not all as dumb as a raccoon."

"Did you think four flares constituted smoking them out?" Hawk asked.

"Hawk, what are you planning on doing?" Mia asked.

"I'm going to smoke them out," he said. "Everyone get ready."

After moving closer to the cabin again, Hawk ripped a swath of fabric from the bottom of his shirt. Then he poured out half the bottle of bourbon before shoving the cloth halfway inside. He lit it and then hurled it through the conference room plate-glass window.

Within seconds a fireball set the room ablaze.

"It won't be long now," Hawk said, hustling back to his position. "Once they exit, we should be able to pick them all off."

Hawk watched the blaze rip through the cabin, spreading from the conference room to an adjacent office within a minute.

"Not much longer now," Hawk said.

Smoke billowed from the roof, flames crackling as they consumed the back of the structure. Even from his position fifty meters away, he could feel the heat.

With the intense flames rendering useless any night vision goggles, Hawk figured that the attackers would do the sane thing in a situation like this. They'd spread out and try to escape, each man on his own. And Hawk, Ryder, and Big Earv would be ready. Mia could handle a gun as well if necessary. Hawk had put the odds in his team's favor—and he couldn't imagine any way the hostiles could regain it.

But he hadn't considered every possibility.

Seconds later, the front door burst open and Hawk lined up his shot. However, by the time he squeezed the trigger, the other three men had fled the cabin and were storming toward him.

When Hawk took aim at the first man, it revealed his position to the others. They split apart and fired on him, bullets hammering the trees around him and stitching lines in the dirt.

"They're all coming this way," Hawk said.

"On my way," Ryder said.

"Copy that," Big Earv chimed in.

But Hawk knew it would be too late. The attackers knew where he was and saw an opening if they could put him down. The woods behind Hawk were vast, providing the men with a way to vanish. All they had to do was kill Hawk. Ryder and Big Earv would never pose much of a threat before it was too late.

Hawk took aim at one of the men and felled him with three shots. He cursed, realizing he was running low on ammo. He wheeled toward one of two remaining attackers rushing toward him and fired. A cloud swept in front of the moon as Hawk prepared to fire. His first two shots didn't hit their mark as the man maintained his blistering pace.

Hawk maintained visual on the silhouetted man and fired again. This time, the bullet slowed him down as he grabbed his shoulder. But it didn't stop him.

Hawk fired twice more, one of the shots hitting the man in the chest. He pitched forward, falling face first into the dirt about twenty meters away.

The wind swept away the clouds, allowing the full strength of the moon to again light the open field. Hawk turned and fired on the other approaching man, but the gun just clicked.

Damnit.

Hawk reached for his K-bar when he realized he still had the flare gun in his pocket with one more flare remaining.

It wasn't the kind of bullet he would've preferred, but it was better than nothing. Hawk took cover behind a tree as the remaining hostile bore down on his position, firing his gun and shredding the surrounding trees.

Hawk knew if he didn't take a chance soon, his odds of surviving would dwindle. With a deep breath, he peeked around the edge of the tree and took aim at the man. The flare sizzled as it streaked through the night before slamming hard against his chest. In response, the man screamed and then stumbled to the ground about five meters away.

Hawk pounced on the opportunity, flying toward the man splayed on the ground. He made a move toward his gun, but Hawk kicked dirt in the man's face, delaying the hostile's ability to get the weapon trained on target. As he groped for the gun, Hawk kicked the man in the head. He tried to scramble to his feet, but Hawk unleashed another powerful kick, this one connecting with the man's side, cracking ribs as he spun onto his back.

Hawk clutched the hilt of his K-bar before driving it into the man's chest. He tried to scream, but nothing came out as his eyes met Hawk's.

"Who sent you?" Hawk asked.

The man grimaced and grunted, his face contorted in a pained expression. But he remained tight-lipped.

Hawk pinned the man down with a knee and loomed over him. "I can make this fast or slow. It's up to you. Now, this is the last time I'm gonna ask: Who sent you?"

The man glowered at Hawk, eyes narrowing. Blood streamed from the corner of the man's face as he gasped for breath.

Then he tried to speak. "Ki ... ki—"

"What?" Hawk asked, leaning closer.

"Kiss ... my ... ass."

Hawk slid the knife out of the man's chest, his shirt soaked in blood.

"You had your chance," Hawk said. "Now, it's just gonna be painful."

The man grinned and stammered as he spoke. "They're never ... gonna ... stop coming. You—"

The man sucked in a breath through his nose and slowly shook his head.

"You don't ... know ... who you're ... messing ... with."

"Obviously, you didn't know either," Hawk said as he snatched the man's gun off the ground.

"Hawk, report," Ryder said.

"I took care of them," Hawk said. "But you might want to double check and make sure one of these rat bastards didn't slink off into the night."

"Copy that."

A few seconds later, Hawk heard a gunshot. And then two more.

"They're all dead," Ryder reported.

"All but this one," Hawk said, looking at the man still fighting against the inevitable.

Hawk took the man's gun and shot him in the head.

"Now they're all gone," Hawk said. "And we need to get the hell outta here before the next wave arrives."

Hawk began walking away when he heard an electronic beep. He turned around and searched the dead man, finding a cell phone. There was a text message waiting, but the phone required a thumbprint to open. Hawk wiped the man's thumb clean and depressed it to the phone. Once it opened, he read the text.

Report ASAP.

Hawk smiled and typed a response.

Targets all eliminated.

Good work. Here's the next target.

Hawk gasped as he stared at the image on the screen. It was a picture of Robert Besserman along with a briefing on him. Hawk removed his phone from his pocket and dialed Alex's number.

"Hey, where did you send Besserman?" he asked.

"Oh, thank God, you're okay," she said.

"Yeah, we took care of them. Sorry. I forgot you knew."

"Is everyone else all right?"

"Yeah, the team's fine. We handled these guys. But I just picked up one of their phones and whoever is handling them wants them to go after Besserman next.

"Whoa. Who do you think's behind all this?"

"I don't know. It seems like it'd be an odd thing for Fang to do, but I wouldn't completely dismiss it."

"That doesn't sound like him though."

"No, but I need to warn Besserman. Where is he?"

"I–I don't know. I just told him he needed to find a new hideout. He said he would but didn't tell me where he was going. He just said it was far, far away."

Hawk cursed and kicked at the ground. Suddenly, he felt like they were fighting a ghost.

THIRTY-FIVE

TANGIER, MOROCCO

THE PROTOCOL FOR STAYING AT THE AGENCY'S Moroccan safe house required a strict adherence to a lengthy list of rules, foremost among them that the place was never to look like anyone was there. Besserman knew the location of all four safe houses, only three of which were documented at the agency. The fourth one was unknown except to a handful of field officers working in the Middle East as embedded agents. If someone within the CIA was hunting down Besserman, the Tangier hideout, one located on a quiet street with mostly vacation rentals, was the most secure.

But it still remained vulnerable—and Besserman knew it.

Besserman brewed a cup of coffee and peeked through the blinds at the back of the house facing the Mediterranean Sea. The back porch looked inviting as comfortable deck chairs faced the water. The sun had just risen, peeking over the horizon, creating an environment he craved. He imagined himself sitting out there with a book, nursing his coffee, while a gentle Mediterranean breeze wafted by.

It's not happening, Bobby.

At least, it wasn't supposed to happen. In a moment of internal rebellion, he questioned whether anyone could see him on the deck. Tall fences separated the properties on either side of Besserman and the only way anyone could truly see him was if they were watching from the water. And as Besserman stared out across the water, there wasn't a sailboat or any other vessel within a mile of him. That made the back porch all the more tempting.

This isn't the time for weakness.

Besserman sighed and stepped back from the window where the blinds were to remain drawn at all times. He considered walking back to his car to retrieve some of his gear, but knew that too was against the rules. All cars were to be parked two blocks away at a park. Unless being actively slept in, beds were to be made to exact specifications. Safe house occupants were only to enter and exit in the darkness and take inside everything they needed initially for their stay. Every scrap of trash and food was to be taken out Thursday evenings before the cleaning lady arrived on Friday mornings. The woman who scoured the place every Friday was supposed to be unable to determine if anyone was actually staying there—just in case she was an informant. It was a trick the CIA had deployed countless times for decades around the world, making the agency wise to how others might turn the tables on them.

With all that was happening, Besserman could only sit and wait. And it felt like dying a slow death. He'd never been one to run from a fight, but this wasn't a fight. This was an ambush, a framing that Jun Fang had undoubtedly arranged. At best, the agency's command would be assumed by Steve Pickens, who clearly wanted permanent control. At worst, the CIA would remain rudderless while it sorted out how to proceed with its leader accused of murder abroad. Either one of those results would be detrimental to the agency, an organization that Besserman would always fight hard to protect. But at the moment, all he wanted to do was clear his name. Yet he felt helpless to make that happen, like a kite trying to withstand a hurricane.

He needed some help.

Besserman looked at his watch and sighed. It was just past 2:00 a.m. on the east coast, meaning if he called someone he'd rouse them from their sleep. He would've rather waited, but he couldn't. Despite escaping with his life the previous night, he knew it wouldn't be long before someone came for him. He was destined to endure this cycle until he was killed. And he knew the odds were stacked against him. Eventually, someone would succeed. The only way to stop the next wave of assassins was to prove his innocence and then go on the offensive.

Hawk's gonna kill me, but he'll get over it.

The phone rang three times before Hawk grunted upon answering his phone.

"I would ask you if now was a bad time, but that'd be ridiculous," Besserman said. "I know it's a horrible time."

"Are you all right?" Hawk asked, perking up. "Is something wrong?"

"At the moment, no. But I can't say that's the case for my life in general."

"You woke me up to tell me this?"

"I'm sorry," Besserman said, contrition evident in his voice. "I really just need to talk."

"Don't you have a counselor or a therapist you could've called?"

Besserman drummed his fingers on the desk in front of him. "They cost money—plus, I doubt they can really help me with my problem."

"You'll have to be more specific," Hawk said. "I understand you have a number of problems right now."

"I'm going to get straight to the point. I want to clear my name ASAP. And I can't do that on my own."

"I know. There's an epidemic going around, in case you

haven't heard. Just tell me what you want me to do and I'll try to help."

"I need you to see if you can find the footage that shows where I really was at the time of the explosion. Think you can do that for me?"

"I don't know. I just—"

"Call Ferdinand Bertolli with Italian intelligence. Tell him you're doing this for me and you want copies of all the CCTV footage from Venice the night of the explosion."

"And you think he'll just give it to me?"

"You never know if you don't ask. But we've been friends for a long time, and I did get him World Cup tickets for Italy's knockout round match the last time the U.S. hosted the event. If he balks, be sure to mention that favor."

"Okay, okay. So, where are you? The team was wondering."

"Tangier. How's the rest of the team doing?"

"We're hanging in there. Had a little trouble of our own earlier tonight, but we managed."

"I want to hear more about that later, but—"

Besserman stopped when he heard what sounded like a vehicle outside the front of his house.

"Hold on a second," Besserman said. "I need to check something."

"Problems?"

"I'm not sure yet."

He peeked through the blinds and noticed a black sedan out front with two men who appeared serious as they checked their weapons.

"Shit," Besserman said.

"So, trouble?"

"I've got some visitors. Two men with guns."

"Just stay calm," Hawk said.

Besserman hustled to the back bedroom, grabbing his lone weapon off his nightstand before shutting himself in the walk-in closet. He looked at the bed and sighed. He'd forgotten to make it. He worked quickly to tuck the sheets in and make it look as if nobody had been there. He scooped up his dirty clothes and go-bag then shoved them into a drawer in the dresser located in the walk-in closet. Satisfied that the place looked empty, he closed the closet door and climbed into the crawl space.

"Bobby, are you still there?" Hawk asked.

Besserman exhaled as he sat down. "Yeah," he whispered. "Still here."

"What's going on?"

"Two guys with guns just rolled up. Not sure who they are, but I'm not going to answer the door to find out."

"Stay on the line with me until they're gone."

"Copy that."

Besserman set the phone aside as he turned toward the front of the house. He heard approaching footsteps along the walkway followed by a knock. The men waited a moment before knocking again.

Another beat.

Then more knocking.

There was a slight pause before they smashed open the door, the frame splintering as debris clanked against the concrete.

"They're coming for me," Besserman whispered.

"I'm sending someone there," Hawk said.

"If they find me, it'll be too late."

"Just hang in there."

Besserman steadied his breathing, his hand wrapped tightly around his Glock 17 and trained on the hatch leading back into the house. If he saw even a sliver of daylight, he prepared to unload on them.

As the gunmen swept through the house, Besserman thought about what he could've done differently. He could've allowed the CIA to capture him and explain the situation. It might've been better, but given Pickens' thirst for power, he doubted it would've been worse than what was about to happen to him—getting pulled out of a crawl space like a coward.

Just like Saddam Hussein.

The thought sickened Besserman. Had he been a coward? Or had he been smart? He doubted he had any chance at a fair trial in a Russian court if the Italians extradited him. And who knew what would happen in an Italian court? History had shown that U.S. citizens struggled to get a fair trial there either.

No, he'd done the right thing. But somehow, someway, someone had found him.

There has to be a traitor at the agency.

Besserman was certain he'd been careful to avoid getting tracked to the safe house. A spy seemed to be the only logical explanation. Hardly anyone knew about the Tangier location. Yet, there were two men traipsing through the house searching for him that suggested it wasn't quite the secret he thought it was.

"Hawk," Besserman whispered, "if I don't make it, tell Rebecca I really did love her."

"Hey, Bobby. None of that talk. You're gonna be fine. I called some men. They're on their way."

"They won't make it here in time. Just find Fang and make sure that bastard pays, okay?"

"No more, Bobby. I'm warning you."

"You're one of the best I've ever worked with. And it's been a pleasure knowing you."

"Bobby!"

"They're almost here," Besserman said as he heard the men enter the bedroom. "Say a prayer."

He placed the phone down and turned the volume all the way down.

With another deep breath, he put both hands on the handle of his weapon and trained it on the crawl space hatch.

I'm not going down without a fight.

∿

Hawk cursed under his breath as he listened. He wanted to say something, but he understood that it might give away Besserman's position. So, he just listened—and waited.

Each second that ticked past felt like a minute. He could hear the stomping of feet.

And then—

Shouting, screaming, yelling.

Gunshots. Lots of gunshots.

Silence.

"Bobby? Bobby, are you there?" Hawk called.

More silence.

Then a click as the line went dead.

THIRTY-SIX

LOS ANGELES

MORGAN MAY SAT UP AND SWEPT HER MATTED HAIR out of her eyes, early morning sunlight streaming through the window. After rubbing her eyes, she heard a knock at the door and smelled freshly brewed coffee. She flung her feet off the side of the bed and put on a pair of plush bunny slippers.

Morgan opened the door and saw her friend Jackie holding out a steaming mug.

"Thought you might want this," Jackie said.

Morgan took the coffee. "Thanks. You always know exactly what I need."

"That's what rooming with you at the Gamma Phi Beta house will do for you."

"At least our partying days are over."

"Thank God for that."

Morgan made her bed and got dressed before joining her sorority sister in the living room. Jackie had graciously invited Morgan to stay with her until everything got sorted out, an invitation she readily accepted.

"Now, just to be clear, you can stay as long as you like," Jackie said, "but how long do you think this situation will take to resolve?"

Morgan took a sip of her coffee before responding. "There's no telling, to be honest. I can't really dispute the narrative that's taking place or else I risk outing myself as the director of a group that operates clandestine agents in the field."

"What you do is legal, right?"

"Legal-*ish*. But we definitely don't do anything illegal, at least by CIA standards."

"So, lots of gray area?"

"That's a good way to put it. But we're actively fighting threats to this country's national security."

Jackie picked up a tablet off the kitchen table and handed it to Morgan. "You might want to read this."

Morgan's eyes widened as she read the headline aloud: "A Presidential Sweet: Records show think tank advisor Morgan May visited White House seventeen times over the past six months."

"What the hell is this? I was just—" Morgan said before stopping.

"What? Just doing your job?"

"Yeah, but meeting with the president is what I do."

"The article does mention that," Jackie said. "But it also said that the most any other advisor not on the president's cabinet or official advisory council visited the White House during that same span was three times."

Morgan sighed.

"Why don't you just come clean?" Jackie asked.

"Why would I? Or even better yet—why do I have to?"

"To spare the President? So you can go back to your job in peace? You tell me."

Morgan shrugged. "Bullock can navigate these tricky waters on his own. He's been through far worse and emerged stronger because of it."

"It'd save him some emotional pain, maybe even his marriage."

"That's not my responsibility, though I do feel bad for him. We'll just see how it plays out. This whole thing may blow over. You know how the news media is."

And as a meteorologist for L.A. news station, Jackie was well versed in news cycles and the short spans they often ran.

"But this is a massive story," Jackie said. "It's on par with the Monica Lewinski scandal with Bill Clinton, at least that's what I heard some of the veteran reporters saying in the newsroom this week."

"And you know what? Clinton survived that scandal politically. The Lewinski affair might be how people remember his time in office, but he's still somewhat regarded as a good president, depending on who you ask, which is better than other leaders who are universally reviled."

"Well, I trust you know what you're doing, so I won't bug you about it. But I do wish I could help you more. I know this has got to be a difficult time for you."

"If you only knew."

Jackie gave Morgan some information about where to find everything she might need before heading off to work. Finally left alone, Morgan propped her feet up on the ottoman and leaned back, staring at the ceiling and contemplating what to do next, if anything. Her team had just survived an attack from a group of mercenaries and details of her personal life were being dragged into the public. Everything she'd worked so hard to build felt like it was crumbling.

Her phone buzzed with a Washington number that seemed familiar to her.

Who is this?

Morgan hesitated to answer, fearing it might be more bad news. The number didn't belong to anyone on her team, which gave her pause. But she took a deep breath and accepted the call.

"Morgan, this is Emma Washburn," a friendly voice said. "Do you have time to talk right now?"

"Time is pretty much all I've got these days," Morgan said.

"I can't imagine what you're going through, and I know it's got to be tough, but I just wanted to reach out on behalf of President Bullock and see how you're doing."

"Would you believe me if I told you I was fine?"

"I'd probably think you were lying."

"Yeah, it's hard to fake how I feel right now. And I just want to get back to doing my job more than anything."

"What if I told you there was a way to speed things up a little bit?"

Morgan sat up straight. "I'm listening."

"Now, I'm sure you heard the report showing guest logs with you visiting the White House over a dozen times in the past six months."

"Seventeen times," Morgan said. "The report I read said seventeen."

"So you've seen them. Good. Now, I believe you could come clean and just tell a trusted reporter what those meetings were about. And that might end everything."

"I've got a better idea," Morgan said. "What if you helped find the CCTV footage of me at the Washington Nationals game that night? Or at least, figure out who hacked my phone and my friends' from that night and deleted all our photos. That would go a long way in proving my innocence."

"You know nobody would believe that."

"Probably not, but I'm not sure how credible any report would be, even with proof, after what Jun Fang just did to us. He completely fabricated an affair and showed it to the world. And everybody wants to believe it's true because we all love a good scandal."

"That's why a public confession will go a long way."

"A what?" Morgan asked, her jaw dropping. "I'm not confessing to anything. I didn't—"

"Calm down, Morgan. I'm not asking you to admit to something you didn't do."

"Then what do you mean?"

"I mean, I'd like for you to consider admitting that you do more than just run a national defense think tank."

"You want me to admit that I'm running a black ops division under the auspices of the CIA?"

"You can word it however you like, but something that would help people understand that your visits to the White House were official and necessary."

"You realize you're talking about burning me, right?"

"That wouldn't exactly *burn* you."

"Yes, it would. Bad state actors would come after me, people who might suspect that I was in charge of some group who meddled in their country, maybe even killed one of their own during a mission. You're talking about me admitting something where the natural consequences would be painting a target on my chest and inviting assassins to take me out. So, I'm going to pass on that idea."

"Come on, Morgan. The president really needs you. His marriage is falling apart. The longer people go on believing this lie, the more difficult it will be to come back from this."

Morgan sighed. "All right. The best I can do right now is tell you I'll consider it. But just know I'm not happy about this, nor do I think it will get the desired result you're chasing."

"Unless you try, you never know."

Morgan sighed, exasperated. "I'll call you back later."

"Thanks for considering this. I know it's a big ask, but—"

"Yeah, yeah. Save it. I'll call you later."

Morgan ended the call and tossed her phone on the couch. She paced the floor for a few minutes weighing the pros and cons. If she admitted what Emma Washburn was asking, it'd be the end of her career in intelligence. And she wasn't sure she was ready for that.

But Bullock might reward her with a nice job in Washington. While a nice sentiment, that's not what she wanted either. There had to be another way, but she was stumped.

She picked up her phone again and called her uncle.

"How's my favorite niece?" Blunt asked once he answered.

"Uncle J.D., I'm your only niece," she said.

"And still my favorite. Nothing you can do will knock you off that pedestal."

She chuckled and shook her head. "You know the only thing worse than bad dad jokes?"

"No. What?"

"Bad *uncle* jokes."

"If you're calling me to ask for some money, you're not buttering me up the right way."

She snorted. "I don't need your money. But I was hoping for something a little more valuable—your advice."

"Hmm. In that case, the answer is yes—by all means, assassinate Jun Fang."

"Whoa. That escalated quickly, but that's not what I was calling about. Well, not exactly."

"Okay. Go ahead. Lay it on me. What wisdom do you seek from this long in the tooth beach bum?"

Morgan proceeded to explain the situation and the options she'd come up with—stay quiet or admit to something that would end her career.

"Oh, Morgan, haven't I taught you better than that?"

"I'm not sure I understand. I didn't do it."

"No, no, no. I know you didn't do anything with Bullock. Besides, I doubt you could stand to be that close to him. Every single time I've been around him, he reeks of garlic. It's like the man is afraid of vampires or something and bathes in the stuff every day."

Morgan laughed again. "Okay, what did you teach me better about?"

"About the danger of binary thinking. There's always more than two options."

"I've been racking my brain trying to think of another one, but I'm stumped. It's why I called you. I knew you'd come up with something."

"Oh, I've got an idea all right. And it's not just about proving that this was a hoax. It's also about exposing what Fang's done."

She couldn't resist the smile creeping up around the corners of her mouth.

"Tell me," she said. "What did you have in mind?"

THIRTY-SEVEN

NEW YORK | LAGUARDIA AIRPORT

MAX SCHEFTER SAT DOWN AT HIS TERMINAL AND loosened his tie. Fingers covered in chili, he adjusted his headset with the back of his hands and then pushed his glasses up the bridge of his nose with his knuckles. He took the final bite of his chili dog before wiping his hands with a napkin.

He'd worked as an air traffic controller for more than two decades, securing his spot as LaGuardia's most senior ATC, evidenced by a full head of gray hair and an ample gut from regularly eating airport food court fare. He made clear to everyone in the tower that the Jets were his favorite NFL team, the irony not lost on him. Whenever he landed a plane safely, he kissed his index and middle finger together and slapped the faded Jets pennant on the side of his terminal. It was the little things that kept him going in a demanding job with a high turnover rate.

But Schefter didn't just enjoy his job—he thrived in it, feeding off the stress. His favorite days were when a weather front blew in more quickly or more powerfully than expected, turning the skies over Queens into something akin to a kettle of vultures. Everyone was shouting instructions, doing whatever it took to get

242

their planes down safely. But Schefter never raised his voice, remaining psychotically calm at times when the tower was on the verge of erupting.

He saw the flight number of the next batch of planes he'd be receiving from approach and heard the number he was looking for.

"Tower, Delta 2582, ILS 22," the approaching captain said.

"Delta 2582, winds 180 at 12, number 2, cleared to land runway 22 ," Schefter said back, his reply smooth yet clipped.

"Cleared to land, 22, Delta 2582," the pilot confirmed.

Schefter jumped to another plane. "American 123, winds 180 at 12, cleared to takeoff Runway 13. American 124, Runway 13, line up and wait."

Then he added his final instruction to the previous Delta pilot.

"Delta 2582, left when able, left on Bravo, ground point seven."

He glanced at his list and prepared to speak with the next incoming plane. But then his computer screen blinked and all the flight numbers disappeared.

"Shit. What the hell is going on?" Schefter said, leaning forward to peer at his screen. "Did anyone else just lose their planes?"

"Negative, Max. Probably just smudges on your glasses from those sticky fingers of yours," said one of the other controllers.

"Stick it up your ass, Kyle. Nobody asked," Schefter growled.

"As a matter of fact, *you* asked me, dipshit."

Schefter ignored the dig, knowing Kyle was right. He had asked, but no one else seemed to have the problem but him.

Then a second later, the screen flickered back, all the flight numbers returning.

"You all right, Max?" asked Brian Randall, the tower's operations supervisor.

"Yeah, I guess. Something weird just happened though."

Then Kyle slapped the side of his monitor. "What's going on?"

"Problems, Kyle?" Schefter asked.

"You gave my computer some virus, Max. Probably migrated through your chili dog cheese farts into my motherboard."

The comment drew a round of chuckles from the other ATCs.

"You can always go on the roof," Schefter said. "You can inhale the fresh jet fumes while you talk in sign language to your pilots."

Kyle spun and flipped a middle finger at Schefter. "You understand that?"

Schefter shook his head and returned his focus to his computer as he began directing the next plane coming in on approach.

"Anyone else having issues?" asked another ATC.

"Okay, show of hands," Randall said, "who's software is glitching?"

Suddenly four hands flew up in the air. Then Schefter's screen blinked again and all the call numbers disappeared.

"Okay, we need to put everyone in a holding pattern until we get this figured out," Randall said. "We can still see all the planes on radar, correct?"

"Affirmative," one of the ATCs said.

"Hang in there, everybody. We'll figure out what's going on."

Schefter's phone buzzed with a text from a friend of his who used to work at LaGuardia but had landed a position at the tower as the Dallas-Fort Worth airport.

Is your software glitching?

Schefter gasped, recognizing the fallout of every airport in the country dealing with a computer issue.

Yeah … just started. It's chaos.

244

And you love it, don't you?

For once I'm actually starting to stress out.

For the next ten minutes, LaGuardia ATCs worked to keep the planes circling overhead without incident. Then Randall stood in the middle of the room to give an update.

"We just figured out what's going on," he said, hands on his hips. "It's a Nexus software issue, something to do with their most recent update. The company is recommending to immediately revert to the previous operating system and to wait on a more permanent fix."

Schefter grumbled as he began the process of downloading the old Nexus operating system. It'd take at least a half hour to download and install, which was an eternity in ATC time.

"Might as well go grab another chili dog, Max," Kyle chided.

Schefter hated Kyle and his personal digs, but he liked the idea. Approach would be handling the traffic building up over the city until his computer was back up and running.

And all the stress had made him hungry anyway.

He asked if anyone wanted anything and took a few orders of his fellow ATCs, yet making sure to ignore Kyle's before hustling to the food court.

As Schefter was descending in the elevator, his phone started buzzing with alerts. He opened one of the alerts from a news site he followed. The software issue was worldwide and causing untold chaos.

THIRTY-EIGHT

ARLINGTON, VIRGINIA

Hawk removed his earbuds as he ran along the dirt path meandering through a wooded local park. He needed to think without any competing ideas in his head. No music. No podcasts. No audio books. Just a clean slate to consider all the moving parts Jun Fang had set into motion and figure out where he was going with them. The Alliance appeared poised to advance part of their agenda, and Hawk sensed he was running out of time to stop it.

Most troubling to Hawk was the fact that CIA Deputy Director Steve Pickens seemed to be working in concert with The Alliance. Whether he was doing so intentionally or unwittingly didn't matter. The end result was the same. But it mattered if Hawk wanted to find out if there were other assets The Alliance was manipulating in order to realize their new future.

Hawk considered who else was involved—and it was frightening the amount of access The Alliance had to some of the most dangerous mercenaries, tech geniuses, and scientists. Fang hadn't become as rich as he was without developing an extensive network of experts and leaders in their respective fields. No, Fang was a visionary, a man intent on implementing his ideas on the world, and doing so in a way that most people wouldn't even notice. In short, he was a magician, distracting observers with one hand while devising a diabolical plot in the other. But Hawk had figured him out. He'd peeked behind the curtain and seen the secret to the trick. All Hawk had to do now was figure out a way to show the world how Fang was doing it—and hope it would accept the truth.

Hawk hustled up a steep hill, calves burning, lungs searing. When he reached the top, he stopped and interlaced his fingers, placing them on top of his head as he tried to slow his breathing. He paced for another minute or so as he caught his breath. Then he looked across the other side of the hill, which opened into a large clearing. A handful of people jogged, while others walked, some with a friend, some alone, some with a dog. Hawk reminded himself that while keeping his family safe was his primary motivation, he was also doing it for these people too, the ones who just wanted to live their lives in peace and enjoy walks in the park.

Hawk's phone buzzed with a call from Alex.

"Hey, honey," he said as he answered. "I was just thinking about you."

"Good things, I hope."

"Always."

After a brief small talk, he asked if she had a reason for her call or if she was just checking in.

"Actually, I wanted to tell you something very important," she said.

"Go on."

"I think I know how Fang intends to get his Trojan software onto every security camera."

"Really?"

"Yeah. Did you see the news about the debacle at airports nationwide last night?"

"I've been a little busy," he said. "What'd I miss?"

"There was a glitch in the Nexus operating system that

affected dozens and dozens of towers across the country, almost bringing flight traffic to a halt."

"And what's the solution?"

"Nexus encouraged everyone to download the previous update *and* they plan to deliver a *new* update within the next few days designed to fix all the issues."

Hawk shook his head. "So that's how Fang's gonna do it."

"Exactly. Nexus is going to play right into his hands, if they haven't already."

"Good catch. I'll call Morgan and see if she can help us get the message to Nexus."

Hawk ended his call and immediately called Morgan.

"Do you have any idea what time it is?" she asked as she answered the phone.

"Sorry," Hawk said, "but this just couldn't wait."

Morgan groaned. "All I wanted was just one more hour of sleep—or at least not waking up while it's still dark outside."

"You'll be glad you did. Trust me."

"Okay, Hawk. What is it?"

Hawk related everything Alex had just shared.

"Alex figured it out," Morgan said. "Great. Now, why did you feel the need to let me know this information right away?"

"Because you can help Nexus stop this."

"Me?"

"Yeah," Hawk said. "I remember seeing pictures of you within the last year where you posed with Nexus CEO Brad Chilton."

"At the security conference in Vegas?"

"That's the one," Hawk said. "You two looked chummy. I'm sure he remembers you."

"Maybe he will, though I wouldn't count on it. But I'll give him a call."

"Thank you," Hawk said, digging into the dirt with the toe of his shoe. "Let me know when you hear back."

Hawk ended the call, pocketing his phone before resuming

his run. When he returned to his car, he climbed inside and cell rang again with a call from Morgan.

"That was fast," he said.

"It's not good news though."

"Why? Did you talk to him? What'd he say?"

"I called his personal assistant, and she told me that I'd have get on his schedule like everyone else. Then I told him it was emergency and needed to talk to him right away. But he as Chilton if he'd heard of me but apparently he didn't remem me and sounded irritated that his assistant was interrupting hii"

"Great," Hawk said. "We've got a guy who's going to The Alliance amass untold amounts of power, and he's anno that someone is trying to warn him."

"Yeah, that sums it up."

"So, now what?" he asked.

"Get the team, get on a plane, and get to Seattle to talk Chilton face-to-face."

"And if that doesn't work?" Hawk said.

"Then you know what to do."

Hawk thanked Morgan for trying before ending the cal quickly texted the team and told them to meet him at the ai in two hours.

THIRTY-NINE

WASHINGTON, D.C.

PRESIDENT BULLOCK, ARMS FOLDED ACROSS HIS CHEST, studied the flat screen monitor on the far wall of the conference room. He tilted his head to one side, squinting as he pursed his lips. His mind whirred as he considered what to say to the Pentagon officials gathered in the room.

"How accurate do you think this intel is?" Bullock asked, his tone sharp.

"It's rock solid, sir," one of the generals said.

"Then send a team in there right now," Bullock snapped. "We can't allow a group of rogue terrorists to lug a nuclear missile around the planet."

"We'll get a team prepped and ready to go, sir," another general said.

"I want a full report as soon as the mission is completed," Bullock said as he glanced at his watch. "I have another meeting I need to get to, but I trust everyone understands what needs to happen here."

"Yes, sir," the leaders at the table said as they began gathering their papers and getting up.

As the advisors filed into the hallway, Bullock looked toward the door and saw Emma Washburn standing with her back to the wall just inside the room. She wore a faint smile, something he hadn't seen on her face for at least the past week. He was sure he hadn't smiled in at least that long either.

Once they had the room to themselves, Bullock approached her. "What's that look for?"

She hugged a stack of papers against her chest, her smile broadening. "Have you ever heard the expression, 'There's more than one way to skin a cat'?"

He nodded. "If you've spent a day in the South, you've heard it. But it's not one I use much anymore. When I was running for Senate once, I used that phrase at a campaign rally, which apparently had a whole group of ladies wearing shirts with 'Cat Ladies for Buchannan' printed on them."

"You probably lost their votes then, didn't you?"

"Let's just say my campaign office was flooded with calls and emails for the next two weeks from pet advocates condemning my words and painting me as a monster," he said. "Cori and I even posed with our Tabby cat named Leo for some campaign pictures, but it didn't seem to stem the tide. Eventually, the furor just died down, but it was rough for a while. So, why do you ask?"

"You know that problem we've been trying to solve?"

"Did Morgan May agree to admit why she visited the White House that many times?"

"Like I said, there's more than one way to skin a cat?"

All the color drained from Bullock's face as he imagined the worst case scenario. "She didn't—"

"No. She's fine. But apparently her team found a very creative way to cast doubt on the validity of the images."

"And how'd they do that?"

Emma paused for a moment, wincing before she continued. "It's probably not how you would've preferred this situation to be dealt with, but it's already proving to be effective."

"Emma," Bullock said, drawing out her name and eyeing her cautiously, "what did Morgan do?"

"I'm not sure she's *personally* responsible for this, but I know her team is the only one who could pull this off."

"Emma, you're making me nervous. What'd she do?"

"Would you rather I just show you?"

"I don't know," Bullock said. "I'd rather you just get straight to the point."

"I know the suspense is killing you," she said. "But this is just one of those things that's better shown than told. It would sound so much worse if I said it aloud."

"Emma, stop teasing me and tell me what she did."

"Just sit down while I catch the lights."

Emma dimmed the lights and navigated to a video online and pushed play. A news anchor began describing what she explained as an inordinate amount of videos of President Bullock with scores of other women.

"What the hell, Emma? Why are you—"

"Just keep watching," she said, pointing to the screen.

Bullock grumbled as he turned back around and the video continued. Images of Bullock with private parts blurred out appeared on the screen, one right after the other of Bullock with women who had different color hair and skin tone.

"I think I'm going to be sick," he said.

"Just keep watching," Emma insisted.

The anchor turned somberly toward the screen and resumed her report. "Now, what you just witnessed is likely faked. In fact, every single image you've seen of Bullock with other women is likely faked. Now, you might be asking how our investigative team came to that conclusion, and the truth is that we used multiple digital forensics experts to determine the authenticity of these videos. And every single one of them determined that all of these videos were real with no AI involvement. But what makes that impossible is that all these videos were filmed in the exact same location with the exact same time stamp. And if you look closely enough, you can tell that Bullock is in the same room doing the same thing at the same time in every video. To do that in real life would be virtually impossible. Now, to prove the point, our production team overlaid each image on top of one another. And as you can see by this footage—" another video popped up on the screen as she continued, "—the only thing different in these images are the faces of the women. Even the hair is the same with the exception of the color."

Bullock looked wide-eyed at Emma. "How did they—"

"I interviewed an intelligence official earlier today who agreed to speak with me on the condition of anonymity, and he told me that there has been rumblings on the Intelligence Committee on Capitol Hill that this type of technology existed now and would threaten the trust the public has with what they can see. In drawing our conclusions, we believe that it's highly unlikely that President Bullock performed these acts with all these women, as it would be physically impossible. But bad state actors could certainly skew this and try to embarrass Bullock by releasing this type of footage to the public. With all the politically charged ads that have been unleashed on Bullock, our team has rated this video as likely false and we're warning viewers not to believe it."

Bullock grunted. "Great. She might as well have come out and announced it was real. Because if her network is saying it's a lie, everyone's going to believe the opposite."

Emma turned the channel and found a news program on the other side of the political aisle parroting the claims.

"Everybody's saying it," Emma said. "And if you can get those two networks to agree on a certain narrative, the entire nation just might believe it's false."

"Especially since it is," Bullock said.

"Yes, and it saves you from having to explain all of Morgan's visits to the White House," Emma said. "We can just continue to say that she's a trusted advisor of policy and we're glad that this matter has been resolved."

"We can say that, but I think we need something a little more convincing that just a statement from your coms teams."

A knock at the door snared their attention, and they both turned to see who was there. The door pushed open and Cori Bullock poked her head inside. She glanced at Bullock before turning to Emma.

"Can we have the room, Emma?" Cori asked.

"Sure," Emma said before leaving and shutting the door on her way out.

Bullock locked eyes with Cori and braced for another verbal attack. Deep down, he only cared what she thought about everything.

She tucked her hair behind her ears, moving closer to him. "I know the truth."

"Are you sure?"

She nodded. "I saw the reports. Now, I'm just laughing at that video."

"What do you mean?" he asked, his tone full of relief, his question genuinely curious.

"It's obviously not true," she said before leaning in and speaking softly. "I also studied the original video a little more closely. That's not what you look like in your birthday suit."

"I'm hoping you meant that as a compliment."

"I did," she said with a tight smile. "And now I just feel awful about what I said to you."

He held his arms wide and beckoned her to him with a slight gesture. She padded toward him and wrapped her arms around his waist, burying her head into his chest.

"I understand how it looked. And I can only imagine how much pain you endured because of it, how you thought that I did that to you. I would never—*ever*—do anything like that to you."

"Deep down, I know that. But it was just too hard to argue with what I was seeing. And then what the experts were saying too. It's like I couldn't do anything but believe it was true."

"Yet it was all a lie," Bullock said.

"I know. Please forgive me for how I acted."

Bullock squeezed her more tightly, acknowledging that he'd forgiven her. "It's gonna be okay. But there's still one more thing we need to do."

"Which is what?"

"We need to stand together and show Americans everywhere that we are united and will not allow these kinds of people to bully us or shame us or distort the truth."

She drew back and locked eyes with him. "I can do that."

"You sure?" he asked. "If it's too much, we can definitely video tape our joint statement. It might be even kind of apropos, right?"

"It would. But this is something we need to do together, live, in front of a national audience. We need everyone to know that anyone could be a victim to this kind of video distortion. And that you're going to do everything in your power to push legislation through Congress that will severely punish whoever knowingly attempts to smear a person's reputation like this again."

"I like how you're thinking," Bullock said.

Then Bullock gave her another hug before she bounded toward the door.

"I feel like I can go to garden club again," she said with a grin.

Bullock removed his phone from his pocket and texted Kip Hughes the good news.

> Your secret is safe again.

That's what I like to hear. And I've got something you'll like to hear too: I've just secured another ten million in fundraising.

> Indeed. Thanks so much.

Bullock slid his phone into his pocket. He'd just skirted past a political scandal—and someone was going to have to pay for what they did.

And he couldn't wait to make sure that was the case. But it'd have to wait.

There were still more pressing issues to attend to, chiefly The Alliance.

FORTY

SEATTLE

AFTER A ROBUST DEBATE AMONG THE MAGNUM GROUP team about how they should approach Nexus CEO Brad Chilton, they concluded instead of approaching him as a group—which might create issues for them in the future by linking them to each other—Hawk should go as the sole representative. As they made the drive from the airport north along state route 509 toward downtown Seattle, they went over the best ways to convince Chilton of the dangers of sending out an update that hadn't been fully vetted. Mia contributed a few ideas using her expertise as a hacker and computer genius that she felt might alarm him. But all they could hope for was that he listened and took them seriously.

Ryder drove, interjecting occasionally to complain about the road's potholes and dense traffic that moved at the speed of Louisiana mud through a sieve. Hawk took in the shared ideas as he stared out the window at the Puget Sound that looked like a sheet of glass beneath gray skies. He fingered the thumb drive in his pocket, the one Mia had prepared that contained a program designed to identify the program Quantum Glitch had created. If one of Fang's operatives had already installed the program, it would be a clear demonstration of the danger Nexus posed if it released its update. This looming conversation had risen to the front of his mind, but it hadn't pushed out the other things he'd be thinking about, especially the status of Besserman. Was the CIA director still alive? Hawk felt hopeless when it came to Besserman. He'd grown tired of seeing good men and women become casualties in a shadow war with ambitious men who sought to leave their mark on the world through might and power. It was a concern that he had to set aside for the moment.

As they bumped along talking about how to handle Chilton, Ryder groaned as he looked at his phone.

"That doesn't sound good," Big Earv said.

"It's not," Ryder said. "I subscribe to alerts from Nexus on social media. And our pal Brad Chilton just announced that the wait is over and quote, 'tonight we will release the latest update at Midnight PDT'. So, not good at all."

"At least my detector should come in handy," Mia said, glancing at Hawk.

He pulled the device out of his pocket and held it up.

"Once you plug that into a computer that has the code embedded in it, that program I wrote will identify it and eliminate it, if that's what you want."

"Of course that's what we want," Ryder said.

"Or you could want to isolate it, study it, and use it on your enemies," she said.

"Which reminds me," Big Earv said, squinting as he looked at Mia. "You didn't have anything to do with—"

"What? The furor online today about all the videos of President Bullock? Moi? Little old me? Never."

Ryder shook his head as he regarded her in the rearview mirror. "I don't need a special program to detect that you're using a heavy dose of sarcasm there."

She shrugged and grinned. "You never know."

As the team continued to banter back and forth, Hawk grew more focused. He rehearsed in his head how he was going to address Chilton and create enough concern for the Nexus CEO to pause the release of the update until they could be certain it was clean. The assignment was relatively new for Hawk. When he'd been asked to make persuasive arguments in the past, he was usually encouraged to use a weapon and plenty of force. But he knew compliance wasn't something he could compel in this case. He needed Chilton to want to help on his own. And it needed to be an earnest desire to help too. Otherwise, it'd be lip service to get rid of Hawk at best, or at worst, it'd be a complete disregard of the warning.

Ryder eased their rental SUV off the ramp and onto surface streets leading into downtown Seattle. He navigated the city's steep inclines, dodging pedestrian traffic that seemed to come from any direction at a moment's notice. Hawk noticed large swaths of the sidewalk were lined with homeless people, some of them sleeping next to trash bags and grocery carts. But as they went deeper into the heart of the city, he noticed an increased amount of police presence, which seemed to coincide with cleaner streets.

Ryder circled through a parking garage before coming to a stop.

"There's a coffee shop across the street," Hawk said. "Wait there until I'm finished. If this doesn't go our way, we're going to need to act quickly."

"What's plan B again?" Mia asked.

"How about just say a quick prayer that it doesn't come to that," Hawk suggested.

Hawk, who was dressed in a three-piece gray suit with a cool blue tie, stopped to snap a picture and send it to Alex. She responded with a text that included a bunch of emojis that suggested she liked his dapper look.

Once Hawk reached the lobby, he checked in with an administrative assistant. She scanned his driver's license and then handed him a badge, directing him to a security guard who would escort Hawk to the top floor. The glass elevator provided a majestic view of the Puget Sound and the surrounding Seattle area. Pine trees blanketed sloping hills, which seemed to melt into the water. Pleasure boats, tour boats, fishing boats, ferry boats, and barges chugged along the waterways, adding even more energy to the already bustling city. Islands dotted water and bridges crossed it.

Hawk checked his watch. It was two o'clock in the afternoon, ten hours until the release of Nexus's new update, which had been nicknamed Prime.

The guard ushering Hawk to the office on the top floor barely blinked as he stood still, hands clasped in front of him. He didn't seem to feel the need to make small talk, and Hawk appreciated the silence. He needed to clear his mind so he could make such a clear case for pausing the update that Chilton would have no other choice but to agree.

Once the elevator came to a stop and the doors slid open, the guard gestured toward the lobby in front of them. Hawk mouthed a thank you and then walked up to a counter where a woman with a tightly-wrapped bun and wearing a headset signaled for him to approach her.

"Are you Mr. Hawk?" she asked.

He nodded.

She stood up and smoothed down the front of her skirt before walking around the counter.

"Follow me," she said. "I'll take you right in to see Mr. Chilton."

She opened the door and announced Hawk before beckoning him inside. She scurried out, closing the door behind her.

Hawk scanned the office, which provided a sweeping view of the city as well as the area west of Seattle.

But no Brad Chilton.

"Mr. Chilton?" Hawk called. "Are you here?"

Nothing.

"Hello? Mr. Chilton? This is Brady Hawk. I'm here for a meeting with you, scheduled for two."

After a few more seconds, the silence was broken by the sound of a high-pitched motorized whine. Hawk thought he could tell the direction the noise was coming from and craned his neck around the corner, straining to see into another section of the office. As he did, he narrowly avoided getting bowled over as Chilton zipped around the corner on a One Wheel wearing a brown aviator jacket, a leather helmet, and a pair of goggles that looked like they were from the 1920s. A pair of antennae with purple glittery balls on the end bounced back and forth wildly on flimsy coils.

Chilton whipped the One Wheel around and gasped.

"Oh, I'm so sorry," he said, placing one of his hands flat against his chest as if in shock. "I didn't see you there, and I almost ran you over. Are you all right?"

"I think I'll live," Hawk said, shrugging off the near collision.

Chilton glanced at his watch. "Would you look at the time. I'm so sorry. I just got carried away and forgot when my next appointment was. Now, remind me again why you're here?"

Hawk had heard Chilton was eccentric. But seeing him in person was jarring compared to the vague descriptions warning that he was a little odd.

Odd doesn't begin to describe this guy. This might be harder than I thought.

Chilton hopped off his One Wheel and strode over to Hawk with an outstretched hand. The two men shook after officially exchanging names.

"Again, please accept my apologies," Chilton said, gesturing toward a seating area that included two small couches and a pair of chairs. "Now, I understand you have some serious business to discuss."

"What led you to believe that?" Hawk asked.

"When the president calls in a favor, you tend to imagine it's a serious matter."

"It is, in fact, very serious."

Hawk proceeded to explain what was happening with the images on security cameras—and any other camera that contained the virus. He thoughtfully explained why it was so dangerous, using the recent situation with the president as an example.

"Wait," Chilton said, extending his hand and tilting his head to one side, "wait just a minute. What kind of situation with President Bullock are you referencing?"

"The one where video emerged that made him look like he was being unfaithful to his wife? I'm sure you at least heard about it?"

Chilton sucked in a breath through his teeth and shook his head. "No, I'm afraid not. I vowed a long time ago to not waste my time reading or listening to the news. I have people who summarize what's happened over the last week, but I don't daily immerse myself in the mindless minutiae of hearsay, gossip, and speculation."

"And you're probably better off for it," Hawk said. "But if you don't know what happened, it's a lot."

Hawk proceeded to tell Chilton about Bullock's troubles, which drew a few gasps.

"But that's all gone now. However, what's not gone is the threat that the same organization that framed some key U.S. leaders will have the power to do this to anyone if they have managed to embed this Trojan software into your new update releasing tonight."

Chilton got up and walked over to his One Wheel, activating it and circling the room on the device.

"Mr. Hawk, are you aware how much Nexus is worth?"

He shrugged. "I have no idea, nor do I—"

"Three point one trillion dollars. Now, I'm not sure if a government worker like yourself—"

"I don't work for the government. I'm an independent contractor."

"Whatever. That doesn't matter. What matters is that you understand that when a company is worth literally trillions of dollars it has state-of-the-art everything."

"Never underestimate a man desperate for power."

"Oh, I don't. I don't ever underestimate anyone, which is why Nexus server farms contain the most robust security in the world."

"I don't care how secure you think your facilities are, this man —Jun Fang—he will find a way to get what he wants. And if you don't have an elite team guarding your primary facility tonight, the world—and especially *your* world—may wake up tomorrow morning and be gone for good."

"Mr. Hawk, you act like they're going to blow the place to smithereens."

"Most of history's most destructive weapons never detonated. And this one won't either. By the time you see what's happened, it'll be too late."

"Well, I appreciate this little chat, Mr. Hawk, but I hate to inform you that you wasted your time. My facilities are the most secure in the world. And nobody is getting on them without proper protocol being followed, which means nobody who hasn't been extremely vetted by Nexus will ever set foot in one of our most crucial buildings. Now, if you'll excuse me, I have real matters to deal with, like the launch of Prime at midnight."

"You're making a big mistake," Hawk said.

He wanted to stay and take another pass at convincing Chilton, but the eccentric CEO buzzed away on his One Wheel, disappearing around the corner. Hawk felt a strong grip yank his arm toward the door. It was the security guard.

"Come on, Mr. Hawk," the man said. "It's time to go."

Hawk didn't utter another word until he exited the Nexus headquarters. He promptly pulled out his cell phone and called Ryder.

"How'd it go?" Ryder asked.

"Round up the team," Hawk said. "It's time for plan B."

FORTY-ONE

TANGIER, MOROCCO

As Robert Besserman regained consciousness, his eyes fluttered open to the sterile white ceiling of a hospital room. A rhythmic beep chirped in his ear while an oxygen machine produced a steady, low-pitched hiss. His head throbbed in pain, though he couldn't remember what from. He strained to recall what events had led him to wind up flat on his back in a hospital.

There was the assault on the safe house. Men pouring in with weapons. Shouting. Shooting. Screaming. It was all a blur. Those fleeting moments of chaos served as an impassable trail, like a door bricked up with no way through. The abrupt ending frustrated Besserman.

Am I dead?

He'd felt this way once before, but he eventually concluded that he was still very much alive. Just like now.

But who was keeping him alive? And why?

As he pondered the answer to those questions, angst stirred in him. The intermittent beep pulsing from the machine by his bed quickened, serving as an immediate reminder that he needed to calm.

Then he looked down at his arms and tried to move them. They barely budged, not as the result of a wound but due to the leather straps pinning his wrists to the bed's railings.

I wish they would've just killed me.

Moments later, a doctor ambled into the room, his face mostly shrouded by a surgical mask and cap. The doctor flicked on a pen light and peered into Besserman's eyes.

"Can you tell me where I am?" Besserman asked.

The doctor grunted and then licked his thumb before turning the page and scribbling a check mark, accompanied by a mysterious high-pitched noise. Besserman didn't know what to make of the sound that came from the doctor's closed mouth. Was it one of satisfaction? Disapproval? Disappointment? Or was it exactly what he expected?

Besserman wanted to speak again, but his throat was dry. All that came out was a slight gurgling sound, drawing another mysterious reaction from the doctor. He nodded his head and widened his eyes before scratching a quick note in a comments section on the paper clamped to his clipboard.

The doctor grabbed a small plastic cup and filled it with water. Then he clicked a button on a control box hanging from the bed, engaging the bed's function that raised the back and allowed Besserman to sit up. The doctor held the cup to Besserman's lips and tilted it forward. Besserman gulped down the liquid, restoring his ability to talk.

"So, Doc, are you gonna answer me? Where am I?"

The doctor drew back and stared at Besserman like he had three heads. He muttered something in another language, prompting Besserman to wonder what language was being spoken. With his brain still in a fog, he couldn't access his full memory.

Was it Mandarin?

The only reason Besserman cared was because he thought maybe it would provide him with some answers. He was in

Morocco when the gunfight began. Where would they—whoever *they* were—have taken him? And why?

"Please, Doc. I need to know."

The doctor recorded a few more notes on his clipboard and exited the room.

Seconds later the door eased open again, this time for a pair of nurses. The women fussed over him, checking his pulse, taking his temperature, fluffing his pillow—and doing so with all the grace of Tasmanian devils.

Besserman tried again. "Who are you? Where am I?"

They both ignored him, not even giving him the slightest indication that he was being heard.

I must be dead. It's the only explanation. And this feels like hell.

Besserman tried once more, but the woman left quickly, leaving him alone again to ponder his reason for being there. Aside from a few aches and pains—none of which he remembered getting—he felt fine. His vitals sounded normal, though he wished he could see them. But he was bound to a hospital bed in a cruel fashion.

Maybe if I go to sleep, I'll get all the answers when I wake up.

Besserman concluded that was his best option. Nothing else he said or did mattered.

Five minutes later, his meditation was interrupted, this time with a familiar face, one that almost underscored his belief that he'd been ushered into the afterlife—Steve Pickens.

Besserman's deputy director squinted as he hovered over him, darting back and forth to inspect his face.

"How ya feelin', Bobby?" Pickens asked.

"I'd be feeling much better if I wasn't tethered to this bed," Besserman growled.

"Don't worry. I'll get you out of there. It was only for your safety. The doctors didn't want your hands to go flailing everywhere while they were doing surgery on you."

"Surgery? Where the—"

Besserman stopped, no longer needing an answer to his question with the searing pain shooting up his shoulder.

"That's right, boss. A round caught you in the shoulder before you fell and knocked yourself unconscious. Fortunately, we were able to engage the team sent to assassinate you just in the nick of time."

"You knew where I was?" Besserman asked.

"We had a feeling you might be here."

"Now what are you going to do with me?"

"Well, I'm gonna take you back to Langley so you can run the agency."

Besserman cocked his head, confused by the response. "You sent people to kill me."

"I never sent anyone to kill you, Bobby. Why would I do that?"

"You're an opportunist."

"True. But I'm also a patriot. And I highly doubt anyone would promote me to director if I was the one responsible for finding you—and I failed. No, I was trying to protect you by bringing you home before someone else got a hold of you, like the Albanians who almost assassinated you for what happened in Venice."

"Why would they—oh, no. This is a mess."

"Not so much anymore," Pickens said. "As soon as those tapes were released of President Bullock with all those women—and the women just had different faces but everything else about their encounters were *exactly* the same—people realized that AI detection software is useless for whatever it was that was distorting reality on security cameras. Whatever was used to create the videos was another generation or two ahead of AI."

"But how did everyone assume that the same technology was used on the security footage from Alexander Nikolaev's boat?"

"Turns out that Nikolaev's eldest son Yuri was behind it all. He found out about the technology and put it on his dad's ship and used it to frame you so he could get all of daddy's money,"

Pickens said. "The problem is he forgot about one camera. And that camera captured Yuri's face planting the explosives on the ship and doing the exact same movements you were recorded as doing by all the other cameras. Digital forensics experts determined that the footage with you in it was manipulated, while the one with Yuri wasn't."

"Makes sense," Besserman said as he rubbed his freed wrists. "But I apparently still have a hole in my shoulder because of it."

"You'll be fine," Pickens said. "Doc already signed you out."

Bullock eased off the table and stood, stopping to scan the room. "Where are we, anyway?"

"That's not important," Pickens said. "What's important is that we get back to Langley in one piece—and you are no longer a wanted man, at least for the wrong reasons. Everyone at the agency, however, is dying to get you back to work."

Besserman had other questions, many other questions. But they could wait. He wasn't dead—and he wasn't being hunted by his chief deputy.

And for the moment, that was what mattered most to Besserman.

FORTY-TWO

LEAVENWORTH, WASHINGTON

THOMAS HANEY ACTIVATED THE SELF-DRIVING FEATURE on his Tesla as he headed north along a ribbon of U.S. Highway 2. The car hugged the side of the road up against the craggy rock face while a single lane and a sturdy guard rail separated him from the raging Wenatchee River. When he first bought his Tesla, he loved letting the car navigate home so he could enjoy the scenic views offered on the drive. But after eight years of the same commute, the breathtaking vistas had become too familiar. Instead of marveling at the natural beauty surrounding him, he stared at his phone, thumbs pounding out a snarky response to an online debate about the position of William Shatner's *Star Trek* movies in the pantheon of sci-fi blockbuster.

Haney smiled as he fancied his clever response, saying it aloud as he hammered it out: "Shatner's movies will not only live long and prosper, but they will continue to make fans at an exponential rate, like tribbles." He added an exclamation point, serving to further emphasize his point as well as mark his enthusiasm. The debate would undoubtedly resume at lunch the next day in the Nexus data center breakroom.

He sighed and put the phone aside as he peered down the road. A few cars zipped past him headed in the opposite direction, but it was relatively quiet. The sun had already faded behind the mountains and dusk was starting to settle. But he thought he'd have just enough daylight once he arrived home to throw the ball to Spock, his spunky golden retriever.

Even before he came to a stop in front of his house, a modest brick home nestled against the mountain on two wooded acres, Spock bounded toward him, tennis ball wedged between clenched teeth. Haney chuckled and patted Spock on the head, who dropped the pale green ball already drenched with his slobber.

"Somebody's ready to play," Haney said, as if it were a new revelation to him.

"Somebody else wants to play too," said Haney's wife Nora from the stoop of their home. She winked at him and licked her lips.

"In a minute, honey," he said, fiddling with his Nexus security badge that still hung around his neck. "I need to give Spock some attention."

She stamped her foot, her face contorting into a pout. "Some of us humans need attention from you too."

Three years into marriage and Haney was already starting to wonder if he should've stayed single. He loved Nora, but felt incapable of satisfying all her emotional needs. Haney was an extreme introvert who needed an inordinate amount of time alone and had spent forty-two years prioritizing his many things over his relationships with other humans. And as much as he knew it wasn't normal, Haney still saw Spock's needs as ones that needed to be met immediately upon returning from work.

Haney snatched the ball off the ground and hurled it into a large clearing. Spock spun and broke into a full sprint in pursuit of the bouncing object. He snared it before it stopped moving and then raced back to his owner.

"Good boy," Haney said as he knelt next to Spock and rubbed

his belly as the dog rolled over on his back, panting with tongue lolling.

The game of fetch continued for another five minutes before Haney went inside the house. He drew in a deep breath, inhaling the aroma of his favorite soup—potato kale.

"How was work?" Nora asked, tension in her voice.

"It was—work," Haney said. "Same old, same old."

"Don't I know that," she quipped.

"Honey, is everything all right?"

She sighed while ladling soup into a bowl. "Not really, but if you can't figure it out, there's no use telling you."

Haney shrugged, uninterested in delving into Nora's mysterious answer. He figured if whatever was bothering her was all that important, she'd tell him.

She placed a bowl of soup on the kitchen table in front of him and returned to the stove to get herself a serving. They said nothing as they ate, the tense silence broken only by the clanking of spoons against porcelain.

"That was good," he said before getting up and placing his bowl in the sink. He returned to the table and kissed her on top of her head before shuffling out of the room.

"Did you want to do something tonight?" she asked.

"Nah," he said. "You can read your book. I'm tired and just want to unwind."

Haney meandered back to his office, slumping into his chair and turning on his computer. He planned to spend the rest of the night like he did most evenings—playing video games online with strangers half a world away.

NORA HEARD the door click as her husband retreated to his office. She fought back tears as she cleaned up. As she put away the leftovers, she pondered why his disinterest in her still bothered her so much. This near-nightly routine had become the worst part of her day, a painful reminder of his consistent rejection of her. She felt duped, even betrayed.

How did I fall in love with someone like this?

Haney had been so different when they were dating. He was fun-loving, spontaneous, adventurous. Now, he was just a bum. She wondered if he'd always been that way and she had just over-looked it somehow.

There was a part of her that wished she'd never met him, or, at least, never married him. His job at the Nexus data center was as dull as he was, which explained why he liked it so much. He didn't have to think, not that he was much for introspection anyway. If he ever did talk to her following a day of work, it would be about his conquests online the previous night where he and three other strangers conquered Nazi German forces in an online video game. Just mind-numbing activity.

She'd tried to get his attention by wearing negligée when he arrived home from work. It excited him a few times, until it didn't.

Nora wiped down the kitchen table and left the room. Another date with action spy Hank Thomas in the latest novel in the series, On the Brink, awaited her.

If I can't have a real man, at least I can read about one.

As she passed through the living room, she noticed the front door was slightly ajar.

Thomas!

She growled as she walked over and shut the door and then twisted the deadbolt. While they didn't have any children, Nora felt like she was a single mom sometimes with her aloof and childish husband.

She grabbed her book, flipped to the page where she'd left off, and began a new Hank Thomas adventure. Hank was hunkered down in Afghanistan, taking fire from all sides as his commanding officer barked impossible orders.

Bang!

Nora was so immersed in her book that it took a few seconds

for the noise to register. She paused and thought about going back to check on him. But that wasn't an unusual sound when he was playing one of his war games. She thought he probably just had the volume turned up too loud, so she kept reading.

But after another minute or two, she didn't hear anything. And it started to bug her.

She slid a bookmark into her book and walked back toward her husband's office.

"Thomas, are you all right?" she said as she walked down the hall.

No response.

"Thomas, are you still playing your game?"

Still nothing.

When she reached the door, it was shut. She knocked on it and then opened it without waiting for a reply, figuring he probably had his headphones on.

And she was right. He was sitting with his back to the door, the top of his balding scalp with headphones arched across it. She drew closer and called his name again before tapping him on his shoulder.

When he didn't move, she glanced at the screen and noticed it was not moving.

Then she saw why.

She gasped, her hands going straight to her mouth. She wanted to scream, but nothing came out. Her knees felt weak and she toppled to the floor, inches away from the blood pooling beneath his chair as it dripped from his torso.

The gunshot wound had obliterated Haney's chest. His head was tilted back, eyes open with a thousand-yard stare.

As if the scene wasn't gruesome enough, she noticed his index finger had been severed.

Then she found her voice.

∾

AN HOUR LATER, the assassin adjusted his synthetic mask a final time before approaching the entrance to the Nexus data center. He stealthily eased a plastic bag out of his pocket and removed Thomas Haney's finger. Placing the finger on the security pad, he swiped the access badge through the reader and waited.

He waved at the guard on duty, who gave him a cordial nod, and then meandered along the courtyard that cut through a cluster of buildings, each one housing thousands of servers. Weston checked over his shoulder before taking a moment to set up his first backup plan for escape. While he hoped he wouldn't need it, the most important thing about every job he took was surviving it.

After he'd finished with that task, he commenced a search for a terminal to upload the secret code and embed it into Nexus's new software update.

FORTY-THREE

LEAVENWORTH, WASHINGTON

Parked atop a ridgeline, Hawk straddled a black Yamaha XT250 and looked at the half-waning moon beaming through the trees on the opposite side of the mountain. Twilight had faded and more stars were visible with each passing minute. Keeping track of the new ones was how Hawk decided to pass the time when the Nexus data center parking lot was still. He hadn't seen any movement on the access road off the highway in over an hour and was starting to wonder if they'd made a grave mistake.

"What if they're going to sneak the embedded code in some other way?" asked Ryder, who was also sitting on a twin bike a few meters away. "This is Quantum Glitch we're talking about here. He's pretty damn smart."

"I'm not ruling out the possibility that we screwed this one up, but the window to do this is incredibly narrow. And this is Nexus's main data center. All updates are hosted here, which means this is the only site that matters in their global network. And according to every expert, they'd have to be here to do it."

"And what if he's got somebody on the inside doing it for him?"

"It'd be too easy to catch them," Hawk said. "Everybody that works here knows that every keystroke they make is being recorded and attributed to them. You know that. We've already talked through all these scenarios."

"But maybe we missed something. I mean, nobody's come or gone since the last shift ended. And from what Mia was able to gather, there's not another shift change scheduled until after the update is released."

"Patience," Hawk said.

After a few minutes of silence, Hawk turned his attention in the direction of a car engine rumbling along the access road.

"Looks like we might be in business," Hawk said over the coms.

He peered through a pair of Pulsar Merger LRF XP50 thermal binoculars at the approaching vehicle and read off the license plate number along with the make and model of the car.

"My man is driving a Tesla," Ryder said. "I need to work at a Nexus data center."

"You'd be bored as shit," Mia said. "Trust me."

"I'm sure of that," Ryder said. "I really just want a Tesla."

Hawk watched the man exit his vehicle and walk toward the security check point.

"Mia," he said, "find anything yet?"

"Still searching," she said. "Patience."

Ryder laughed. "Good one. Hawk hates it when he gets a dose of his own medicine."

"All right," Mia said after a few more seconds. "Found it. The car's registered to a guy named Thomas Haney."

"What's he do for Nexus?" Hawk asked.

"Senior data specialist."

"So, he'd have access to the updates?" Ryder asked.

"I imagine so," Mia said. "He's a veteran software engineer and oversees the implementation of Nexus operating systems, according to his professional bio on social media."

"Get me his cell number," Hawk said, his eyes locked on the employee as he continued moving toward the security gate.

Mia read off the number and Hawk dialed it on his phone. The man didn't answer, but a woman did a few minutes later.

"Hello?" she asked, her voice shaky.

"Uh, yes, I was trying to reach Thomas Haney. Is he available?"

"No," the woman stammered. "He can't come to the phone right now."

"Is he there? Because it's kind of an emergency."

"I said he's not available," she snapped.

"Mrs. Haney?"

"Yes?"

"Look, this is really urgent," Hawk persisted. "It's actually a matter of national security."

"He's not coming to the phone, not now, not ever."

Hawk was taken aback by her comment. "I'm sorry, I didn't mean to upset you."

"He's dead," she hissed. "He's dead."

"I'm sorry, what?"

"I just found him dead," she blubbered. "In his office. Shot himself in the chest with a shotgun."

Hawk looked at Ryder and nodding knowingly as he pointed at the facility below.

"I'm so sorry," Hawk said. "I didn't know."

"I called the cops," she said. "They still aren't here. I don't know what to do."

"Okay," Hawk said. "Just stay calm and don't contaminate the evidence just in case he didn't actually shoot himself."

"Who else would've done it?" she asked. "Nobody came into the house. Oh, God, you don't think I—"

"No, no. Of course not. I—"

"Who is this? Are you a cop?"

"I'm investigating a potential national security breach," he said. "And I think your husband could be connected to it somehow."

"I know Thomas isn't the most patriotic person, but he would never do anything like that."

"I don't think he would either, but I do think someone might have used him unwittingly."

"What do you mean?"

"Can you tell me if his car is in the front yard?"

"Of course it is. I saw him drive it home and—"

"No," Hawk said. "I mean, is it there right now?"

"He's dead. How could it drive off?"

"Just check for me, please. It's important."

After a few seconds, Hawk heard her breath hitch. "It's gone. His car's gone. How could—I don't understand."

"I think I do, Mrs. Haney. And I'll make sure you get an explanation soon, but I've gotta stop something from happening."

"What did you say your name was again?"

"Agent James," Hawk said, protecting his identity, just in case she was a good actress and in on it. "Take care. I'm sure the cops will help sort it all out soon enough."

Hawk hung up.

"Well," Ryder said, "is that our guy?"

"I think so," Hawk said. "At least, that's his car. But according to his wife, he's dead."

"How?"

"Gunshot to the chest."

"Damn. These guys aren't messing around."

Hawk dialed Brad Chilton's number. The Nexus CEO picked up after three rings.

"Who is this? And how did you get this number?" he said.

"This is Agent Hawk. I'm calling to let you know that your data center in Leavenworth is under attack."

Chilton laughed. "Please, forgive me, Agent Hawk, but that's patently false. My security is extra tight tonight, and there haven't been any reports of any attacks on the data center there."

"Then explain to me how one of your senior data specialists is dead at his home, but his car just pulled up and I watched him enter the facility."

"I'll explain it by telling you that you have no idea what you're talking about."

"Don't be a fool, Mr. Chilton. There will be grave consequences if this operating system update releases at midnight."

"You're absolutely right about that. My stock will plummet in the morning as everyone will assume we're having more problems. The company's valuation will take a massive drop, as will my personal net worth, and all my opponents will dance on my grave. So, unless I hear otherwise, I need to warn you to back off and quit trying to make something out of nothing."

"You're making a big mistake."

"You are the one making a big mistake," Chilton said. "And if you dare set foot on any Nexus property, I'll make sure you're prosecuted to the fullest extent of the law. I can assure you, too, that you don't want to tangle with me. I'm very well connected as someone in my position is prone to be. This is your final warning."

The line went dead.

Hawk pocketed his phone and cursed.

"He wasn't listening to you, was he?" Ryder asked.

Hawk shook his head and glanced at his watch. They had less than three hours before the update was scheduled to be released.

"We're gonna have to go in another way. Go grab your gear."

FORTY-FOUR

LEAVENWORTH, WASHINGTON

A HALF-HOUR LATER, THE SKYDIVING PLANE HAWK HAD arranged to have on stand-by had reached a sufficient height. The Cessna 182 hummed as it approached the space over the target. The near lack of moonlight provided ample cover for the jump, but it wasn't perfect. If one of the guards on patrol was looking skyward, he might see the duo descending.

Hawk couldn't take any chances in this scenario as they only had one shot. That's why Big Earv was sitting behind a boulder with an RPG about two hundred meters from the Nexus data center. He was ready to light up a few vehicles in the parking lot to draw away the guard's attention. It was bold, but necessary to avoid any unnecessary confrontations.

"How is it up there?" Mia asked over the coms.

"A little chilly," Ryder said. "Other than that, we've got a nice view of the place."

"Have fun," she said. "Just let me know when you two hit the ground."

"Copy that," Hawk said.

The captain signaled for them to jump, and Hawk and Ryder

dove out within a few seconds of each other. Hawk studied the target through his night vision goggles and then looked at his watch. After forty-five seconds, his chute deployed. Ryder's followed right after him. Hawk steered the chute toward the quad space in the middle of the data center.

"Are you watching for us now?" Hawk asked over the coms.

"I'm watching, but I don't see you yet," Big Earv said.

"Patience," Ryder said.

Hawk chuckled. "Now you're learning, kiddo."

Another minute passed before Big Earv keyed his mic. "I see you now."

"Then that means the guards might be able to see us," Hawk said. "Time to get this party started. Big Earv, will you do the honors?"

"I thought you'd never ask."

Hawk removed his goggles to save his vision and then a few seconds later watched the fireball erupt in the parking lot. Another twenty seconds and another blast.

He watched guards rush toward the scene and then scan the mountainside for the source of the incoming fire. He was close enough to see two of the men pointing, but not in Big Earv's direction.

"I think you're safe," Hawk said. "But I'd get out of there if I were you."

"Copy that."

Less than two minutes later, Hawk and Ryder hit the ground. They came to a stop and then gathered up their chutes and stuffed them in a sack, hiding them in a trash can near the edge of the courtyard.

Several guards poured out of the data server buildings, rushing toward the flames lapping the night sky. Hawk saw one of the doors nearest to them swing open and a guard dart out. Hawk sped toward the door and thrust his hand into the small opening, wedged his finger between the corner of the door and the frame. He tugged on it and flung it open before gesturing for Ryder to join him. Once inside, the two men split up, maintaining radio contact.

"How many people should be here right now?" Ryder asked. "This place is a ghost town."

"Not many," Hawk said. "I only counted about two dozen cars in the parking lot. There's space for at least five times that. And I'm betting from what I've seen, most of the cars belong to guards."

Hawk hunted for the rogue man who'd stolen Thomas Haney's identity and security badge, an endeavor that was fruitless for the first ten minutes. Wandering up and down rows upon rows of shelving units with servers slammed together, Hawk considered that maybe there was a better way to conduct the search.

Wires dangled from the face of the machines, while lights flickered back and forth signaling some sort of activity. The only sound was that of whirring fans, working hard to keep the computers from overheating, and an occasional distant footstep. It was a vast sea of computer components working in concert with one another, and not a soul in sight.

Hawk eased out into the main aisle and looked as far as he could see. He estimated the back of this particular building was about three hundred meters away. A scooter or a golf cart would've come in handy, but it wasn't an option.

Where is he?

His coms crackled to life with Ryder's voice.

"Have you seen anything yet?" Ryder asked. "This is like trying to put socks on a rooster."

Hawk snickered. "Who the hell puts socks on a rooster?"

"That's exactly my point. You'd have to be crazy to do that, just like you'd have to be a few fries short of a Happy Meal to think you could search this enormous facility for one person. By the time we find him, it might be too late."

"Just keep looking."

"I know, I know. Be patient."

Hawk smiled but didn't say anything, resuming his intense hunt. He decided to pick up his pace, running as stealthily as possible down the rows, head swiveling from side to side as he checked the rows on both sides of the center aisle.

Still nothing.

Then as Hawk entered the back third of the building, he heard the click-clack of someone pecking away on a keyboard. He strained to hear the direction it was coming from. An aisle up ahead on the left. Although he couldn't tell which one, he knew it was nearby.

Almost as soon as the sound perked up his ears, it stopped.

Hawk crept closer toward the direction he'd last heard the noise. He poked his head around the shelf of servers and looked toward the end of the aisle and noticed a man hunched over a keyboard, his fingers whirring again.

"Excuse me, sir, but you need to stop what you're doing," Hawk said, training his weapon on the man.

Then with the emphatic tap of one final key, the man stopped and turned toward Hawk.

"Fine, I'll step away," he said, raising his hands in a gesture of surrender.

Hawk's brow furrowed as the man's voice sounded familiar.

"Who are you?"

The man offered a faint smile. "As you can see on my badge right here, I'm Thomas Haney. Who the hell are you?"

"Thomas Haney's dead," Hawk said. "I just talked to his wife."

"You mean my wife, Nora? I think you're a little mixed up."

Hawk heard footsteps behind him, thundering down the aisle toward them.

"What's going on?" Ryder asked over the coms. "Four guards just entered the building, so get ready for company."

Hawk eyed the man closely, his mind churning through his memory bank as he tried to recall the man's voice.

"No, I don't think so. Why don't we go back outside and test the security panel again with your fingerprint?"

"I don't think that's gonna happen," the man said nodding toward the center aisle.

"I know you're lying," Hawk said. "And I know what you're doing."

"Do you now? Well, I was just doing my job, which I just finished."

The man winked at Hawk.

"Now, if you'll excuse me," the man continued, "it looks like you've got some people who want to talk to you."

Hawk turned to see the guards rushing toward him.

"Don't move," one of the security guards said. "Hands where I can see them."

"Ryder," Hawk said over the coms, "time for another distraction."

Hawk raised his hands in the air.

"Drop the gun and kick it over here," one of the guards instructed.

Before Hawk could comply, a series of booms outside the building shook the ground, distracting the men as they turned in the direction of the explosions. That moment was all Hawk needed to slip away from the guards and dart around the corner after the impostor, who was racing toward an exit about twenty meters away.

"Come back," one of the guards shouted.

Hawk ignored them and pursued the man out of the building. The impostor hit full stride within a few seconds and banked left, turning down another row of server buildings. Hawk pumped his arms, heart hammering in his chest as he continued his chase. The man turned down another row, entering a maze of lookalike structures comprised of nothing but white aluminum siding.

Mia's voice came over the coms. "I need someone to tell me what's going on. I'm still not online."

"Sorry. Ran into some issues," Hawk said between gulps of air. "Working on it."

"If you don't get me connected to the system quickly, I'm not going to have time to stop the update."

"Copy that. Ryder?"

"I'm here," Ryder said.

"You still in the building?"

"Affirmative."

"Good. Stay put. I'm gonna need your help there in a minute."

Hawk gained ground on the man, drawing within about thirty meters of him. As he rounded a corner, Hawk followed the impostor toward a 12-foot high chain-link fence bordering the back of the Nexus property.

The man leaped onto the fence and started clambering up it. He'd almost reached the top before Hawk pocketed his gun and then jumped high on the fence, climbing up fast enough to snare the man's foot. With a violent tug, Hawk pulled the man back. He kicked at Hawk, smashing him in the nose, blood gushing out. But Hawk brushed off the blow and kept scrapping, grabbing, yanking. With two fistfuls of the man's pants, Hawk put his full weight into pulling the man off the fence.

They both tumbled to the ground in a heap, Hawk using his parkour skills to soften his landing and roll up into a standing position. But so did the impostor. Hawk reached into his pocket for his weapon, but the man kicked it loose, sending it skidding beneath a thin gap at the bottom of the fence.

Reeling from the loss of his gun, Hawk tried to regain his focus. The man delivered a body blow and then looked for a knockout shot at his head. But Hawk blocked the attempt and delivered a few of his own. As the men exchanged blows, Hawk noticed a seam around the impostor's neck. Lunging toward the man, Hawk scratched at the seam and managed to wrap his fingers around a swath of plastic. With a hard pull, the mask ripped.

Hawk took a step back, surprised by the half-revealed face of the man in front of him.

"Sid?" Hawk asked. "Sid Weston?"

"Brady Hawk," Weston said.

Hawk resumed fighting, leaning back and hitting Weston with a roundhouse kick. Weston responded with a leg sweep, knocking Hawk to the ground. Before Weston could capitalize, Hawk rolled away from his opponent and returned to an upright position.

Then Weston backed up, creating a sizable gap between them.

"I'd really like to finish this, but I'm afraid that's not possible," Weston said. "I need to get going."

"You're not going anywhere," Hawk said. "I know what you were doing."

"Well, I *am* leaving now, and you're not going to stop me."

Hawk glared at Weston. "Don't be a coward."

Charging toward Weston, Hawk drove his shoulder into the man's torso and sent him staggering backward. Weston broke Hawk's grip, forcing him to the ground. Before he could get back to his feet, Weston was nearly over the fence.

Hawk wasted no time in trying to scale it, but he froze when Weston spoke from the other side.

"I wouldn't do that if I were you," he said. "Alex and J.D's life depends on it."

Hawk's eyes narrowed. "What are you talking about?"

"They've been detained."

Mia squawked over the coms in Hawk's ear. "Come on, Hawk. I need you to get me connected or else this mission is over."

"They've got nothing to do with this," Hawk said to Weston. "Release them right now."

"You're right. They're *mostly* innocent, especially your son. But I knew you were trying to stop this, so I needed some assurances that you'd back off, just in case you actually got close enough. And, congratulations, you did."

"Sid, I swear I'm going to kill you."

Weston reached down and picked up Hawk's gun and pocketed it. "I don't think so, especially if you want to see your wife and son alive again. I mean, I could just shoot you now, but who would I pin all this and Thomas Haney's murder on?"

"You're a dead man."

Weston laughed. "Now, you make sure that update goes out and I'll release them. Understand?"

Hawk said nothing.

"I'll take that as a *yes*," Weston said before he spun and hustled toward a motorcycle near a dirt road about twenty yards away.

"Come on, Hawk," Mia said over the coms. "We're running out of time if you want to stop this thing."

Hawk sprinted along the fence back toward the main server building where he'd encountered Weston.

"Hawk, are you all right?" Mia asked.

"I'm coming back," he said, "but they've got Alex and J.D."

"Who's *they*?" Ryder asked.

"Sid Weston. He's a freelancer who I worked with years ago when Firestorm was in its infancy. But Weston abandoned the organization for more profitable missions. And now he keeps questionable company."

"There's no one more questionable than The Alliance," Mia said. "So, what's his play?"

"If the update doesn't go out, he's going to kill Alex and J.D."

Mia sighed. "So are we done?"

"Not if I can help it."

Hawk spied the open door ahead with Ryder poking his head out and gesturing for him to hurry.

"You're going to kill the update—and then I'm going to kill Sid Weston."

Hawk handed the device in his pocket to Ryder.

"Help Mia get connected to the server, and do it fast before the guards find you."

Ryder dashed back inside, while Hawk sprinted toward his motorcycle in the parking lot. When the guard at the gate saw him running toward him, he ordered Hawk to stop. But Hawk dug into his rucksack and tossed a flash bang toward the man. The combination of the loud noise and burst of light stunned him enough to help Hawk easily avoid any attempt to detain him.

Hawk raced toward his bike, straddled it, and ignited the engine. After putting on his helmet, he goosed the accelerator and took off, the back tire kicking up a cloud of dust as Hawk tore out of the parking lot and headed toward U.S. Highway 2 in pursuit of Weston.

"I'm already in," Mia said over the coms. "I'll make sure this update doesn't go anywhere. You go get your man."

As Hawk headed north on U.S. Highway 2, Big Earv sent another RPG toward the other side of the property, creating another fireball that illuminated the night sky. The blast didn't hit the building, but it wasn't intended to. Just another distraction to help Ryder escape.

"You out, Ryder?" Hawk asked.

"Almost," came the reply.

"Help Mia however you can. I'll meet you guys once I take care of this bastard."

Hawk crouched low on the bike and leaned forward. He spotted Weston up ahead as he raced around a bend in the road.

FORTY-FIVE

THROUGH THE VISOR ON HIS HELMET, HAWK LOCKED IN on Weston. The freelancer zipped north along the stretch of asphalt and appeared in complete command of his bike, hugging tight corners and accelerating out of them. With each passing mile, he distanced himself from Hawk, who was fighting to stay close. Unsure of how far Weston might go, Hawk realized the possibility of losing him was real. But it was also unacceptable.

As Hawk drove, he mulled over Weston's next move and conjured up a way to possibly outsmart him.

"Mia, how's it going?" he asked.

"I'm still trying to find the update in the system," she said.

"Once you find it, changes of plans."

"You realize it's getting late, right?"

"I know, but instead of killing it, I want you to remove the code and release it," Hawk said. "That'll at least buy me a little bit of time."

"We've only got about a half-hour before it launches. That's cutting it close—if I can even find the damn thing."

"Just keep working and keep me posted."

"Copy that."

If Sid wants the update released, he'll get it.

Hawk considered for a moment that Weston could stay true to his word and let Alex and J.D. go after the update was released. But that wasn't a risk Hawk was willing to take. After all, Weston had made this whole situation personal by involving Hawk's family—and that wasn't something he could just let go.

Ten minutes later, Hawk approached a fork in the road. He wasn't sure which way Weston had gone. If he stayed on U.S. Highway 2, he was heading west toward Seattle where maybe he would catch a flight anywhere in the world. But if he took the fork east on State Route 207, he could disappear in the woods. Or maybe even go back toward Montana through the panhandle of Idaho.

Hawk hesitated for a moment.

What would I do?

Hawk knew that he'd want to disappear in an untraceable manner. Utilizing air travel would make him more trackable. But the mountains of Eastern Washington or Idaho or Montana? A trained soldier like Weston could vanish forever. And it's exactly what Hawk would choose if he was in the same situation.

Hawk leaned right, taking State Route 207 toward Wenatchee State Park.

"How's it coming, Mia?" he asked over the coms, desperate for an update.

"Still working on it," she said. "I've located the update, but I'm struggling to find all the lines of code. If I can't find them all, I'm going to delete the entire update so it won't go out. But keep your fingers crossed that it doesn't come to that."

"I believe in you, Mia," Hawk said.

Big Earv's voice boomed through Hawk's ear piece. "Where are you?"

"I'm up near Lake Wenatchee State Park. I think our guy is trying to pull a Houdini on us."

"Too bad he's being hunted by a relentless bloodhound," Big Earv said.

"Did you get Ryder out?"

"He's right here with me," Big Earv said. "Now go finish that bastard."

"I'll do my best."

As Hawk crossed a bridge, he looked to his left and saw the headlight of a motorcycle. He stopped and watched for a moment. The mystery bike came to a halt and the light was extinguished. Hawk watched, straining through the darkness to see if it was Weston. A shadowy figure rushed toward the water and cranked a jet ski.

That's gotta be him.

Hawk sped forward and wound to the public boat ramp. He spotted the Tesla that Weston had been driving. Hawk dismounted and sprinted toward the edge of the water where several jet skis appeared to have been tied to one another at one time. But the cord tethering them together had been severed. Hawk grabbed the jet ski on the end and used a knife to jimmy open a locked compartment behind the seat. He found a key inside and inserted it into the proper slot, cranking the engine. Hawk whipped the jet ski around, sending a rooster tail of water into the air.

The shallow riverbed leading out of Lake Wenatchee and into the river made for a rough start. Hawk bumped the hull against rocks and nearly flipped at one point before regaining control and his nerve as the water deepened.

Being unfamiliar with the contours of the river, Hawk relied on the bright headlight piercing the darkness to stay on course. The vacation cabins lined the banks on both sides and security flood lamps emitted enough ambient light to give Hawk a better sense of the water's boundaries. He passed several people sitting around campfires along the banks, enjoying the cool late summer night.

Hawk's jet ski sliced through the water and around a bend opening into a large straightaway. Red tail lights illuminated the back of Weston's craft. Hawk couldn't determine exactly how far away he was, but he was visible on the water for the first time since he started chasing him.

Mia's voice came through Hawk's earpiece.

"Can you hear me now?" she asked.

"Yeah," he said. "Have you been trying to reach me?"

"For the past half-hour. And we didn't get any response."

"I'm still alive and kickin'. Traded in my bike for a jet ski and headed south on the Wenatchee River."

"I've got good news," she said. "I fixed the update. All the lines of code are gone. The Prime update is going out in five minutes without Quantum Glitch's world-changing code."

"Great work. Now, send Chilton a message to let him know we saved his ass and then head this way."

"You need help?" Big Earv asked.

"Hope not, but I will need a ride home. Track me on my phone."

Hawk skimmed across the water, Weston's red light getting closer as his jet ski appeared to stall in the water. Looking up along the ridge, Hawk noticed a sign that suggested they'd entered a section of the Wenatchee River near the city of Plains.

But Weston's jet ski seemed to stall.

What the hell?

Then Hawk saw it—the calm water had given way to a roiling cauldron of white water rapids.

He tried to slow down, but it was too late. His jet ski hit the rapids, bucking left and right, nearly tipping several times. He opened up the engine, but it coughed and sputtered, unable to propel the craft out of the choppy water. Both powerful jet skis had been rendered to little more than unnavigable dinghies at the mercy of the Wenatchee.

Hawk fought to stay on as Weston removed a gun—Hawk's gun—and opened fire. Hawk counted with each muzzle flash before Weston had emptied the magazine. As Hawk flailed through the rapids, clinging to the handlebars, he realized he could lose Weston at any moment. One rock against the hull, one fallen log—and Hawk's craft would capsize, leaving him power-less to catch Weston.

Hawk cajoled his jet ski every possible way he could to get it closer to Weston's. And after Hawk fought for another half-minute like he was bare-back bronc busting at a Montana rodeo, he drew close to Weston and then leaped for his jet ski.

Hawk crashed onto Weston's craft, destabilizing it further. It swayed from one side and then to the other, the current spinning them around like a top before shooting through a rapid backward. Hawk thought they were almost free of the rough water before the hull of the jet ski hit a submerged boulder, jolting both men loose and into the water. Seconds later, they hit another patch of unforgiving water, pinballing the men through a brutal rapid.

Hawk scrapped to keep his head above the water as the current banged him against rocks, tossing him left and then right. For seconds at a time, he couldn't keep his head up, the churning river forcing him below the surface. Whenever he reemerged, he coughed up water and tried to regain his bearings. He felt like he was blindfolded in a boxing ring with a dozen other fighters taking shots at him. As the relentless current battered him against the rocks, he wondered how much more he could take.

Then the water fell calm.

Hawk staggered to his feet and looked around only to notice Weston sloshing toward the shore. After waiting a moment, Hawk followed suit, the water making his bruised legs feel like they weighed a hundred pounds each. He gritted his teeth as he willed himself forward.

When he reached dry ground, he scanned the woods but didn't see Weston.

Where the hell did he go?

Hawk trudged forward, ignoring the chill that had suddenly come over him, and continued his search for Weston.

Seconds later, Weston jumped out from behind a tree clutching a knife. He swiped at Hawk, who parried away the jab.

But Weston slashed Hawk's right quad before darting into the darkness.

Hawk looked skyward and screamed, bracing for how bad the cut wound would look. When he looked down, he saw a six-inch gash in his leg, blood spurting from the spot of the laceration. He heard plodding footsteps trampling branches and leaves and turned to see Weston heading deeper into the forest.

Hawk grimaced and let out another shout in frustration.

He couldn't stop now, not with Alex and J.D. still held hostage—at least as far as he knew.

"The update went out," Hawk said, setting his jaw. "Are you going to keep your word?"

The freelancer stopped and turned back toward Hawk. "Are you going to kill me?"

Weston turned and ran.

Hawk clenched his fists and chased him into the woods.

FORTY-SIX

THE CLOUDS PARTED, ALLOWING MORE OF THE FOREST floor to be illuminated by the moonlight streaming through the pine trees. For a moment, this development excited Hawk, giving him hope that he'd be able to better see Weston. But the freelancer seemed to have vanished in the woods.

Hawk found a tree and sat down, leaning against it to take a break. Every muscle in his body seemed to ache, either from exhaustion or bruises sustained in the Wenatchee. He touched his ribs, the mere action of reaching for them painful. They were tender and even the slightest pressure lit up his pain receptors.

Reaching into his rucksack, Hawk grabbed a couple of pills for the pain. At the moment, it didn't matter. His adrenaline and drive to finish the job, to save his family, overrode any pain he was experiencing. But later when it was all over, it would matter. Yet given the circumstances, he just hoped there would be a later for him.

Hawk knew he'd crawl over broken glass for his family, but willpower wasn't the issue at this point in his pursuit of Sid Weston. No, for Hawk to survive the night, he needed to outwit Weston. But as Hawk sat resting at the base of a tree, he remembered that Eastern Washington was Weston's home territory. He'd grown up outside of Spokane and had told Hawk a story or two about his adventures in the woods. Weston was on his home turf, and Hawk felt lost.

All Weston had to do was remain hidden and wait out Hawk. The only way to get a fair shot at Weston was to draw him out. But Hawk had nothing—or did he?

Hawk worked through all the possible responses in his mind. He had one move, and Weston could respond several different ways. However, Hawk was getting desperate and he had to do something. He had to play the only card he had left before it was worthless.

"It's over, you know," Hawk cried.

No response.

"The update failed. Did you know that?"

The truth is nobody would've known it yet since the update went out as scheduled, just without Quantum Glitch's secret code.

Hawk waited anxiously, hoping Weston would respond.

Still nothing.

"What'd they do to you, Sid? What threats did they make?"

Finally, the rustling of leaves—and a strong reply.

"You made a big mistake, Hawk. You just killed your family. Congratulations."

Hawk identified where the voice was coming from. He eased around the tree and looked where he thought Weston was. But the woods were quiet again.

Hawk felt his K-bar knife still strapped to his belt. But the weapon wouldn't help unless it was a fight in close quarters. The goal was to lure Weston into that fight and take a chance. Otherwise, Weston would just run out the clock and it wouldn't matter what Hawk had done. This was his desperate play and he could only pray it worked.

"I know that's a lie," Hawk said. "I know you've already had them killed."

"No, no. They're still kickin'."

"I don't believe you, Sid. You never were a good liar. So, now you're dealing with a man who has nothing to lose. May God rest your soul."

"You're crazy, Hawk. They're still alive. You still have a chance to save them. But you're gonna have to restore that update as it was and reissue."

"Not gonna happen, Sid. You know I can't do that."

"Can't or won't? I'm betting it's the latter—but when you find their bodies, just remember it was you who did it to them."

Hawk paused, a smile spreading across his face as he remained shielded behind the pine tree.

"Okay, okay. Is there a way I can save them?"

"Surrender and let me take you in."

"Take me in?" Hawk said. "Take me to who?"

"No, no, no. We're not playing that game."

Hawk took another glance and noticed the moonlight glint off a shiny object next to a tree. "But it seems like we are."

Hawk waited and watched again, confirming it was indeed a cell phone.

"If you come out now, I won't send this text to my handler telling him to go ahead and kill your wife and son. But all I have to do is press the send button, and it's over for you. And there's not a damn thing you can do about it."

Hawk reached into his ruck and felt for his throwing stars, the only thing he had left capable of striking from a long distance.

"Why would you do this to me, Sid? I mean, you know my family. You even saw them in the airport recently and played with J.D. Now, you're gonna allow him to be killed? And for what?"

"It's nothing personal, Hawk. It's just a job, a lucrative one that will set up me and my little boy up for life."

"So, you're calling it quits after this?"

"That's the plan."

"Even if you get a shit ton of money, Sid, you'll be spending it on personal protection. Because I swear to you, if my wife and son are killed, I'll hunt you until my last breath."

297

"That's why I'm gonna kill you too tonight."

Hawk could feel the rage coursing through his body. He wanted to rush out into the open and charge Weston. But despite the overwhelming anger, Hawk took a deep breath, pausing to consider that baiting him might be Weston's plan.

"Think about your decisions right now," Hawk said. "Think about your future."

"I already have. Time for you to think about yours—or at least your loved ones. Come out now and at least save them."

Hawk could see just a sliver of Weston's hand holding a phone around the corner of a tree about twenty meters away. It wouldn't be an easy shot, but he had to try.

"This is your last chance, Sid. If you wanna live, surrender. I promise to go easy on you."

Weston laughed. "You've got a brass pair, Hawk. I'll give you that much. But I see that you're not willing to budge. And I'm not going to waste any more of my time. Your wife and son are going to die."

Hawk eyed Weston's hand, sticking out ever so slightly from the side of the tree. In a move reeking of desperation, Hawk slung a throwing star toward the thin target. The weapon whizzed within inches of Weston before lodging deep into the pine tree behind him. He drew back, moving away from the attempted strike.

But Hawk had predicted what Weston would do and approached him from the other side of the tree. By the time Weston figured out what was happening, Hawk had whipped another throwing star at him, this time finding its mark.

Weston looked down at the device buried in the right side of his chest. He didn't yelp in pain but instead just stared at the exposed blades, too stunned by the hit. Weston reached for his knife, but Hawk was already on him, flinging another throwing star into the center of his chest. He staggered backward as blood gushed from his chest. Hawk had missed the man's heart—and it seemed like it was on purpose.

Hawk rushed within a few feet, the hilt of his K-bar secure in his hand.

"Drop the phone," Hawk ordered.

Weston looked up and sneered at Hawk. "What difference does it make now anyway?"

"You're gonna kill my little boy now for what? Because you can? Because it'll make you feel good before you die?"

Weston laughed and bared his teeth, now stained amber. "You're taking all this so personally. I told you it was just business."

Hawk watched as Weston's thumb hovered over the send button on his phone.

"Don't do it," Hawk said.

"You messed up this time—messed up really good. And now you're going to spend what's left of your life thinking about it."

Hawk, determined not to blink so he didn't miss anything, studied Weston's hand. After a couple of tense seconds, Weston's thumb flinched.

"No," Hawk screamed as he lunged for Weston. Putting a shoulder into him in a diving motion, Weston dropped his phone, toppling to the ground along with both men.

Hawk glared at the freelancer, who drew back a blade and swung toward Hawk. But he blocked the attempted blow, the sudden jarring stop shaking Weston's knife free.

Weston reached to the side groping for his phone. But Hawk brushed it away and then rolled on top of Weston, blade inches from his throat.

"Go ahead," Weston said through gritted teeth. "Do it. Just get it over with."

Hawk huffed. "I warned you that it didn't have to be like this."

"Just shove the blade through my neck and end it, damnit."

Hawk shook his head. "I have some questions first."

"Kiss my ass."

"I'll make a deal with you, Sid. You tell me who's giving you your marching orders and I'll make sure your son gets taken care of financially. It's the best offer you're gonna get from me, so you better take it."

Weston winced. "Damnit, I hate you."

"Last chance," Hawk said.

Weston set his jaw. "Remington Steele."

"What did you say?"

"I said, Remington Steel. That's the guy's name."

"That's bullshit," Hawk said. "That's a character's name from a stupid TV show."

"That's all he told me. I swear it. He mentioned something about being part of some alliance. He works at the Pentagon. You can try to reach him through my phone, but that's all I know. I promise."

Weston coughed up more blood, this time darker red. His fight had almost left him.

"You'll take care of my little guy?" he asked, his voice weak.

"Yeah," Hawk said. "I'll take care of your little guy. But I've got one more question for you first."

"No more questions," Weston said, almost in a whisper.

He reached for Hawk's wrists and pulled down on them, driving the blade into his throat. Within seconds, Weston's head lolled backward and his body went limp.

Hawk withdrew the knife from Weston's throat and climbed off the man, the dirt on the forest floor mixed with blood. He picked up the cell phone and typed a short text to the number Weston had been interacting with discussing Alex and J.D.

> Release them. He cooperated.

> Done

Hawk had hoped for something more in the response from the texter. But he realized that was unrealistic. And he certainly wasn't going to turn the tables on them without knowing if his wife and son were yet safe. There'd be time for that later. And time to mourn Sid Weston, even though the bastard had nearly killed his family. Maybe there'd been more to this job to disseminate a dangerous computer program. Maybe it wasn't just about money for Weston. Hawk would never know now about Weston's true motivations. But he didn't care. He'd gotten the information he wanted—the information he *needed*—out of Weston.

"How's it going?" Mia asked over the coms.

"I'm still alive," Hawk said, "which is more than I can say for Sid Weston."

"Did you take care of him?" Big Earv asked.

"More or less," Hawk said. "I'll explain everything later. In the meantime, get your asses over to me. I'm freezing—and I want to go home to my family."

Hawk found a fallen tree and sat down. He clasped his arms around his body in an attempt to stifle the chill that had become glaringly evident now that his adrenaline had subsided. He fought back tears—tears of pain, tears of regret.

But he couldn't fend off the tears that welled up once he thought about Alex and J.D.

Fifteen minutes later, his phone buzzed with a call from his wife.

"You okay?" he asked before devolving into a blubbering mess.

"We're gonna live, though I don't know what it's going to do to J.D."

"He's resilient," Hawk said. "He'll bounce back before you know it."

"How did you—"

She stopped.

"I can tell you everything later," Hawk said. "I just want you and J.D. to know how much I love you both. I'd do anything for either one of you."

"We know," Alex said.

"I'll call you in a bit when we're on the road," Hawk said.

"You need to hear every last word of this."

FORTY-SEVEN

LOS ANGELES

HAWK STARED AT THE NEW FLOOR-TO-CEILING TV screen in the Magnum Group conference room as he sat in a chair, his feet propped up on the desk. He reached for the bandage on his leg and winced as he adjusted it. A panel of experts assembled in a cable news studio were discussing the dangers of artificial intelligence and how it was reshaping the way humans think.

Ryder entered the room and stopped by Hawk, inspecting his leg. "They gonna have to amputate that thing?"

Hawk grunted and shook his head.

"It looks uncomfortable," Ryder said. "Maybe you would've been better off with backup."

"We got the job done," Hawk said. "That's all that matters."

"I'm not sure I want to get jobs done that result in me being out for a while."

Big Earv chuckled as he slapped Ryder on the back, joining the men.

"You don't ever end up that way because you're not as tough as Hawk," Big Earv said. "You would've baled on the job."

Ryder glowered at Big Earv. "Watch it."

Big Earv broke into a smile before playfully jabbing Ryder in the chest.

"It's all right," Hawk said, eyeing Big Earv. "You don't have to defend me. I can take care of myself. Besides, I'm not offended by anything this newbie says about me. His brain hasn't caught up to his mouth yet."

"Is that so?" Ryder asked.

Hawk shrugged. "If I said it, it's so," he said, before pointing at the screen, "unlike these people, who wouldn't know the truth if it was a flying ju-jitsu kick to the chest."

"Is everyone still trying to break down the big threat that was exposed earlier this week?" Big Earv asked.

Hawk nodded. "Apparently, these people are now concerned about AI and the danger it entails. There's only one guy on this panel who knows anything about AI, and he seems to have some insider knowledge on what just happened. It's a little suspicious, to be honest. I mean, if this was all classified like we were told last week after stopping Nexus's Prime operating system update, how the hell does this guy know so much?"

"Maybe he's got some inside sources," Morgan May said as she approached the trio of men.

"You weren't his source, were you?" Hawk asked.

"Believe it or not, I did go on a few dates with that guy when we were in grad school," she said. "He's a fair-minded journalist, and a good one at that. He always does his research."

"You didn't answer the question," Hawk said with a wry smile.

"Maybe I'm getting ready to announce my senate run," she said.

"No," Big Earv said. "If you're leaving us for politics, I'm walking out that door and never coming back."

"Oh, calm down," she said, waving at him dismissively. "You're so dramatic. It was a joke, all right?"

Big Earv set his jaw and shook his head subtly. "Sorry, but I've had it with all the bureaucracy bullshit. I don't want to work for anyone else. You're my last stop on this crazy train."

Morgan smiled. "I guess I'll take that as a very high compliment coming from you. And, don't worry, I'm not interested in politics. They're the necessary evil for us."

Everyone spun and turned toward the screen as the panel began discussing President Bullock's alleged affair, a story that was sparked by AI-like generated images. The B-roll footage played while the guests talked about Bullock and the video that fooled even the best digital forensics analysts.

Morgan laughed and shook her head. "If only I did look like that."

"Don't wish for something you're not," Mia said as she strode into the room. "By the way, I think you look better than whoever that woman was posing as you in that video."

Dr. Z entered the room on a One Wheel, his bowtie mechanically twirling around.

"Hawk, have you ever seen these things? You've gotta get one."

Hawk groaned and shook his head. "If I never see one of those things again, I'll die a happy man."

"What do you have against these machines?" Dr. Z asked. "They're incredible."

He rolled through the room, gliding around the table before coming to a stop and collapsing into a chair. But he continued before Hawk could answer.

"I use it when I walk Astro," Dr. Z said. "I was beginning to wonder if I'd ever be able to keep up with him, but now I don't lose him whenever Mrs. Hawthorne's cat gets loose and taunts him from the top of her fence."

"It's a long story," Hawk said. "Just not my favorite contraptions, especially when you're trying to talk to a certain CEO who's flying around the room on one."

"I believe I can see how that would be frustrating," Dr. Z said.

Morgan clapped her hands. "Well, now that pretty much everyone is here, let's get started. I've got a busy day."

Robert Besserman and Rebecca Fornier joined the meeting via teleconference along with Alex. Once everyone was either seated or connected, Morgan wasted no time in getting down to business.

"Director Besserman had something he wanted to share first," she said.

Besserman thanked the team for their help and promised to provide better protection of their identities in the future. Morgan had been exposed, but the agency's office worked diligently to mitigate the potential damage and keep her legend as a policy wonk intact. Hawk wondered if Besserman really could control stories in the future. Sometimes covers were blown no matter how hard one worked to protect them, something Hawk had witnessed several times during his career.

"Well, I'd like to begin by thanking all of you for your support during this trying ordeal," Morgan said. "Both Director Besserman and I have experienced one of the most traumatic things any person could endure aside from witnessing a gruesome death or attack. To be accused of doing something you didn't do —and something you'd likely never do—is a special circle of hell I wouldn't wish upon anyone."

"Even your worst enemy?" Hawk asked.

"No, I'd definitely wish something like this on Jun Fang. He deserves every bit of it. But he's not going to be a problem for a while."

"What happened to him?" Ryder asked.

"Gone. Vanished," Morgan said. "However, Fang's assets have been frozen or seized in various countries. In exchange for a lesser prison term, Nikolaev's son confessed that Fang was the person who approached him about conducting the operation to kill his father, suggesting that it would serve a two-fold purpose of getting him all his father's inheritance money *and* framing a high-level CIA official."

"So the whole thing was a planned setup?" Big Earv asked.

Morgan nodded. "And they would've gotten away with it if you guys hadn't worked so hard to expose the truth, which is an endeavor that's getting increasingly more difficult in this day and age."

"Now what?" Hawk asked. "Is The Alliance dead since Jun Fang has been rendered toothless?"

"Not exactly," she said. "Remember Felix Vogel?"

Hawk nodded.

"Well, he appears poised to take over the organization, according to our sources. But regardless of who's running the show, we still have to beware of Fang. He's not going to like that we exposed his little pet project with Quantum Glitch, so I imagine he's going to be gunning for all of us."

"Then are we going after Vogel?" Ryder asked.

"Not yet," Morgan said. "We still have plenty of investigating to do with some of the evidence we collected, starting with Sid Weston's phone. We're trying to track down the person who kept giving him detailed instructions. Whoever it is, it's a powerful person—and preliminary indications suggest he works at the Pentagon."

"His name is Remington Steele," Hawk said. "At least, that's the man's alias."

"Right," Morgan said. "But there's still more to learn from Weston's phone."

"I'm still on it," Mia said, raising her hand sheepishly. "Making progress, but it's slow going."

"We have people within our own intelligence community who are actively trying to sabotage us for the sake of The Alliance," Morgan said. "That ought to tell you just how high the stakes are. And I can promise you that we're going to stop this."

Hawk eased to his feet, pushing off the arm rests and bouncing on one leg until he steadied.

"I don't want to just stop these guys," Hawk said. "They

threatened my family, even my seven-year-old son. And now they've poked the bear. Who's with me?"

Every hand in the room shot up as all eyes were on Hawk.

"Good," he said. "Glad to know I can count on every single one of you. This whole thing with The Alliance has become incredibly personal for me. And I want them stopped no matter what."

Morgan looked around the room and smiled. "I think it's safe to say that we're all with you, Hawk."

He looked every person in the eye and nodded, a ghost of a smile dancing on his lips.

"Of course they are," Hawk said as he sat back down. "Everyone here wants good to prevail."

"Well, now that we've got that settled," Morgan continued, standing and pacing the floor, "there's a new threat I want to tell you about, one that's going to require the best in all of you if we're going stop it."

"You're never getting anything but my best," Hawk said

Morgan smiled. "What about the rest of you?"

The group collectively nodded, determination evident on their faces.

"Great. Then let's get to work."

THE END

To continue reading in The Phoenix Chronicles, order **LOYAL TRAITOR** now. Or to read more novels from the Firestorm world, check out the Brady Hawk series also available on Kindle Unlimited.

NEWSLETTER SIGNUP

If you would like to stay up to date on R.J. Patterson's latest writing projects with his periodic newsletter, visit the website www.rjpbooks.com to sign up.

ACKNOWLEDGMENTS

I am grateful to so many people who have helped with the creation of this project and the entire Phoenix Chronicles series.

Brooke Turbyfill was a big help in editing this book and this series.

Also a big thanks to Dustin at Alpine Adventures in Washington who helped me with the climactic scene along the Wenatchee River.

I would also like to thank my advance reader team for all their input in improving this book along with all the other readers who have enthusiastically embraced the story of Brady Hawk and The Phoenix Chronicles.

ABOUT THE AUTHOR

R.J. PATTERSON is an award-winning writer living in southeastern Idaho. He first began his illustrious writing career as a sports journalist, recording his exploits on the soccer fields in England as a young boy. Then when his father told him that people would pay him to watch sports if he would write about what he saw, he went all in. He landed his first writing job at age 15 as a sports writer for a daily newspaper in Orangeburg, S.C. He later attended earned a degree in newspaper journalism from the University of Georgia, where he took a job covering high school sports for the award-winning *Athens Banner-Herald* and *Daily News*.

He later became the sports editor of *The Valdosta Daily Times* before working in the magazine world as an editor and free-lance journalist. He has won numerous writing awards, including a national award for his investigative reporting on a sordid tale surrounding an NCAA investigation over the University of Georgia football program.

R.J. enjoys the great outdoors of the Northwest while living there with his wife and four children. He still follows sports closely.

He also loves connecting with readers and would love to hear from you. To stay updated about future projects, connect with him over Facebook or on the interwebs at www.RJPbook-s.com and sign up here for his newsletter to get deals and updates.

Made in the USA
Coppell, TX
27 September 2024

37801215R00194